Pavane

for

Miss Marcher

a novel by

Leigh Verrill-Rhys

Pavané for Miss Marcher

A novel of Maine

By

Leigh Verrill-Rhys

eresbooks.com

3rd Edition Copyright © 2023 Leigh Verrill-Rhys/Eres Books
Cover Design: © 2017 Gwion Dulais
Cover Photos: *Lilies*, Kozh; *Red Gown*, Faestock
ISBN-10: 1-958967-08-9
ISBN-13: 978-1-958967-08-9

---

[1] **Pavane** – a musical term used to describe a slow-paced piece, stately in character, as in Mendelssohn's 'Wedding March', Pachelbel's 'Canon in D' and Ravel's 'Pavane for a Dead Princess'.

Dedication

In memory of my mother, Virginia May Verge Verrill, who introduced me to fiction writers of American history and one of the best story-tellers I have ever known.

Acknowledgments

My brother, US Army veteran and American Civil War enactor, Lt. Thomas A. Verrill, Jr. (RIP), first introduced me to our family's connection to the Battles of Gettysburg, especially Little Round Top and the 20th Maine Regiment. I thank him for the deep pride I have for my family heritage and my home state.

My sisters—Jacklyn, Maxine, Hallie, Celeste—have supported and encouraged me through many years of writing. They have read and suggested and questioned and challenged me at every stage, for which I am always thankful.

One

George Rupert Smith stretched his legs across the gap, toward the bench his sergeant, Morton Pierce, occupied to the full extent of his physical being. Though the train could not progress any slower up the coast, Rupe pressed his back against the upholstered seat as though he could hold the engine back by force of will.

Mort, arms folded across his chest, his bulk stretched the length of the padded seats, slept as if he had an easy heart, had never faced the muzzle of a gun, never doubted returning home. The big man had a lot to answer for in Rupert's final capitulation to the badgering to leave the ranch. The house was built and the range land ready for the cattle they had negotiated out of their neighbor's herd. All good reasons Smith gave to stick to their plan. All good reasons Mort gave to get back to Oslo Hill.

For the wakeful man staring out the carriage window at the rain-soaked countryside, Oslo Hill was the last place he wanted to be and the only place he could be whole again. If he wanted that, he'd be sleeping sound like his traveling companion. If he wanted that, he'd be leaning forward, pushing the inappropriately named Achilles[2] engine with all his might to reach the little town in Oxford County as fast

---

[2] **Achilles Train Engine** – a class of steam engine run on the Boston and Maine Railroad in the 1870s.

as possible. If he wanted that, he'd be dreaming of practicing Law, not a ranch in Wyoming and a smart girl he once knew.

The power of the Achilles engine ground away the miles on the narrow-gauge course toward Lewiston despite all Captain (Union Army – retired) G. R. Smith's efforts to haul the locomotive back to Portland, back to Boston and further back to their starting point in the high grasslands of eastern Wyoming.

Mort Pierce stretched his arms above his head, groaning as he extended each to his sides, hitting his captain in the knee and laughing as he sat up. He chucked his former commanding officer on the calf and expanded every ounce of sinew and muscle, relieving the chinks in his cramped body.

"Remind you of any place?"

"Too much," Rupe answered. "Too much."

"Sorry." Mort dropped his gaze, shaking his head like a demented bear from side to side. "I meant the view out the window."

"That too."

"You'll feel different, Rupe. Take my word for it, once we get there."

"Reserving judgment,"

"Spoken like a lawyer, plain and simple."

"Years of training. Hard to shake off."

"Good an excuse as any, better 'an some." Pierce pressed his shoulders back, straining the buttons on his shirt front. "Mind if I show some good spirits? Being as I ahn't been home for more 'an eight years."

"Long as you don't expect the same from me."

"Never fear. I've come to expect the opposite, even when there ahn't no damned good reason."

Rupert smirked, turned his gaze back to the window, waved the mist out of his face, inhaled the fragrance of the spring rain deep into his lungs along with the scent of lilacs.

"Eleven years, almost to the day."

"Ay-yuh," Mort yawned.

Opening the house on the Hill reminded him of all the damned good reasons he had given for never coming back. Oslo Hill hadn't changed a mite since he'd last seen the village green back in 'Sixty-one. What high-minded thoughts he had all those years ago, on *that* April day.

Like so many, he'd been certain of returning home in time for the Christmas pageant, take Susan Hamlin for that hayride he'd threatened the year before, make sure his mother had the foxtail collar for that tatty coat she insisted was just as good as the day his father bought it for her, make good on his contract to join that law firm in Augusta.

Following his dad into law and perhaps taking the next step into politics had been his fervent plan, the dream he'd thought was written in stone.

The floorboards of the veranda creaked under his heavy-heeled boots. Until that was fixed, he'd be awake all night. The front hall smelled of furniture polish and pine. He'd expected rot and must. The credenza gleamed, standing up to the scrutiny of his parents, staring at it and the painting of decadent red lilies his mother loved from across the wide entry way. Not a speck of dust on the painting's gilt frame or on the plain oval frame around the lithograph of the elder Smiths marred the scene.

It was as though he had been gone for less than a day. The first impression of his childhood home could not have cut deeper. Mort's hand on his shoulder reminded him that years had passed. Years of deaths that could never be forgotten and longing that could never be requited. What fools they had been to believe that glory and valor had meaning.

In the spring of that vainglorious year, Rupert Smith had sat on the back of the thoroughbred Arabian his father had purchased for him as a commissioned officer. The sun was in his eyes, even beneath the brim of his hat with that outrageous white plume waving like a damsel in the breeze as his newly formed regiment commandeered the green, trampling the lawns with their stamping hooves and stiff boot heels.

Susan and her silly classmates from the Girls' Academy waved handkerchiefs and fans, one moment in awe, the next giggling, then chattering and clucking like the Snyders' barnyard hens. His chest had doubled in breadth with all the admiration. The thought of that day—if he'd known how many of his regiment were to die in that first year of war, if he'd known how long the agony was to drag on, if he'd known what cost to his parents his absence proved—could he have done any different?

"Looks like someone's been busy. Wonder if there's a meal awaiting us in the pantry." Mort stepped out from behind him, but Rupert held him back with a hand at his elbow.

"Everything's just as it was. Somehow. Someone's been taking care of the place."

"Seems so, Rupe. Must have known you were coming home."

"How? I never said I was. I didn't tell anyone, here or down in town."

After his parents died—first his mother, and a few months later, his father—Allan, a former classmate at Bowdoin, wrote to say that the house was locked up, awaiting his return. He had dreaded even walking up the front steps, expecting worse than a creaking board, expecting dust as thick as his fingers, expecting the scampering of mice and rats, broken windows, howling complaints from the attic.

"Maybe that woman your mother wrote about—."

"The house has been closed up for more than five years."

"All the same, feels like it's been waiting on you, just the way your folks wanted it."

"Damn it all, Mort, they've been dead all this time. Trust you to make it worse."

"There ahn't no call for you to feel bad, Rupe, nor for you to go blaming me for you not coming home. That's on you but you know damn well you had your reasons."

"Evie."

Mort looked at him like he'd drifted away to the clouds.

"That's the name of the woman Mother wrote about. Always saying what a Godsend she was, how she helped out with everything, the garden, the house."

"So maybe she kept doing it."

"Makes no sense unless she was getting paid somehow. I'll see what Allan has to say about it. He's coming by tomorrow to finalize the—. I should have been here for them."

"Ay-yuh, like I should have left you in that hell camp when I got the chance to escape. And the Arne boys should have gone home to their farm when their tour of duty was up. Rupe, you could no more come home than any of the rest of us. That's the way it was."

Lucky to be alive. It never felt that way in the last months of the war. Sure, his wound hadn't festered like some of the others and sure, he hadn't lost a limb. He was a whole man. Still, that didn't change the way he screamed at night, never out loud for fear the prison guards would put an end to his complaints and his misery with a musket ball or a bayonet. More likely the bayonet or a club, why waste lead on a half-dead man?

On the nights the moon was full, he pulled the letter from his pocket, careful that he didn't damage the fragile folds any more than he had already with his constant reading and pressing it close. What could a girl be thinking writing to a man about goodness and nobility when all the other girls were swooning, pouring heaps of praise on their "brave soldiers" and writing anonymous love letters to boys they'd never look at otherwise. This girl seemed to write personally, to him. He shared the other letters, even Susan's gushing news of the village and her new bonnets, but he kept this one letter private, to himself.

None of his boys would have appreciated the high ideals and allusions to Greek philosophers—he hardly understood them, especially on the darkest nights, when the cries of the boys from home for their mothers and their wives and their sweethearts made him weep.

Through the first years, other girls had sent miniature portraits with locks of their hair tied in pink and white ribbons. Lieutenant Smith shared these among his troops as well. Some were so pretty, a man's heart could be captured forever with a dream of that precious visage gazing up at him, those innocent lips pressed against his cheek. Some of his boys went to sleep at night with the tiny locket clasped hard in their grimy hands against their hearts as though to keep her safe from harm and in hope the gesture could keep them alive until dawn.

Rupert Smith had no need of a portrait to keep the face of one girl close to his heart. His relief at the news of Susan Hamlin's marriage made clear what he had kept a secret even from his own thoughts, he loved that passionate girl for whom "doing what was right" meant she had no love of gallantry or glory or valor but that he, George Rupert Smith, believed that what he did was right.

Of that, he was no longer certain, had not been certain for most of the long years that battles raged on, ceaselessly claiming the lives of his boys and those of men he might have called his friends if not for what they believed to be right being in conflict with what he believed.

On the day he killed his last man, on the day he was wounded and taken prisoner, thrown into a wagon with other wounded men and taken to a camp where only the strongest and most determined had any hope of survival, on that day he saw it all for what it was and had always been, from the dawn of existence, from the raised fist of Cain, just as that girl saw it.

Keeping her letter and those from his parents close to him had been his shield against the incessant siren call of Death, fortifying his will to live and return to a life that was more than he had dreamed of and had no taint of the past. While the prison camp existence ate away at his body, their letters became the muscle and sinew of his humanity. And at the end of all the bloodshed and carnage, news of his parents' deaths reached him by letter held at his regimental headquarters until his release and delivered as he waited, with Mort, the Arne brothers and the fourteen-year-old kid from Kentucky for transport away from the gates of Hell.

Mrs. Moffatt expressed her condolences with gentle phrases but the blow damned his soul to purgatory. Going home as he was, starved and half-mad with the banshees of inhumanity howling in his mind, with nothing more to show for his sacrifice than a promotion to Captain, no longer the man of ideals and ambitions, became impossible.

"When Lila Snyder told me she had seen Rupert, I thought she must have had too much sun at the church picnic." Susan Hamlin Miller tipped her fan in Mrs. Moffatt's direction with a decisive click of the ivory slats. The silk threads holding the filigreed ribs together was only a little frayed on the plain side but the front of the fan was as fresh as the day her late husband presented it to her. The child-sized fan made another satisfying click as the young widow flicked her wrist in her practiced way. "I have waited until I spoke to you before venturing to call at the Smiths' house, in case you had an intention to do so."

The windows of Mrs. Moffatt's front parlor looked onto the residential street facing the church square, half a mile from the renamed Lincoln Street where the Smiths' house stood across the road from the Oslo Woods.

"I should think not, Susan. Although you are a widow and perfectly within the bounds of proper neighborly concern, you are only recently bereaved."

"Yet, Rupert and I were such friends, surely——."

"He will have much to do to get that old house in order. After all, no one has opened a door or a window since poor George followed dear Margaret to the grave." Mrs. Moffatt leaned forward to tap her guest on the knee with her equally elaborate fan. "Mr. Giles will surely have all the news we could possibly need. He will be attending to Captain Smith's requirements and arranging the workmen."

"I've heard that at least one neighbor has not shown him such courtesy."

"No need to say. Cathryn has taken her efforts to fulfill the wishes of Captain Smith's parents very seriously. They would not have wanted her to continue but she will do as she pleases. That child has been a caution ever since her own parents passed away. If it weren't for her charitable works, I am certain she would have many more lectures from the Pastor than she does."

"She is no child," Susan replied. "There are but a few months between us."

"I have a soft heart when it comes to our Cathryn, as you know. Living alone for so many years in Snyder's old cabin cannot be an easy life for a young woman."

"For that, she only has herself to blame. After all, what call had she to go all the way up to Boston to nurse? There were plenty of brave wounded soldiers in Portland."

"Dear Susan, no good can come of that argument. Boston had a fine military hospital close by. Where but to the finest would a young woman intent on following Clara Barton's[3] good example go?"

Susan Miller née Hamlin stroked the edge of her fan along her chin. "You are right, of course. Cathryn and I have always been friends and I err on the side of caution but only from concern."

"Naturally. But, Portland would have been no better for her. Poor child. She is her own worst enemy. She will do as she will, without regard for semblance or sense. Be that as it may, she is our own dear and we have a duty to ensure her name and character are not further besmirched." Mrs. Moffatt tapped her fingers on the starched doily covering the arm of her chair. "Therefore, I think it best that I, together with Pastor Jorgens, call on poor Captain Smith to offer heartfelt condolences on behalf of the whole village population."

Susan glanced beyond the lace-covered window in the direction of her thoughts, toward the Snyders' farm and their tenant's meagre cabin, plunked down at the gate of their property without regard. "As it is properly settled, I will postpone my singing lesson with Cathryn no longer. I have sorely neglected my voice these last weeks."

Cathryn controlled the giddy, giggling girl until she safely closed the door of her cabin and leaned her back against the cross-brace. George Rupert Smith had come home. Alive. That sum total of her knowledge was sufficient to cause the giddy, giggling girl to emerge from years of anxiety. Through the years his parents kept her informed of his career in the war and the blind faith of the months they knew he was a

---

[3] **Clara Barton** established medical battlefield services to the U.S. Army, raising donations and supplies to provide assistance to wounded and dying soldiers and support for doctors during surgery. Many women joined Barton on the battlefield to offer nursing care.

prisoner, she had kept his well-being in her nightly prayers and her daily thoughts.

She shared George and Margaret Smith's fears for their only son, heard every heartbreaking sigh and woeful, whispered concern. The day they were told of his capture and imprisonment, the pain worked through their hearts, wearing their hope to nothing as surely as her own parents had lost their battle against dashed expectations for themselves and their daughter. Amassing their wealth in heaven, John and Hazel Marcher had no earthly goods to pass to their only child, trusting their daughter would find her way with God's help.

Though Cathryn had no expectation that the most handsome, most eligible young man in the county before the war had any knowledge of her, she had come to know him better than even his former fiancée through his parents' love of him.

She had never been one of the giddy girls who thought the volunteers were gallant, that the war was a short lark interrupting their spring dances. Though she knitted scarves and mittens for the soldiers with Susan and the other girls, after her first attempt, she was banned from writing to any of their chosen correspondents. Her missives, in their opinion, were destined to depress the poor boys so they'd never want to come home again.

Instead, along with her parents until their deaths, and Rupert's folks, with a few others in the village, she secretly hung quilts[4] in the woods to aid runaways following the

---

[4] **Quilts** – messages hidden in patchwork-patterned quilts aided runaway slaves to navigate, believed to have been coded in traditional African symbols that also strongly resemble the 18thC patchwork patterns of Welsh immigrants to Pennsylvania which influenced the Amish. See *Hidden in Plain View: A Secret Story of Quilts & the Underground Railroad, Making Welsh Quilts, The American Quilt, American Patchwork Quilts.*

North Star[5] toward their new Canaan. George and Peggy Smith shared parts of Rupert's letters with her as she helped them through the months stretching into years. Her initial admiration for their only son—a beautiful, proud and goodhearted man, destined for brilliance in the future— gradually became tainted with sorrow for the suffering he witnessed. Once she had garnered her own experience of the full nature of war, she knew his letters spared them the worst of his knowledge. Admiration and sorrow melded over the years of the war and the slow withering of the Smiths' hope of ever seeing their son again into an abiding care.

At their deaths, she prayed they could now watch over him and be heartened and content. She had, along with the rest of the Oslo Hill residents, expected Rupert Smith to return to his home town. Susan Hamlin Miller had been made a widow and Mrs. Moffatt surely had made her favorite bachelor aware of that news, as sad as it was.

His unexplained absence had eventually been accepted by even the giddiest of the young women whose chances of marrying had been dashed by the carnage. Though many young men did return to the county, resumed their former occupations and settled into family life, few were unscathed. Spring dances held no allure for them after the summer of eighteen-sixty-three in the fields of Pennsylvania.

She had always since thought well of George Rupert Smith but when they passed one another on the sidewalk in West Oslo a day after she learned of his return, she saw a different man from the young idealist she had known nine years before.

---

[5] **North Star/New Canaan** – the Underground Railroad, following the North Star to Canada which, through the British Emancipation Act (1833), had abolished slavery throughout the Empire, Canada's own anti-slavery bill was passed in 1793.

Though he seemed not to see her and she walked past without acknowledging him, she recognized the expression in his gaze, one she had seen too often in the eyes of soldiers she had nursed through wounds and disease, some unto death. Rupert Smith, though long away from war, had not healed.

She had not expected him to recognize her. He had not often been in the village as a young man. His parents sent him to the Young Men's Academy in Oxford, then on to Bowdoin College to study for the Law. At Christmas and Easter, his strong baritone rose above the other male voices at the church services, often in perfect harmony with Susan Hamlin's top soprano. Although, like Cathryn, he had been an only child and was now alone in the world, the similarities ended there.

Her parents lived in a one-bedroom rented cabin, the same one she returned to after the last soldier left the military hospital in Worcester. She attended the local school, a one-room class for the village children, until she was fourteen when she began playing piano for the church and teaching piano to the children of local families to help support her mother and father.

Though the Smiths were not as wealthy as the Hamlin family, they were well-respected and their son had always been considered among the most handsome, friendly, down-to-earth and eligible young men. Though Susan and Rupert were expected to merge their fortunes, he showed little interest in the village girls. Rupert attracted their admiration though he never courted it. His intention to seek a career in the legal profession and public office were accepted as givens—until the war.

At the door of the Giles residence, Cathryn waited for the maid to answer but the lawyer's daughter, Megan, ran ahead and yanked the door open. The little girl threw her arms around her piano teacher's waist, pulling her into the foyer toward the door of the front parlor.

"Miss Megan, you know you're not supposed to open the door," the maid, Mary Cook, scolded.

"I knew it was Miss Marcher," Megan whined, holding Cathryn's hand.

"All the same, a rule is a rule, you know your father wouldn't be happy if you opened the door to a stranger."

"Miss Marcher isn't a stranger."

"I'm sorry Miss Marcher," Mary murmured, "but Mr. Giles is particular, especially since there's been some strangers seen in the village."

Cathryn replied with a smile and submitted to Megan's insistence that her lesson was to start as soon as her teacher removed her bodice jacket. Though the fashion for hoops had passed, Cathryn still wore the full skirted dress she had made seven years before, hitched up at the back in a bustle, the gathers hidden by a wide bow.

Allan Giles considered his position in Oslo Hill society as that of protector and strangers were anyone he had not personally introduced to the village elders, Mrs. Moffatt and Reverend Jorgens. Although he and Rupert Smith had the same opportunities, went to the same academy and started at Bowdoin in the same year, ten years had passed. Allan earned his degree, established his practice in East Oslo and bought the second biggest house on the Hill when the owners moved closer to their offspring in Augusta. His assumption of leadership was never questioned.

Though his proposal to Cathryn after her parents' deaths tainted their previous friendship, creating an unpleasant distance, their civility toward one another was a necessity of village life. Soon after Cathryn's refusal, he won the hand of the elder daughter of the Coffin family, Nancy. His bride-to-be became aware of the tension and eventually learned of the proposal from one of the many gossiping inhabitants of the Hill. Nancy also responded to Cathryn by maintaining a civil distance, tinged with superiority. As far as Nancy was concerned, Cathryn was employed to provide a service, nothing more, ending their otherwise amenable relationship.

Neither was the case with their seven-year-old daughter.

Megan launched into the song, *Kindernacht*, she was learning for the Summer Fete without waiting for her singing teacher to settle at the piano, Cathryn folded her hands in her lap, allowing the seven-year-old her moment of impatience. As Cathryn flexed her fingers ready to accompany her student, the door from the foyer opened and Allan Giles entered, sat in the arm chair behind her, crossed his legs and applauded when his daughter completed the verse.

"Excellent, my dear."

The little girl's pleasure at the parental approval did little to relieve Cathryn's displeasure at the intrusion on the lesson and she remained silent until Megan returned to her position at her teacher's side.

"Remember to stand straight, Megan," her father admonished, "I am not paying Miss Marcher her fee for you to slouch through the lesson."

Cathryn took a deep, imperceptible breath, flexed her hands over the keyboard. "Use your breath to sustain your note, Megan."

"I'm trying."

"That is no way to speak to your teacher," Giles reminded his daughter.

Cathryn cared not so much that Allan Giles had proposed to her—she had many proposals from young men while they were on her hospital ward—but that he had proposed to her on the assumption that because she was penniless, she had no other option. Her refusal had come, not because she disliked him—though she had grown to dislike him very much since the proposal—but because he assumed she welcomed his attention because she was poor.

For no other reason than her own stubborn pride, she refused to be seen as a charity case.

The lawyer's constant belittling of his daughter to rile Cathryn had become a sad pattern. Tormenting the child to punish her for enjoying her singing lessons with the woman who had rejected him was more than sufficient reason for Cathryn to be overjoyed she had not married him. Doubly so since he made Nancy, his wife, as miserable as he strived to make his daughter.

Though Nancy had no love for Cathryn, she gave the teacher her grudging respect for her musical ability to correctly instruct Megan to sing without straining her young voice. The child's eager and generous desire to sing her very best gratified Cathryn whose own voice languished for lack of opportunity. Though she compensated by teaching others to be at their best when they sang for an audience, she sang to herself with a quiet ache in her heart.

"Support your voice with your tummy muscle," Cathryn murmured. Megan glanced at her stern-faced father and, rather than answer her teacher, she drew a long slow breath, without raising her shoulders or any other bad habit and sang a pure middle A note.

"Is that right?" Allan asked. "Did she get it right at last?"

Cathryn counted the beats in the following bar with her fingers tapping soundlessly on the ivory keys before she said, "Megan is rarely off key. Her voice is as perfectly pitched as any human being can hope."

"Do not praise her too highly, Cathryn. We do not want a prima donna in our midst."

"Mr. Giles, please. I have only a few lessons with Megan to prepare for the Summer Fete Concert. It is unfair to expect the child to perform without proper preparation."

"You forget who pays for her lessons, Miss Marcher. I have every right to ensure I am getting worth for my investment in my daughter's ability."

"I only ask that you refrain from comment until the lesson is concluded."

"I will do as I please in my own home, Cathryn."

"Yes, of course." Cathryn faced the music on the stand in front of her and rippled across the keys playing the B-flat scale over several octaves until her breath came easily, soothed and restored, before she nodded to her pupil to begin the Schumann lullaby once more.

Megan had not finished the first phrase before her father demanded, "What language are you teaching her?"

"The music is written for the language of the composer, German."

"Are there no English words? Who in Oslo Hill will understand what she is singing?"

"They will understand the purpose of the song. The meaning is in the music and the vocalist's interpretation."

"You give these villagers too much credit, Cathryn. Teach her to sing in English or do not teach her at all."

"Papa!"

"Do not complain, Megan. I am not paying this woman to teach what *she* determines is suitable but what is acceptable to me and your mother." He rose from him chair. "Is that clear?"

"Yes, Papa."

"Miss Marcher?"

"Of course."

When he had left the room, Cathryn met her student's tear-filled eyes. "Sing the English words, Megan, but *feel* the German."

Two

Allan Giles tapped the back of the envelope lying on the blotter in front of him. On the other side of his massive desk, opposite him, the man he had hoped never to see again read through George and Margaret Smith's jointly executed Last Will & Testament. From the room down the hallway, Megan plunked incessantly on the piano keys, striking several over and over in the same pattern, doing her best to learn the sequence as well as annoy her father. Allan's only consolation at the time was that her teacher had left before Rupert Smith arrived for his appointment to review his parents' bequests.

"I intend to honor their wishes," Rupert repeated, "of course. Are you sure they gave no indication who exactly they meant?"

"None whatever. I've made inquiries, naturally, but there is no other record of who this person might be."

"Mrs. Moffatt doesn't know? The pastor?"

"Surprisingly, even Mrs. Moffatt could not help. The present pastor, Mr. Jorgens, is new here, Rupert. Poor old Butler retired a year ago and passed away within a week."

Rupe studied the single page for another few moments, every word reminding him of the pain he had caused the two most important people in his life. Coming home had not relieved any of his guilt. He had none of the courage his parents believed him to possess.

"What is this below their signatures? My father has written something."

"No need for that now. You have returned safely so that codicil does not apply."

"What did he mean to do?"

"To be frank, Rupert, your father was somewhat distraught in his last months. Your mother's health and the long vigil before her passing…"

"Say what you mean, Allan. Because I did not return at the end of the war, as soon as I was released from prison."

"That was surely not entirely your fault. Many of our brave soldiers and officers had painful wounds… troubling memories… they chose not to inflict on their families."

Rupert met his friend's gaze for only a moment before he clenched his fist and returned his attention to the document. "My father says here that all his worldly possessions are to be given in their entirety to this person who was to receive my mother's effects should I not return alive."

"That is the gist of it, yes." Allan rolled his ebony-handled pen at his fingertips on the blotter. "Less legal costs and any taxes owing."

"But you do not know who this person is."

"No, I do not."

"What was to happen to the house, land, bank accounts if I did not return and this person was never found?"

"After costs and taxes, the property would be sold, I presume, and the government in Augusta would absorb whatever remained."

"We would not want the government to go wanting, would we?"

"Rupert, that is the way of these unsatisfactorily executed last wishes. If not that Mr. Smith had sat here in my office and wrote that provision before my eyes, it would not have been accepted as a legal statement. However, since you are here and alive, the provision is moot."

"You are absolutely certain there is no one who worked for them or in the village by the name of 'Evie'? One of the young girls, a maid, someone who cleaned, the child of their gardener?"

"As I told you, all avenues of investigation were explored *ad infinitum*, Rupert. No such person has been found and it is more than likely such a person never existed. That was the sorry state of your poor father's mind at the end. I regret that may cause you some discomfort…"

Discomfort? To know that his father and mother suffered heartbreak because he was not fit to return to them was more than a discomfort. There was some solace in knowing that a stranger was able to show them the comfort and kindness he could not but this phantom 'Evie' seemed more an apparition than a living being. How else to explain the devotion of one woman to two suffering souls. Angels, as he knew, sometimes appeared when most needed but not often in the form of someone who might find use of his mother's ivory combs and fox fur muff.

None of these items had been distributed as specified by her final wishes but remained in his parents' bedroom as his mother had left them.

"There is nothing for it but for me to make what effort I can to find this person and ensure she has all that my parents meant for her to have."

"I can assure you, Rupert, every effort has been made. If she exists, or ever existed, this person is no longer in the region."

"All the same, Allan, I will do all in my power to fulfill their wishes. That is the least I can do for them."

The short ride from the lawyer's town office to his parents' house on Lincoln Street—once known to him and everyone else in the village only as the road to Snyder's chicken farm—did nothing to dispel his sense of having grievously failed the only people who loved him as he was, no matter how flawed, no matter how warped by grandiosity and selfish regard for his own future or lack thereof.

Mort rocked on the porch, puffing on a pipe he had carried with him throughout the war, comfortable and at peace with his lot. Rupert raised his hand in greeting as Mort stood and came to the front steps.

"Mostly settled," Rupert said. "I have some digging to do, but other than that we can go right ahead with getting the place ready to sell."

"If that's what you want, Rupe. I'm getting mighty partial to this little place."

"Don't. We've got a ranch and some heifers waiting on us. If we're not back before the snow comes down from the Rockies—."

"That won't be near long enough afore we get this place in good shape."

Rupert looked up at the porch roof, sagging between posts, raw banisters where there had always been gleaming white paint. "Can't be helped. We'll do the best we can."

"You'll want to do the place justice," Mort said, "for your parents' sake."

"Damn you, Mort. You know right where to strike and leave a fellow gasping for mercy. I said, we'll do what we can—the best we can—between now and first snow. Otherwise, we'll be stuck here 'til next year."

"Worse places to be stuck over the winter months, in my opinion."

"And what about the kid? What about the Arne boys?"

"They'll forgive you."

"I don't want to be forgiven. I want, for once, to get something right."

Sergeant Pierce shook his head. "Ahn't no call for you to be making stupid talk like that, Rupe. And 'sides, you ahn't found that pretty girl you told me about when we was sitting in Cahaba[6], no thanks to Sam Jones," Mort spit the name of the second in command of the prison camp at the ground, "all by our lonesome."

"Which one?"

"Well, from what I've seen of the womenfolk around here, there's sure to be more 'an one suits my fancy but I'll bet my eye-teeth there ahn't but one for you."

"That one married."

"I ahn't talkin' about that one and 'sides, she's a widow now, hear tell."

"No use, Mort. And I've got more to think about than courting when courting can't lead to anything but farewells."

"You can't be certain of that, Rupe. Some gals like adventure."

"Most girls don't." Rupe walked into the hallway, dark and cool, too full of memories to be a pleasant relief from his sergeant's attempts to lighten his burden. Prodigal sons weren't always a welcome sight. In a day or two, the whole village would know where he'd been and what he'd been doing instead of coming home like a good son, like a man.

In the kitchen, he pumped a kettleful of spring water and set it on the range. Finding the woman who'd stood by his aging parents and saw them through what may have been the darkest time of the war's aftermath for them, was his only chance at redemption. Whoever she was, she had stood in his place, did as he was meant to do and he owed her what George and Margaret Smith had willed her to have.

---

[6] **Cahaba Prison Camp** – located in the small town of Cahaba, Alabama, this prison camp opened in June 1863, comprised of a brick cotton warehouse surrounded by a wooden stockade. Intended to hold only 500 prisoners of war, the number of prisoners held was over 3,000 by 1865. Lt.-Colonel Samuel Jones was reported to be a cruel drunkard, though the commander of the camp, Captain H. A. M. Henderson, a Methodist minister, was remembered as "often kind."

The house was not his to sell now but he pledged to make certain, if Evie did not want it, the house on Lincoln Street was worth enough to repay her kindness.

When Rupert started to whistle as he made a meal of rustled up cornbread and beans, Mort laughed, tugged on his pipe and the rocker creaked like a drunken sailor cursing the wind.

Church on his first Sunday home in nine years was all the torment he'd expected, even with Morton standing guard, ready to strike at the slightest sign his Captain wanted out. He had dressed in his gray striped trousers, matching waistcoat, and his father's outmoded frock coat, as somber as he would have been attending their funeral. The top hat never got near his head, he carried it on his forearm like a book as he walked toward the whitewashed church, cringing each time the steeple bell rang.

Mort's easy gait, like a strong thoroughbred ready for a race through the fields, kept Rupert from thinking too hard about the service to come. At least, the Reverend Jorgens had no idea who he was and the stares he endured as he walked toward the pew his family had claimed throughout his life were not accompanied by any vocal demonstrations or hails. Although he recognized many of the church-goers and was in turn recognized, he made no eye contact, except with Mort to gesture toward the seats they were to occupy.

The first hymn, the processional, was so ingrained, he sang without looking at the music or words. Susan Miller's voice was clear, coming from behind and to his right. Her voice blended with so many, a natural chorister who preferred the solo role, with whom he had so often harmonized. He fought the impulse to follow her lead, listening instead for another voice. There was no corresponding contralto, the rich depth of feeling that, even ten years ago, promised…

Rupert focused his gaze hard on the hymnal in his hand. Mort, not a natural singer, strove to contend with the bass line but faltered so often, he lowered his voice to a murmur. Rupert picked up the bass line though it was not his most comfortable range. With a wink, Mort raised his voice to join in the last few bars as the pastor took his place and gave a quick nod to the organist perched above him near the side entrance.

For the final notes, for the *Amen*, Rupert forgot to breathe. Mort tugged at the hem of his coat and Rupert dropped to his seat, still staring at the organist. When he realized that Mort had noticed and was looking in the same direction, Rupert closed his hymnal with a snap, folded his arms and concentrated on the pastor.

"Well, I'll be damned," his sergeant declared as they walked out of the church, passing the Reverend Mr. Jorgens without exchanging a word and avoiding every curious well-wisher in their path until they reached the road and could escape to the safety of a brisk cadence back to the house.

"Probably," Rupert replied.

"That's her, ahn't it? That's the one you've been hankering after." When his companion remained silent, Mort clicked an appreciative one-sided smile and winked again. "Ay-yuh. Mighty fine-looking woman too. Sort of skinny though, not much for a man to depend on."

"Who are you talking about?"

"That little songbird, kept flirting with you like all get-out, doing her best to get your undivided attention. If I didn't know better, I'd say you weren't interested."

"I'm not."

"Can't fool me, Rupe. Hard as you try, I know better."

Noam Snyder pulled up on the reins, bringing the old buggy alongside Cathryn's side yard, tipping his cap and wiping beads of sweat from his brow. "Mighty hot for a lady to be working like that," he called out to his tenant.

"Now's the best time," she called back, straightening her back, pressing a dirty hand on her lower spine. "These pumpkins won't win any prizes this year unless someone gives them a hand." She wiped her neck with a handkerchief and wacked at the weeds in her pumpkin patch. "I swear these dandelions know I've got better things to do. They just grow out of spite."

"Pesky things, but make mighty fine wine, when Lila has a mind."

"I'll save what I can for her." She set aside Monday mornings for yardwork. Tuesday morning for cleaning. Wednesdays had once taken her to the Smith house. And, when she could, Thursday morning, her one free day of the week, the coach to Portland waited at the corner of the village square.

"Guess you heard Rupert Smith's come home."

"Yes. I saw him at church."

"Guess there'll be no need for you to be tending that old house now, will there?"

"Guess not," she answered, turning the hoe side-down to scrape weeds from around the smaller pumpkins on the vines.

"He know all the work you did for his folks?"

"No and there's no call for you to go yapping about it either." She straightened and wiped her forehead with the back of her hand. "I suppose Mrs. Moffatt will go blathering when she gets a chance."

"Don't look like he's much in the mood for comp'ny. Walked straight out of the service, straight past all the folks waiting to welcome him back, like some high and mighty."

"Noam, you know better. Mr. Smith isn't like that."

"Guess not but he sure is acting like it." He tsked at his horse, flicking the reins just enough to urge the mare to lift its head.

"He must have a lot on his mind with his folks passing away like that and the house left empty."

"We'll soon find out. Good day to you, Cathryn. I'll be by soon enough to fix that roof."

"I'll have the rent money ready." Her back ached but there were another two rows to hoe and the string beans needed tying up again. Cathryn stretched her shoulders back, twisted her waist a few times and went back to the patch.

If there was anyone in the village who did not know that Cathryn Marcher had been housekeeper, gardener, cook and laundress for the Smiths, she could not name her or him. A simple question to any one of a score of people would let George Rupert Smith in on the secret, not that her relationship to them had ever been a secret. His great-grandfather had a passion for her landlord's great-grandmother and his mother was the cousin of Allan Giles's wife. Cathryn's parents, John and Hazel, attended the same Bible Study class as George and Margaret Smith and shared their abhorrence of slavery, working secretly with abolitionists to assist the Underground Railroad.

When John and Hazel passed away, George and Margaret had already lost contact with Rupert. In a manner of speaking, they adopted her—not to take his place but perhaps to assuage their loneliness and fear. Cathryn welcomed their dependence on her—to compensate for her own loss or so she pretended. Being close to them, brought her closer, at least in an ethereal notion, to Rupert.

She had not been one of the giggly, gushing girls who waved good-bye to the soldiers and their lieutenant on their way to war. But she had been one of the letter-writing club who penned missives every week to their boys from Oslo Hill, knitting gloves and scarves unceasingly through the first winter. Her first letter to Rupert Smith earned ridicule and constant humiliation from the letter-writing and glove-knitting girls' club of the Hill. When the war failed to end in the spring, the club banned Cathryn from ever writing again for fear her letters were depressing the soldiers' spirits with their high tone of nobility and sacrifice.

Other than one absurd letter and, since he had never acknowledged receipt of the letter at any time, Cathryn fervently hoped her words were lost and forgotten.

"They don't want to hear such flappery. They want news of home and such, like stories of how the chickens got into the steeple," Susan had told her in front of the other girls.

"Goodness, yes," Nancy Coffin had laughed. "All this swooning and chatter about grand ideals, I'm sure any brave man would choke on every silly word of it."

Why moments like this always came back to her when she was most peaceful she accounted to her parents. For John and Hazel, amassing praise and wealth belonged to heaven, the true home of every good soul. While she did not disagree, at times a contented moment had its place. Even if it was while a body was chopping wood and wishing one or the other of those girls' head was on the block.

At that instant, the head of her axe flew off and Cathryn hit the block with only the handle. The strike reverberated along her arms and the kick back came so fierce, she lost her balance. She cried out, cursed and flopped to the ground on her backside, cradling her upper body. Hearing a horse trotting up the road from town, she pushed to her feet, found the axe head poking out of a surface root and worked it back and forth to free it.

"Unorthodox," a man's voice commented, "but you always were one for getting to the root of a problem."

Cathryn stared at the heel of the axe, steeling her nerve to gain control of the giggly gushing girl before turning to look at Rupert Smith, leaning forward over his horse's neck, grinning down at her.

Though she had an angry retort ready, she ripped at the axe head and wiped it on her pant leg.

"Fine day, Miss Marcher."

"Fine day to you, as well, Mr. Smith."

She went back to her work but the axe was good for nothing and she put the chopping aside to finish when she had time to repair the tool, not for the first time. Half expecting and half hoping he would leave, Cathryn turned back to hoeing the patch though that job had been finished soon after Noam went up the road to his farm.

Rupert dismounted and picked up the pieces of the axe. "Mind if I have a turn at mending this for you?"

"There's no need, Mr. Smith, but thank you. I've mended that a few times before now."

"All the more reason for me to offer."

"If you've a mind to, it wouldn't be neighborly to refuse. The tool box is over there, on the porch."

"It won't be much good without a new handle. This one is all shot to——. Been repaired once too often, I reckon."

While he hunted around her porch for a suitable replacement, Cathryn dug around her pumpkins, doing her best not to undo the work she'd completed earlier in the day. He had come from town, still dressed in frock coat and trousers, not work clothes. She wore her father's old pants, suspenders and a plaid lumberjack's shirt. He sat on the porch steps, whittling at a tree branch she hadn't gotten around to chopping, stripping what was left of the bark and shaping the handle as if he'd always been a woodsman.

"I'm surprised to see you working like this, Miss Marcher."

"Why?" She straightened her back, resting an arm on the upturned hoe to frown at him.

"I'd have thought, with you being the organist, you'd be concerned about hurting those talented hands of yours."

"I'm not afraid of a little work, Mr. Smith."

"Most ladies——." He met her stern gaze for a moment. "You think I'm rude," he chuckled. "Maybe so. I beg your pardon, Miss Marcher. I'm not accustomed to conversing with anyone, let alone young ladies."

"Most folks have some trouble getting used to the way I do things. This is my home, Mr. Smith, who else will do my work?"

"No gentleman in the village to offer?"

"Most men have their own yardwork to keep them from bothering me," she replied, hanging the hoe on the back wall of the house. "I'm making a pot of coffee. You're welcome to a cup if you want one."

"Much obliged, whittling is thirsty work." He set the handle aside and took up the whetstone, sharpening the axe while she shoved more wood in the firebox of the range.

Somehow, she could not remember Rupert Smith talking like a working man. Had she ever spoken to him to know? By the time he had enlisted and she had been befriended by his parents, she might have heard him talking with one of the village men, or Allan Giles. This tone and pattern of speech was more like Noam Snyder and the lumbermen who came every fall to clear the woods. George Smith had served as a Justice of the Peace. He always spoke in a professional, cultured manner. The war had changed Rupert Smith in more ways than one.

The expression she had seen the first time she saw him after his return was still there, guarded but lingering.

"You're probably wondering what I'm doing up this way."

"I wasn't," she answered. "A gentleman has a right to travel any road he chooses in this county."

His short laugh was more sarcastic than amused. Cathryn dried her hands and set the kettle on the range. She worked the lid off the tin of fresh ground coffee, inhaling deep of the fragrance while she scooped out enough for a small pot.

"I'll tell you anyway," he said, standing outside the back door, leaning on the frame, his hands shoved into his trouser pockets. "I'm headed up to Snyder's to ask him a few questions that no one else in town seems to have any information about. While I'm here, I wonder if you can help me."

"I'll try, but Noam is the fountain of all knowledge up this way. And Lila, of course."

"My parents wrote me a few times during the war.... Most of the letters didn't reach me until the whole nightmare was over, but they mentioned a woman who was helping them with the house. I've asked near everyone in town and up here, but no one seems to know her."

"Odd," she murmured.

"That's what I thought. Every blessed time someone cuts a tree back, this village is talking about it, but ask about a woman helping two elderly people, it's like asking them to pull out their own teeth with a set of rusty pliers."

She laughed aloud, covered her mouth with her fingertips and set the pot on the table. She put a few biscuits and a jar of jam in the center, on a chipped china plate.

"Did they ever mention her, talk about her to you? Maybe you might have run across her? Name of Evie."

Cathryn thought while she laid cutlery and poured two cups of coffee. "No, Mr. Smith, your parents would not have talked to me about her." She held out the plate and cup to him, sorry to see disappointment in his expression.

"Seems she's just gone. Disappeared."

Cathryn carried her cup of coffee to the edge of the back porch and sat down, planting her feet on the ground. "I wish I could help, Mr. Smith."

"I was hoping to thank her."

"Might be she'd be the sort who wouldn't have wanted thanking."

After a few moments, while he devoured the biscuits and jam and sipped his coffee, he said, "How long have you played the organ?"

"A few years. Mrs. Moffatt stopped when her husband passed away and her fingers got too stiff."

"Didn't you play the piano?"

After she had recovered from the surprise that he had ever noticed, she said, "I still do."

"And teach?"

"Yes, I teach sometimes. The children in the village."

"Pays well?"

"Mostly in exchange for what I need."

Rupert set his empty cup on the step and finished the biscuit. "Best damn jam I've had in years," he murmured, apparently unmindful of his language. "Will you be involved in the Summer Fete this year?"

"I usually attend. I help with the cooking and...the rest."

"And the dance? Do you dance?"

"When I have mind to do so."

"Don't you like to dance, Miss Marcher?"

"I've attended all the dances it's been my pleasure to *choose* to attend, Mr. Smith."

"Would that have been when you were in Boston?"

Cathryn glanced at him and looked away toward the pumpkin patch. "Yes, Mr. Smith."

"I'll keep that in mind," he said, rising from the step. Cathryn held her hand out to take the plate from him. He stared at her out-stretched hand, followed the lines of the three prominent veins from her wrist until they disappeared at the cuff of her work-worn shirt. "I'd best be on my way to Snyder's before I wear out my welcome. I've left my horse out the front. Hope that doesn't cause you any embarrassment, Miss Marcher."

"It shouldn't, Mr. Smith. Noam and Lila will be having their dinner about now. But, if you don't mind waiting half an hour outside, they'll welcome you."

"Have you already had your dinner, Miss Marcher, or have I kept you from it?"

"Neither. I don't order my activities according to a timepiece."

"Rebellion or independence?"

"Both," she answered.

He laughed, his headful of brown curls thrown back, laughing out loud, as though he had nothing in the world to worry him. Cathryn carried his plate and cup into the kitchen, wondering what she'd said this time that he found so amusing. How many other ways could she prove to be laughable? She set the dishes in the sink and worked the small pump.

"Thank you for the hospitality. I haven't had a taste of any home cooking as good as that since I left here. Much appreciated."

"You are welcome. Thank you for trying to mend the axe."

"I'll finish that job when I'm up this way again. I'll be going now."

She kept her back to him, painfully aware of the state of her clothes and the bird's nest of her hair. "I'm obliged, but there's no need. I can manage."

"Best be careful for now. That edge is sharpened up pretty fierce."

"I will. Thank you." The giggly, gushing girl fought every inch of the way to make a fool of her. She didn't want to be in the yard when Rupert Smith rode back toward town, but she was. A fine spring's day was too precious to waste hiding from a man just because some giddy girl couldn't act right. The Smiths' only son rode by without as much as a glance in her direction. *May be he didn't like what Noam told him.* She wielded her hoe between the rows of crookneck and patty-pan squash. *He's had his fun for the day.*

By the time the sun set over by the Falls, Cathryn was worn down to the bone. She drew all the curtains, closed and locked all the doors, heated some water from the well and took a bath in the little cold store by the pantry.

She had a lesson to prepare for the Sunday School and some cakes to frost for the social hour after the service, but after that, there was nothing to keep the giddy girl occupied. She set Cathryn's heart to racing every chance she had. To defend herself, Cathryn sat down at her desk in the narrow bedroom and opened the box containing the proof she—for once in her life—had been an admirable young woman who had won the devotion of another man. Though he had never captured her heart, she had given Jericho Colson all he needed.

Three

Damned pretty girl, looks good in those dungarees. Too good. Rupert swung his leg over the saddle and turned the horse he'd ridden since leaving the Cahaba prison camp, easing the ache as he rode past her property at a canter. The one couple who knew all there was to know about everyone and anyone in the county had no information about this woman, Evie, who haunted him, compounded his guilt about his parents' passing and proved his self-pity worthless.

On the first step of the house on Lincoln Street, Mort's deep voice halted Rupert's entry into the front hall. Another man spoke in a modulated tone. *The Reverend Jorgens.* Rupert took a long drag on the pine-scented air and stepped toward the sliding doors of the back parlor. He hesitated as his hand reached for the handle at the sound of a woman's voice. *Susan.* The thump of his boot heels had announced his arrival.

"That must be Rupert now," Susan Miller said.

"Might be," Mort replied. "Could be the cook."

Before Rupert could escape, Susan exclaimed, "That's his horse out front, isn't it? I was *certain* I heard that majestic animal's hoof beats coming along the street."

Rupert removed his wide-brimmed hat and tossed it over the newel post before he slid the door aside. Striding toward the widow, he bowed over her extended hand, supporting it with his index finger but did not kiss her wrist though she held her hand in expectation. Instead, he withdrew his support and turned toward the pastor.

"To what do Morton and I owe this honor, sir?"

"A neighborly visit, Captain Smith. Mrs. Moffatt and I had intended to express the good wishes and joy of the residents of our little village at your safe return. However, Mrs. Moffatt was unavoidably detained and Mrs. Miller graciously offered to speak on the elder lady's behalf."

"Thank you. Both," he added, bowing toward the widow. "There was no need for such formality, I assure you. Mort and I are well accustomed to the village by now, but we do appreciate your gesture."

"Mrs. Miller was just telling me about the Summer Fete. Seems you and the lady make a fine show of singing duets for the entertainment of the folks hereabouts."

"Ten years ago, perhaps."

"Oh, Rupert, please don't slight your wonderful voice. I'm sure with a little practice——."

"Reverend, has Sergeant Pierce offered you any refreshment? Mrs. Miller, may I get you a cooling beverage?"

"Thank you, Captain Smith," Mr. Jorgens replied, "but I will have to return to my duties soon. The church wardens' meeting is this evening."

"I regret I was detained," Rupert replied. "My inquiry regarding a personal matter took longer than I expected."

"Ah yes, I was told you had visited our organist earlier."

"Were you?" Rupert glanced at Mort who could not have known any of his movements that morning. His sergeant shrugged and shifted his long legs.

"Very little happens along this road that someone in the village doesn't see and report, Captain," Mr. Jorgens chuckled. "We have vigilant angels who watch over us."

"That must give you all a deep sense of security."

"Most assuredly, Captain. Very much so." The pastor rose to his feet, clasping his low-crowned felt hat with both hands. "I regret we did not have a longer chat."

"As am I," Rupert answered, extending his hand to assist Susan Miller to stand. "Perhaps another time, Mrs. Miller."

"Oh—. Of course," Susan sighed, gathering the narrow skirt of her afternoon dress, smoothing the ruffles of black lace. "I sincerely hope we will be able to renew our success as a duet, Rupert. The people of the village so enjoyed our efforts."

"If you wish, Mrs. Miller."

"Of course, this will also benefit poor Cathryn."

"How so?"

"Miss Marcher depends," Mr. Jorgens offered, "on her earnings from musical instruction, Captain Smith, and has since her parents were taken from us, as well as the meager stipend the church can offer for her contribution as organist."

"Our church would be the poorer without her," Susan agreed, flicking the slats of her ivory fan together.

"Seems to me," Mort grumbled, planting his big feet on the floor and rising to his full height.

Before he continued, Susan responded with a tinkling laugh, "If only you knew, Sergeant Pierce." With a flounce of her underskirt, she sashayed to the parlor door with the pastor close behind her.

When their peace was restored, Rupert thumped his former sergeant in the shoulder and walked out of the room after their guests had left the porch.

"Guess your search didn't go according to plan," Mort mumbled as his friend climbed the staircase.

"No. It did not."

"You'll find her, Rupe."

"If she even existed."

Cathryn's Wednesday afternoon pupils, the Snyders' two young daughters, waited their turn to sit at the piano in the front room of the farmhouse, swinging short legs and fidgeting while Lila's biscuits baked in the oven and the aroma of fresh lemonade distracted them. Only Prissy had any real desire to play the piano. Polly tolerated the lessons for the reward of biscuits, cream and a tall glass of sweet lemonade their mother had waiting for Miss Marcher when the hour was over.

"How many eggs will you be wanting this week, Cathryn?" Lila asked as soon as the girls were out of the way and the two women had settled at the kitchen table with their glasses of lemonade.

"I will be baking cakes, so a dozen should do this week."

"Cakes? Rupert Smith a'calling?"

"He won't be calling again," Cathryn replied, taking a long drink to conceal her consternation.

"I'd not be so sure. He seems determined to make your acquaintance as far as I can see."

"He's making the acquaintance of all the villagers."

"Hear tell he's striking up with Susan Miller again."

"That's natural. They were almost engaged before the war, weren't they?"

"To hear Susan tell it, that's the way of it. I never heard George or Peggy say a word about such a thing and you know how a mother likes to think she'll have some grandchildren in the future. I'd stake another half dozen eggs on the Smiths wanting Rupert to come home and get hitched to someone else."

"Nancy Coffin? They were always partial to their cousins."

"You are a caution, Cathryn Marcher."

"Why do you say that?"

"Even a blind man could see Rupert Smith is no more hankering after Nancy Coffin than Missus Uppity Miller." Lila leaned back and searched the hallway for her daughters.

"I know that is uncharitable toward a widow but I've seen how she plays on that for sympathy."

"You have a right to speak your mind."

"But you won't be speaking yours on that subject."

"She is my pupil, and my friend."

Megan Giles scooted into the empty seat next to Cathryn as the Sunday School pupils gathered in the room at the side of the church hall. Pastor Jorgens led the prayer to begin the class and left to finish preparation for the service. Cathryn pushed sheets of drawing paper to the center of the low table and asked Aurelius Cook, as the eldest, to give all the children a box of colored chalk. Megan dragged her box to her side but did not take a sheet of the flimsy manila paper.

After she had simplified the pastor's sermon as the lesson of the day, Cathryn took one of the youngest girls into her lap to help her translate the lesson into a picture to give her parents. Megan folded her arms across her chest and glared at the younger girl until she had finished the drawing.

"Why aren't you drawing, Megan? You draw so well."

"Mama and Papa say I need to be taught how to draw well. Will you teach me?"

"I don't draw very well either," Cathryn murmured.

"But you helped *her*."

"The lesson is more important than how you draw." Even though that was true, Cathryn had no faith that either Allan or Nancy would appreciate their daughter's effort to interpret the lesson she had heard. "Drawing is like music, Megan. It is to be enjoyed and practiced, not judged." She plucked a sheet of paper from the pile and chose a blue chalk stick. "Draw anything you want, Megan. Take pleasure in the feel of the movement of your hand."

The child scratched across the paper, back and forth, until the sheet ripped. "I spoiled it! I told you I couldn't draw."

"There is plenty of paper," Cathryn said, laying several sheets in front of her student. Megan chose another color and her teacher beckoned Prissy Snyder to help prepare the lemonade and cakes for refreshment.

"Good morning, Cathryn."

Her back stiffened. "Good morning, Mr. Giles." Annoyed with his persistent familiarity and demands for her servility, as someone he employed, Cathryn turned her attention to her task. Prissy folded napkins on a tray. Cathryn laid her hands flat on the edge of the pantry counter when Megan crept toward her. She gave the seven-year-old a nod and the child stacked cups from the cabinet on another tray.

"Be careful you don't drop those," her father warned.

"Megan and I do this all the time, Mr. Giles!" Prissy squealed, dancing away to the table. Megan gripped her tray and followed with slow steps.

"You have worked your spell on her," Allan murmured, "as you have on me."

"I work no spells, Mr. Giles." Cathryn moved to put the children's table between them, thankful he made no effort to follow.

"If I didn't have the church council, I would stay to help you, but duty calls, Cathryn, as ever. Megan, do remember that you will join your mother after Sunday School."

"I will, Papa."

His excuse for interrupting Cathryn's class turned her back on her father and offered a cup to the youngest girl.

Although he was too early for the council meeting, Allan turned away on his heel. Since the day he had informed her she was homeless and without inheritance—a pauper—he had not spent more than three minutes in her company. Her poverty was an embarrassment to him but his attraction to her was not. Cathryn stared after him for a moment, eyes narrowing.

Aurelius, the eldest boy in the village and the leader in the class, only slightly shorter than his teacher, rapped his knuckles on the table. "Miss, we're waiting for you to say *Grace*."

Her thoughts at that moment were neither graceful nor generous. She credited Allan Giles with his efforts to find Rupert after the death of his mother and father, but she did not credit him with any chivalry. He had married well, within weeks of her refusal to accept his proposal and departure for Boston to serve as an auxiliary nurse in Timothy Wellington's military hospital[7].

"Which of you will say *Grace*?"

"But, Miss…" several of the children said together.

"I will," Megan Giles declared, folded her hands and bowed her head.

Nine of the children followed her example as Megan repeated the thanksgiving they had heard spoken at their family meals all their young lives. Cathryn pressed her fingers together, meeting Aurelius's glare. The fourteen-year-old huffed and did the same, muttering "Amen" with the others. Cathryn kept her gaze lowered for a moment, saying her own silent prayer in memory of the many whose lives ended despite her care and one short thanksgiving for the life of one man spared and returned to his home.

Mrs. Moffatt greeted members of the congregation as she entered the sanctuary, striding along the aisle to her family pew. Once seated, she continued to greet those who followed in her wake. She occupied the pew in solitude, presiding over the assembled villagers while they awaited the arrival of their children from Sunday School and the entrance of the pastor.

---

[7] **Timothy Wellington** set up a hospital in Worcester, MA for wounded and ill soldiers in 1862.

Prissy led the children in single file from the stairway into the foyer and dispersed her charges to their parental care. Aurelius slid into the back pew as their teacher took her place at the organ in the loft.

Rupert, slouched in the far corner of the balcony above the sanctuary, took a long look at people who had aged since the last time he had seen them, recalling the four-year-old Aurelius Cook throwing mud at the pretty Prissy Snyder when she toddled into his play fort and stepped on one of his stick soldiers. Today, the boy was old enough to join the army. The boy's sister, Mary, walked into the sanctuary on the arm of a young man who, judging from his bearing, had once been a military man.

In a few years, Prissy would be thinking of a husband and would have an easier time finding a man fit for the purpose than Allan's maid. While the young man bore himself with pride, his weary expression mirrored Rupert's own. He'd seen death, stared into the depths of evil, seen his own vicious soul and wondered daily why he had survived. With luck, Mary's sweet generosity had shone some light on the darkness tormenting her beau. Otherwise, she was condemned to go into the depths with him.

The congregation rose as one to their feet as the organist played the first bars of the processional hymn. While she was occupied, Rupert left the balcony to follow the pastor and wardens, one of whom was Allan Giles, into the church from the foyer. He dropped into the last pew next to Aurelius and nodded to his sergeant in the pew on the opposite side of the aisle. He winked in response to Morton's frown, glanced at the procession, taking note of Allan's interest in the organist in the loft, perched above them all.

Mrs. Moffatt sang the uplifting hymn, happily swaying with enthusiasm for the tune as the organist played. Cathryn's musical ability imbued every muscle in her body with enjoyment, singing the chorus as she played.

Several moments passed before Rupert noticed that Susan Miller gestured, with growing irritation, for him to join her. She too glanced up at the organ loft, an annoyed wrinkle marring her brow.

A quick glance at Mort and a nod brought the two men to the widow's pew, one on either side of her. Rupert sang in harmony with her, relieved that the hymn had seven verses and an equal number of opportunities for Cathryn to sing the chorus. When the organist sang, he lowered his voice to hear her interpretation, harmonizing with her contralto range. At the same time, his pew companion raised her soprano voice but Rupert was deaf to her effort, tuning his hearing as he had learned to do in battle, to the voice he must hear to complete his mission.

As the hymn came to an end and the pastor raised his hands to signal the congregation to sit, Susan Miller huffed, sweeping her purple underskirt away from Morton's leg. Rupert shuttled a few inches further toward the aisle to avoid her dress, grateful for the excuse. Susan's widened eyes and sudden gasp, was strangely satisfying. Her glance up at the organ loft and immediate frown was not.

Though church was not the place to express his displeasure with Susan Miller née Hamlin, he could not resist the wink over the top of her head that brought a chuckle from Morton.

Though he listened respectfully to the pastor, when the service came to an end, he hustled Susan Miller to the church hall. The young widow jostled her way through the churchgoers toward the pastor, turning only as she reached the clergyman and his wife to scowl back at Rupert. He tipped his finger at his forehead at her and turned his attention to the organist, now serving at the refreshment table. Even though she seemed reluctant to serve him, Rupert persisted.

"Is this, by any chance, one of your cakes, Miss Marcher?" Rupert leaned closer, speaking in a normal tone.

"I don't believe it is, Mr. Smith." She moved away, coming face to face with Mrs. Moffatt.

"Do not believe a word of that, Rupert," the elder woman said over Cathryn's shoulder. "This young woman makes the best Sour Cherry Cake in the whole of Oxford County, if not the State of Maine."

Despite Cathryn's embarrassment, Mrs. Moffatt continued her praise for the young woman until Cathryn sought refuge in the kitchen. The dowager continued serving cake and coffee in Cathryn's place, scowling at Rupert when he smiled in the direction of the kitchen.

"Mind your manners, young man," she murmured. "You have already caused enough harm where Cathryn Marcher is concerned."

"How is that, Mrs. Moffatt? I mean to cause no injury to Miss Marcher or any other."

Mrs. Moffatt studied him for several moments. "You have changed, Rupert. War changes all who are concerned, women as well. Mind how you proceed."

"With utmost caution, I assure you." His beatific smile was meant to assure her but she rapped him on the wrist with her widow's fan.

"Miss Marcher has seen enough trouble for one so young and good-hearted, sir."

"Oh, Mrs. Moffatt, I'm sure Captain Smith has meant no harm at all where our dear, poor Cathryn is concerned."

Although the defense of his action was welcome, the source was as hurtful as if he had himself slighted the young woman. He stood as straight as Amos's plumb line[8] and turned on the speaker, ready to inform her he was capable of being his own character witness when the object of the exchange returned to the church hall, laden with a tray of

---

[8] **Amos's plumb line** proved spirituality and morality were genuine.

more cake plates. Recognizing a better course, Rupert offered to take the burden from Cathryn.

To his surprise, she accepted his offer and returned to the kitchen. Rupert, eyebrows raised, turned to Mrs. Moffatt for guidance.

"Follow me."

Rupert turned on his heel and presented the tray of cakes to the elderly women and men seated around the trestle table at the side of the hall. One man raised a trembling hand but his grip was too weak to grasp the plate. Rupert accomplished the task with one hand, rescuing the whole tray once the gentleman had his dessert under control.

"I have great hopes for you, Rupert Smith."

"In what way, Mrs. Moffatt?"

"Men of your spirit are rare."

"I regret to say you over rate my character, Mrs. Moffatt." Again, he turned on his heel, setting the empty tray on the nearest table, and strode out of the hall, leaving Mort behind.

Mrs. Moffatt gazed after him for a moment before she followed Cathryn into the church kitchen.

"He's a handsome man, I'll admit. Not as handsome as my Tom, in anyway, but still more than worthy of a good study."

Cathryn continued in her task.

"I have never believed you were shy, Cathryn. This man has a peculiar effect on you, my dear, as you have on him. If you want my opinion—."

"Thank you, Mrs. Moffatt, I appreciate your interest but I am not in need of advice."

"Excellent. I am about worn out with my sons on that score. Cathryn, my dear, I have nearly forgotten. You know that you have promised to accompany me to this opera in Portland. I hope you remember."

"I do, Mrs. Moffatt, I am delighted you asked."

"Nonsense. No one in my family would condescend to keep me company on such an adventure. You are the only creature who would understand the thrill of such a night in the theater."

"I thank you all the same."

"I hope you will feel the same afterwards. Now, come away from that sink and sit with me over a cup of coffee and your delicious cake."

Only a few of the older members remained in the hall, chatting amongst themselves as they cleared the tables rather than go to their empty homes. When all the dishes were washed and all the tables cleared, Cathryn bid farewell to the elders and began her walk to her cabin, pleasantly surprised to meet Sergeant Morton Pierce at the church drive's juncture with the road.

"Before you ask, Miss Marcher, I am at liberty as my friend has been detained."

"At liberty?"

"To escort you home, Miss."

"That is very kind of you, Sergeant Pierce, but as you can see, I have company enough to see me home although your company is also welcome."

"You are most gracious, Miss Marcher. More so than some of your neighbors."

Cathryn had no need to ask of whom the war veteran spoke. As she took the arm Morton offered, Allan Giles raised his buggy lash to encourage the mare along the road toward his family's home but raised no hand in greeting to his daughter's teacher nor to the sergeant. Ahead of them, the Widow Miller strolled across the street on the arm of Morton's friend.

"It's not what you think, Miss."

"I have no thoughts on the matter, Sergeant Pierce. Mrs. Miller is at liberty like anyone else in this village, to keep company with whomever she chooses."

"That may be as you say, but I know someone who is not as fortunate," Morton murmured.

"Don't they make a handsome couple?" one of the older women in the walking cadre said to another. "Few are so suited to one another. I'm sure we all agree on that."

The consensus was as she expected among the elders as each departed at the walkway to their respective homes. When the Lincoln Street sidewalk ended and all the elderly had been dispersed, Morton clasped his companion's elbow to steady her footing on the narrowed road to the chicken farm.

"There's more than one here don't agree with that lady."

"Underestimating the opinion of an elder is unwise, Sergeant Pierce."

"Name's Morton, Miss. Mort for short and it'd do me an honor to be considered a friend."

"Thank you. I am honored as well." At the boundary of her rented property, Cathryn asked, "If you have no plans for your Sunday dinner, Morton, Mort, will you join me? I cannot offer a sumptuous meal, not even a repast adequate to your requirements, but you are most welcome."

"Thank you, Miss Marcher—."

"Cathryn."

"Now that will surely rile someone," Mort laughed. "Any time or meal spent in your company, Cathryn, will be elegant beyond dreams." He bowed from the waist and followed her to the front door of her cabin, which he left open for the sake of propriety.

"I know of no one who could be in the least riled by our friendship, Morton."

"I can name several, a few of whom have witnessed your passage through the village from time to time and—."

"Please, Morton, do me the kindness of keeping such things to yourself. I cannot be made responsible for the feelings or wishes of others of which they have not made me aware."

Mort cocked the side of his mouth with a click and a wink. "Well said, Miss. I will honor your request with pleasure. Great pleasure, in fact."

The company suited Rupert's mood not at all. The crystal schooner of Madeira turned on his palate with a gag reflex. Something as simple as a Sunday dinner was roiling through him as though he stood at the gate of a cemetery containing the corpses of all the men he had seen die. The Miller House reeked of all he disliked about the self-satisfaction of those who consider themselves superior. He preferred the stench of the barn, the fragrance of the open range, coffee boiled too long on an open fire. He preferred the work of fashioning an axe handle to drafting a defense brief.

Allan Giles regaled his wife and his hostess with the details of his latest legal triumph. Rupert stood near the parlor window, half turned away, regretting his acceptance of Susan's invitation to join them. If not for his haste to escape Mrs. Moffatt's enthusiasm for his return, he would be walking toward his parents' house, in good company with his friend and perhaps the owner of that broken axe who passed a few minutes before.

Besides that young woman who passed, laughing and chatting happily in the company of Mort Pierce and the older citizens to whom he had served her sour cherry cake, the one other person he might have found some interest in having a conversation with, Megan Giles, had been sent home in the company of the Giles's maid, Mary Cook and her young man.

Four

As a stranger, as a man no one in his present company knew, Rupert longed to get back to the place he was only known as Rupe Smith, a cowboy, a ranch hand, a good man to have on your side in a fight, working the herd he and his friends had bought on the land they owned together. Selling his parents' house was the key step, in respect for them, to take his life in his own hands as they had done. He owed them a good life, a future, not the slow death Oslo Hill now offered.

Much as he resisted a public acknowledgment, Mort had been right. There was no future for him, no happiness, without this confrontation with his former existence. Leaving this to linger, to fester beneath the surface, without resolution, never knowing exactly that his future was not in this place could never release him.

He had still to find this woman his parents had willed many of their possessions to and make good on their wishes. Other than that, nothing else kept him in Oslo Hill.

"Dearest Rupert, you are distinctly quiet," Susan cooed as she clasped his elbow. "Was Pastor Jorgens's sermon so moving or is Allan's tale particularly riveting?"

"Neither, Mrs. Miller—."

"Oh, please. Surely we have been friends long enough for you to call me by the name you once found so comfortable."

"I remember no such name, Mrs. Miller."

"You have been away such a very long time, Rupert, that I hesitate to remind you—."

"I have no wish to cause any distress, Mrs. Miller. As you say, I have been away for many years. We will both be more comfortable if we do not struggle to recover the past." Rupert turned toward the rest of company. Allan swung a decanter from his hand, beckoning his former classmate to join him on the far side of the room.

"No law says a man can't do as he pleases in the privacy of a friend's home on a Sunday afternoon."

Nancy joined her hostess on the settee looking onto the street. Rupert took the drink as the two women leaned their upper bodies closer to one another and Nancy shielded her face from his scrutiny as she murmured something to the widow. Allan cleared his throat and his wife leaned away, glancing over her shoulder at her husband.

"Women's gossip matters very little but they will have their say about others whose circumstances are somewhat less advantaged."

"Of whom do you speak, Allan?"

"No one of whom you need to concern yourself, my friend. Their jealousy is of no consequence to superior minds and talents."

Rupert savored another sip of whiskey. "You've done well for yourself, Allan."

For a moment, Giles stared over the heads of the two women, at the street beyond the window. "There are many ways to be a hero, a servant of our country. You were always destined for the battlefield. I have been destined for the courtroom."

"You will have no argument from me. I meant only what I said. If I had known sooner what I was destined for before the war, it might have made sense to me."

"Tell me what your plans are now you're selling the house."

"Most of them depend on what I can get for the place and the woodlands but I've...seen some land in Wyoming—a ranch." He looked down at his Eastern clothing, a fraud when he was more comfortable now in plaid and denim, a wide-brimmed hat and neckerchief, running a finger around the inside of his collar. Damned necktie. Damned ankle boots. Damned eastern saddle.

"Sounds ambitious," Allan commented, swishing the whiskey around in his crystal glass. "Sounds like you. Steer roping, cattle drives, six shooters."

"You've been reading too many of those tall western tales."

"I've never had a reason to kill a man, Rupert, but I can imagine it takes some kind of rage, an insanity."

Rupert was spared having to make a response when the housekeeper tapped on the door, admitted only after a suitable pause, and announced that the meal awaited them.

"Thank you, Jessie," the lady of the house replied.

Every instinct in Rupert's body resisted the engrained response but the sense of chivalry was stronger and he crossed the room to offer his assistance as Allan presented his hand to his wife. The table had been set formally but with no one seated at the head of the table. Susan's place at the foot was also unoccupied and she took the place next to the seat Jessie indicated for Rupert. Remembering his best manners, he held the chair for her, giving her a curt bow as he waited for Nancy to be seated beside her husband and opposite him.

After Rupert realized they expected him to do so and he declined the honor, Allan bowed his head but it was some moments before he said *Grace*. Sympathetic sighs from the ladies accompanied the momentary silence. He doubted Mort had been subjected to any such expectation, if he was fortunate to spend the afternoon with Miss Cathryn Marcher, with whom, both he and Allan Giles, preferred to be at that moment. Allan extended the *Grace* until Jessie's son brought the roast into the room.

As the boy served the slices of pork roast, Allan snapped his napkin into his lap. "Susan, what songs are you preparing for the Summer Fete?"

"I have not, as yet, decided. There are a several we are considering. One is a duet."

"With Cathryn? As your teacher, of course."

"Oh no, it is a duet for…two voices. A male voice is required."

"Our Megan is also preparing a contribution with Cathryn's help."

"As you would expect, of course, since she is paid to do so. I enjoy the opportunity to offer my meager talent as entertainment, to show my gratitude to my fellow parishioners."

"Miss Marcher is your singing teacher?" Rupert asked.

"Well, yes, she is. One does what one can to help her, of course, after that…episode in Boston."

Allan's jaw hardened.

"That 'episode' was only a rumor, of course, but one can't help—," Nancy began.

"What do either of you know of it?" Allan demanded. "Through the entire wretched mess, you were nicely coddled in your parents' mansions, knitting useless mittens for soldiers."

"Some of those mittens came in handy, Allan," Rupert interjected.

"For what? Cleaning gun barrels? Wadding for the cannons?"

"That is hardly just." Susan folded her napkin. "We all did what we could to help, some went a tad too far."

"Far as in distant," Nancy cajoled her husband.

"Neither of you have any better occupation than to belittle and gossip," Allan replied, patting his wife's hand. "And that is as it should be. Delicate as you are."

"Rupert, I could not help but notice that you still have a fine voice. And a wonderful ear for harmonizing—quite naturally."

"One of the few abilities not driven out by necessity," he replied.

"And which duet has Cathryn suggested you attempt?" Allan asked.

"A Schubert song. Or is it Schumann? One of the German masters."

"I am not at all surprised. Cathryn is a gifted musician, knowledgeable. She puts most of us to shame, does she not?"

"I wouldn't say that, Allan. I may not have spent three years in Boston, but I have a considerable knowledge of suitable music for an audience."

"We have asked Miss Marcher to teach Megan the English words," Nancy said, glaring at the hand her husband clenched on the table. "Cathryn does get above herself at times."

"You seem to have put Mrs. Moffatt into a snit when you spoke to Cathryn, Rupert," Susan commented. "Whatever did you say to her favorite to upset her?"

"Rupert's conversations with Miss Marcher are of no concern to any of us, my dear Susan."

"Well, I beg to differ, Allan. Mrs. Moffatt seemed quite concerned. She is very protective of Cathryn, won't hear a word that isn't high praise for poor, dear Cathryn."

"The man who gets past Mrs. Moffatt will be special indeed. Ever since her parents died and even more so after your own parents passed away—how they doted on Cathryn when she returned from Boston," Nancy prattled. "All that charm and sophistication in our own little town. You would have thought she'd been to Europe on a Grand Tour as Susan did just before her marriage to dear departed Mr. Miller. The way everyone fell all over themselves to invite her to their homes. Half the men and all the boys were in love with her. But she'd have none of them. No Miss Marcher had set her sights very high indeed."

Not one pair of eyes ventured from her face as Nancy Giles spoke. Had Rupert see her husband's expression, he would have guessed if he hadn't already known, that Nancy was speaking for her husband's benefit.

"In fact, Mr. Smith, I mean *Captain* Smith, had you been here, I do believe you might well have been near enough to her expectations."

"I'm flattered you think so, Mrs. Giles."

"Nancy is exaggerating, Rupert. Cathryn Marcher is quite a typical unmarried woman, a bit eccentric as I mentioned, set in her spinster ways."

"Mr. Giles, my dear, you do Cathryn an injustice by such simplistic dismissals. She is a woman of the world, perhaps never married but certainly experienced in matters concerning—."

"We are in mixed company and you go too far."

"I'm interested to know, Mrs. Miller, if you are learning this song in German," Rupert interrupted.

"Of course, but I shall sing it for the village in English. As is proper for our part of the world. Although Cathryn insists it is better to sing a song in the language for which the music was written."

"There, you see, Mr. Giles, what better proof than that of Miss Marcher's sophistication?"

"I have never doubted her suitability as a teacher for amateur singers."

"It is a great pity, don't you agree, *Captain* Smith, that a young woman with so much to commend her, should be consigned to spinsterhood by war. In another time, Cathryn might well have been the first among us to be whisked away in marriage to a very great man. She most certainly had many offers, several young men of my acquaintance were madly in love with her but as I said earlier, her sites were set high. I am sure she would be the first to admit she is wasting away here, despite all her good and kind efforts to fill the lives of others with joy and contentment."

"You mean, to make amends for her behavior, don't you?" Susan added. "It appears to me that guilt is a prime motive for some women to make such efforts to please others."

Though tempted to rise to the defense of his neighbor and the author of his most treasured correspondence, Rupert contained his anger, drawing on his military training to reserve his energy for the real battle to come. What little sympathy he felt was for Allan whose embarrassment at his wife's vehemence toward a woman he so obviously admired was painful to witness. How often did his wife vent her bitterness in company regarding this teacher to take her vengeance on her husband was a matter for their private discussions. Rupert had no experience of such resentment to hazard a guess.

He stole a brief glance at the woman who counted herself among his most intimate group, mocking another woman to affect a prejudice in his mind against Cathryn while the wife of his friend, in an ill-disguised attempt to embarrass her husband, belittled the same woman. *They are jealous.* His mother's familiar admonishment of such behavior brought a thoughtful smile to his weary face and a chill to his heart. *Wyoming can't be this bad.* But he had no assurance that Wyoming residents were any different.

The meal was, for him, tasteless, as familiar as he was with range beef on a spit over an open fire.

"Thank you for your hospitality, Mrs. Miller, but I must get back to the house."

"Rupert."

He ignored that demand in her tone and scraped his chair back on the polished oak floor. His ankle boot heels had a less impressive stomp than his Army-issue Wellingtons but grabbing his hat from the rack served the purpose.

"Welll!"

Rupert answered Nancy Giles's exclamation with the tip of his finger to his brow and click of the door.

The Smith House was dark and silent when Rupert reached the porch. Mort was absent and the spring warmth had dissipated hours before. The walk he took through the woods around the village had not dissipated his resentment toward his friends. His first stop was at the door of his father's whiskey cabinet. The bottle of rye George Smith treasured was too good to waste on his mood and Rupert grabbed the cheapest scotch, splashed a slug into a jar in the kitchen and gulped it down.

He greeted Mort's return with a tip of the glass canning jar and waved him away when Mort stepped into the unlit front room. Before the big man disappeared up the stairs, Rupert asked, "Good time?"

Mort turned to look back, one foot on the first stair, sighed and shook his head and continued up to his room.

"No?"

Mort whirled around at the landing. "Guaranteed better 'an your'n, Rupe." He took two leaping steps down and pointed a finger as his former commanding officer. "Make a decision, Rupe. You're either in or you're out. You find this woman, give her this house and let's get back where we belong. Or," he growled, "don't. Stay here, make a mess of another ten years and break a bunch of hearts. Up to you."

Rupert gripped the glass jar hard but resisted the impulse to throw it at the wall. Instead, he gulped down the rest of the cheap whiskey and stood. "You're right."

"Which is it gonna be?"

"I'm finding this woman."

"Good. I'm gonna get some sleep."

"What did you two talk about all night?"

"Weren't you, if that's what you're worried about. Miss Marcher's too gracious to talk behind anyone's back."

Rupert looked down at his ankle boots and grinned. "Thought so."

Monday afternoon, Rupert walked into the entry hall of Allan's house and handed his wide-brimmed hat to Mary Cook. The maid bobbed a curtsey to him and, from the dance in her step as she retreated to the back hall, hanging his hat on the rack as she went, he figured she had passed a pleasant Sunday afternoon with her young man.

"What's his name?"

"Pardon, sir?"

"The soldier who accompanied you to church."

Mary blushed and nodded, a shy smile spreading over her pretty face.

"Is he looking for work?"

"Yes. Yes, he is."

"Send him 'round to my place. We'll talk."

"Thank you, Mr. Smith. Thank you."

"What's that about, Rupert? Are you attempting to poach my maid?" Allan held the office door open with one hand and beckoned his client to enter with the other. As Rupert crossed the threshold of the door, Allan shoved the door closed and strode to his desk.

"Not Mary, her young man. I'm going to need some strong backs to get the house ready for sale. That is, if I can't find this woman, Evie."

"If such a woman existed, I've assured you, I would have found her by now."

"So you've said. I'm not doubting your efforts, Allan. I just want to be certain, to honor my parents' last wishes. I'm sure you understand that."

"Of course, especially since you have taken such a long time to return. There must be some lingering guilt...I understand entirely," he added in a rush. "No one knows what you must have suffered in that prison camp. The horror of seeing——."

"No one knows," Rupert snapped. "Except those who were there, who fought for their country, who sacrificed all they had for what they believed was right." He glared at the sheer curtain rising on a breeze at the open window. *What were Cathryn's words?* For the good and the right of the greater—no matter now. "Why have you asked to meet me today?"

"I may have found a buyer for the house." The lawyer pushed documents around on his desk until he uncovered a bundle tied together with a red cotton ribbon. "This gentleman is also a war hero. And an attorney. He's looking for a house, exactly like yours, in this area. He's recently taken an appointment…Well, that's irrelevant. His wife is a native of a town nearby. One of the Springs or Falls in the area."

Taking the bundle in his hands, Rupert thumbed through the deeds of his parents' home without looking at them. "And?"

"I thought you'd want to make an assessment or consider his offer."

"There's a lot of work to be done. The place has been empty for more than five years."

"This gentleman doesn't seem too concerned about that."

"He's seen the house?"

"No, but——."

"I'll think about it." Rupert set the bundle on the edge of Allan's desk.

"There is someone here who'd like to see you."

Rupert glanced over his shoulder at the little girl peeking around the half-open door. Allan's indulgence of his daughter's intrusion raised his suspicions but the child had a bright, expectant smile, along with a fearful glance at her father.

"Well, Megan, what is it?"

Rupert stood and took a step toward the girl when her father's impatient question spoiled her excitement and she retreated into the hall.

"Have you interrupted our meeting for a purpose?"

"I'm sorry, Papa. Mama told me Mr. Smith had come to hear me sing."

"Well, then, Mr. Smith must be indulged, mustn't he?"

"I am delighted to listen, Miss Giles. Lead the way to your music studio."

"Oh, I don't have one of those, just a room," Megan murmured, opening the door to the back room and pointing at the small French grand in the middle of the room. "But Papa bought this for me."

"Didn't your mother have a piano, Rupert?"

"Yes," he replied with a sudden frown. "But I haven't seen it in the house."

"I wonder where it is now. I doubt anyone would have stolen such a large instrument."

"Hers was not as large as this. My father bought it for her from Boston, from a friend."

"Gilbert or Chickering[9], American-made, wasn't it?"

"I wouldn't know the maker," Rupert replied, approaching Megan's European-made parlor grand. "Mother was very proud of it." His frown deepened as a memory of his mother's enjoyment of the iron-frame square grand formed. "I wonder I hadn't noticed it was missing," he murmured.

"There's a reasonable explanation, I'm sure," Allan assured him as he flipped the hem of his broadcloth frock coat out of his way to sit to the side of his imported instrument.

---

[9] **Timothy Gilbert** and **Jonas Chickering** were 19th Century American pianoforte manufacturers.

"Miss Megan, if your father is willing, would you be so kind as to sing for me?"

The child glanced from one parent to the other, hovering at the door of the room. Both, for their own and separate reasons, were enthusiastic but Megan said, "I have no one to play for me. Miss Marcher isn't here."

"I will play for you, my darling," Nancy offered, gliding into the room. Taking a seat on the brocade bench, she spread Megan's song sheet against the mahogany music rack.

"But, Mama, I don't know the words."

"You have been practicing long enough. High time you performed, my dear."

"But Miss Marcher says…"

"Miss Marcher is paid to teach you," her father interrupted, "I would like to know what, if anything, she has taught you on all these jaunts to her lessons."

"Mr. Giles, perhaps it is not for lack of effort on Miss Marcher's part that your daughter is slow to learn."

"If you do not mind, Mrs. Giles," Rupert interjected, "I can play for Megan. I won't need her music."

"How gifted you must be, Mr. Smith. No wonder Cathryn is so taken with you."

"Nancy."

"It's quite apparent, Mr. Giles, she has set her cap at last."

"You must forgive my wife, Rupert. She has these flights of romantic fancy. Cathryn Marcher does not. If ever there was a colder, more antagonistic, less fanciful woman, I have never met one."

Rupert had replaced Nancy Giles at the parlor grand, raised his fingers above the keys as he read the music. As Megan squared her shoulders, standing beside him, he slid the sheet music aside so the child could more easily read the words. As Megan prepared, he read the notes her teacher had written in pencil to help her pupil understand the notation in all the tiny symbols of code that a child understood: spectacles, heart-shapes, rainbows. He played through the tune for his own benefit and nodded when he was ready.

While Megan drew a long breath and released it slowly, he played a few bars for introduction. The child's voice echoed in the cold room with the lullaby but the only person listening without an ulterior motive was her accompanist.

"Superb. Highly commendable, Miss Megan."

"There is no need to overstate, Rupert." Allan said without looking at his daughter. "I will have words with her teacher."

"Quite lovely, Megan, my dear," Nancy disagreed. "Miss Marcher has done a wonderful job and she would be proud. You perform very well."

Megan curtsied to her parents. "Thank you, Mama."

"Cathryn has worked a spell over you, my darling, but it is time for you to go to your room to rest. You have a full day at school tomorrow. You must not be over-excited and fail to sleep well."

"You coddle the child far too much."

As soon as the child had left the room, Rupert stood.

"No, sir, you will not go until you have told us more of this ranch you are purchasing in the west. A great adventurer is our Mr. Smith, Nancy, my dear. No small town will contain him. He has his sights on the wide expanse of our great purple plains. This intrepid explorer has a mind to conquer the continent."

"To accomplish that, I must be at my work, Allan. I intend to be away before the end of August."

"But you will not be here to celebrate Thanksgiving."

"Absurd notion, Nancy. Rupert can have no interest in this passing fashion. Why the ladies persist in honoring our dead President Lincoln's idea of giving thanks when it only creates more work for them and too often reminds us of our terrible losses, I fail to understand."

"As an opportunity to bring parted families and friends together, Mr. Giles, and to show our gratitude for all those who have sacrificed so much for our benefit. You will join us, Mr. Smith, won't you? And I think the time has come, high time, we showed our gratitude to others who lost and gave so much during that terrible time. Indeed, I will invite Miss Marcher tomorrow."

If there had been a time when Rupert had doubted he knew what was in any man's mind or heart, he knew he was wrong, meeting Allan Giles's gaze. There was rage and murder, as well as pain.

"I can make no promise, Mrs. Giles, but am grateful for your invitation. If I am still in residence, I will accept but there are many obstacles. I have commitments to others." He accepted his hat from Mary Cook's out-stretched hand, bowed to his host and strode out, through the village streets and up the rise to his own house where the tasks he had so far avoided demanded his attention.

Five

He lit the gas lamp on his father's desk in the back parlor and untied the cotton ribbon on the bundle Allan Giles had thrust into his hands on their first meeting. Warned by Allan what to expect, he sat back with the first letter, in order of receipt in Allan's office but not in order of postmark. He sorted them in order of his parents' writing, most written in the last year of the war, a few earlier while he fought in another unit, one from his commanding officer after his capture written at the end of the war and after his parents had died and one final one in a hand he recognized, postmarked a week after his father's death.

He read them all in the order they had been written to have a sense of what their lives had been like when his only concern had been for his own life and survival.

How happy we are to know you are safe.

Delighted to hear you will be home on leave, even for a short time.

How proud we are.

How much we miss your wit and good humor.

You must not blame yourself that we will not see you as soon as we hoped.

Sad news for us at home. You will remember Mr. & Mrs. Marcher and perhaps their daughter, Cathryn. Both have passed away this winter. Cathryn is very brave but at seventeen, to be so alone. We do what we can for her.

Much happier news than when we last wrote. Susan Hamlin is wed to Joshua Miller—such a fine man—somewhat in haste as he was home on leave and will have returned to his regiment by the time you receive this. But this other happy news has puzzled both your mother and I. Your friend, Allan Giles, has become engaged to Miss Nancy Coffin. She is a lovely girl and we wish them every happiness, of course, but cannot help but feel saddened for Cathryn. Even Allan's mother was convinced he would ask the Marcher girl—he had been courting her for several months since her parents' deaths.

Rupert read the letter and the passage several times before he decided that it explained enough and the explanation sent a wave of unpleasant pain to his temples and burned his eyes. He glanced at the mantel clock and stretched his fingers toward the next letter, written after his capture.

We have had so little news to raise our hearts since we read your last letter. The Portland News has begun to telegraph a list of casualties each day. Your father goes to the Courier office and returns with a lighter step—your name is not there. We are so grateful but feel so guilty to rejoice when so many others of our friends have lost their sons, brothers and husbands.

There had been days when he wanted death, begged for death to select him, unmindful of what his parents might suffer.

My son. Our beloved child. We have learned today that you have been gone from the care and keeping of your friends for more than two months. Had we but known! May God give you the strength you need to live and return to us. Your mother sends you her love.

Each letter thereafter was written by his father.

You won't remember her, but Cathryn Marcher came last week when your name appeared on the list of the missing in action. Such a kind-hearted girl. She is going up to Boston, as a volunteer nurse. We will miss her sorely.

The six following letters were filled with the names of his classmates who were dead or returned home wounded, the names of widows and orphaned children, and

We continue to hope and pray for your safe return.

The war is over, my son. Your mother and I await your homecoming with lighter hearts.

Three months have passed since peace returned to our country but we have had no word of you. Pray God will help us endure if you have not survived.

We have one candle in our darkness. Cathryn Marcher has come home. She is so changed from that happy girl we knew but says nothing of the horrors she has seen.

Rupert did not have to search deep in his memory for the horrors of hospital wards for the gall to rise in his throat. He was fortunate he was whole but could not erase what he saw in dreams or felt as he woke. His lungs were filled with the metallic stench of blood and rotting flesh. No nurse ever passed a cool hand over his brow while he lingered between wishing for death and enduring pain. No nurse held his hand through the long vigil toward life but he could imagine Cathryn comforting hundreds who would worship her until their dying breath for the simplest drop of water on their lips.

Rupert read his commanding officer's letter to his parents—a letter they had not received—explaining the six months' delay in letting them know he was alive and transferred to a convalescent hospital in Kansas where he was receiving the best of care and would write to them as soon as he was able.

The gas lamp spat and flickered. He stretched his hand toward the last letter, postmarked the same day as his commanding officer's letter, addressed to his regimental headquarters and returned to his hometown and his parents' lawyer. He wondered if Allan had recognized the handwriting but saw no sign the letter having been opened. His hand trembled as he clasped his father's treasured decanter of rye whiskey and filled the crystal shot glass from his mother's wedding set.

When he broke the wax seal, his heart stilled and plummeted to the pit of his gut. Cold, detached, antagonistic? He sank back and swallowed a good gulp of whiskey, apologizing to his father for his lack of respect. He pulled the single sheet from the envelope.

She had written all she had to say to him on one side and he unfolded the small rectangle with his eyes closed and holding his breath. The date was the evening before the postmark and the ink was black. Around the edge of the cream paper was the black border he could not then have expected—a kindness to warn of the letter's content.

Dear Mr. Smith,

She would not have written to him using any other salutation, despite the intention of the letter. Her handwriting was constrained, dense and unfaltering.

My heart is so heavy with loss I know I will fail you. Your parents, my dear friends, have both passed from this life.

Lest you grieve for their suffering, I can tell you that they did not. Your mother slipped away in sleep and, a short time after, you father joined her in rest while praying. Their love for you and their fervent prayers for your return home were and are never-ending. I will continue, on their behalf, to pray you are alive and will soon be well enough to return to your home. May God bless and always be with you in this ordeal and all others.

With deepest, shared sorrow for your loss,
Cathryn Marcher

At that moment, he thanked God he had not received her letter or he would have returned home with all his rage and insanity intact. The man who had told him his parents were dead, a year later, had done him a favor. "Everything there is gone, Rupe. Time to make a new life with what's left of you." And he had, a good life, but what was left of him still had pieces missing.

Rupert folded the letter into its envelope and returned all of them to the folder with the stamp of Allan's law office practice in the corner. Allan Giles couldn't have known Cathryn had written to him or the letter would have been removed. Allan's resentment toward her was fierce, he could see that but he wondered why, if Allan had been the one to end the courtship and Cathryn was the one wounded. The answer was plain, even to Rupert Smith, who had never been known to concern himself with anyone but his own ambitions.

Another glorious spring day greeted Cathryn when she woke at five, to make muffins for her breakfast and pump water for her garden. Her vigorous squash gave her hope for at least one to become the pumpkin pie to be auctioned at the Church Harvest Festival. But first, she had to decide what gown she would wear and what suit she would travel in to Portland to attend the first opera performance of the spring touring season.

Mrs. Moffatt had not divulged which opera or who the singers were, nor the company, but none of that mattered. She had not been to the opera nor had an occasion to dress with any semblance of elegance since leaving Boston and the opportunity was enough of a treat on its own.

Her choice of gowns was not extensive. She had one in green silk crepe and the other in deep purple velvet—both had been gifts from a woman who had no need of them, whose friendship Cathryn had treasured during her years in Boston. Both were outdated fashion but with a stitch here and a flounce there, she was confident only the most critical attendees would notice.

While she watered her vegetable garden and her muffins baked, she practiced her vocal scales in the dark behind the house, waking the jays and thought for a moment she heard another voice but when she lowered her volume, there was only the jays and the splash of water from her can. Wishful thinking.

Mrs. Moffatt had arranged to collect her in the late morning. They were staying at a hotel, having supper, attending the opera and returning by carriage on Saturday afternoon. Mrs. Moffatt had promised a chance to visit the shops and Cathryn had already decided her purchase with the money she earned from conducting the ladies' choir through the spring months, preparing for the Church Summer Fete. Never mind that the ladies would consider her decision decadent, if not downright sinful.

She finished her chores and was waiting at the road when Mrs. Moffatt's carriage appeared at the bend in the road from town.

"I could have walked down," she said as she lifted her satchel into the vehicle.

"Nothing of the kind, Cathryn. You would be tired before our adventure began and this will be an adventure, I assure you—something we all deserve more than once before we are too old to enjoy them." Mrs. Moffatt patted the seat beside her. "Tell me all you have done this week, all your accomplishments and pitfalls. I am eager to know and so weary of tiresome complaints. You know, I have not heard more than one joyful tidbit since Sunday."

"Which was that?"

"Oh no, young woman. First you will entertain me on our journey and, perhaps, if I am in a generous mood, I will return the favor."

Cathryn regaled her companion with feats and failures, antics and agonies of her pupils with anonymity until the carriage entered the driveway arch of the hotel and they were shown to their rooms. Mrs. Moffatt had the bedroom and Miss Marcher was to sleep on the day bed in the anteroom.

After a light supper, they dressed, assisting one another as ladies' maids. Mrs. Moffatt requested a hotel carriage rather than her own and they were delivered to the theater early enough to be shown to the dowager's box but Mrs. Moffatt preferred to linger in the foyer to be seen and observe.

Cathryn sipped a glass of wine, stepping aside as her benefactress enjoyed the social limelight.

"There you are, young man."

"I beg your pardon, Mrs. Moffatt. I took advantage of the fine evening to walk from my hotel."

"Cathryn?"

"Yes, Mrs. Moffatt?" she replied, as she composed the giddy, giggling girl and turned toward the dowager, praying she did not betray her state of mind or disgrace herself, glad she had chosen the sedate green silk crepe gown. "Hello, Mr. Smith." His warm smile was unexpected and she blushed in response to the intensity of his gaze.

Rupert bowed over her extended hand, supporting her gloved fingers as he kissed the top of her wrist. By her response she was not displeased, neither was she surprised nor moved in anyway other than—detached. Eleven days had passed since he read her condolence letter to him.

Though he had both ached for and dreaded seeing her again, made excuses for his absence from all engagements that might bring him near her, longed to encounter her by chance as this was meant—at least by him—to seem. He suspected Mrs. Moffatt's motives but, unless Cathryn was a better actress than he believed, she was as indifferent to his presence as he was agitated.

"Good evening, Miss Marcher."

"Isn't this delightful? You must join us, Rupert, unless you are accompanied, of course."

"I am not."

"You have no objection, I'm sure, Cathryn."

"I have no objection at all," Cathryn succeeded in saying before she turned her head away to find some sobering image to calm the absurd bubbles of elation threatening to make a fool of her.

"Good, then it is settled. If I may take your arm, Rupert, we can enjoy the spectacle of mankind from my box until the performance begins."

Cathryn followed, glad of the distance and the moment to compose her behavior for the rest of the evening. At the box, Mrs. Moffatt urged her to take the forward seat. Rupert Smith sat behind her and she prickled with nervous excitement, fearful she would betray her delight each time she glanced around the theater. *Does he object to being trapped here? Should I have protested he might prefer his own arrangements rather than allowing Mrs. Moffatt to insist he sit with two unaccompanied women? Perhaps he came to meet someone and we have spoiled a tryst.* Cathryn was so engrossed in his discomfort she lost interest in the tragic story played out on the stage and eventually gave up any pretense that she felt for the star-crossed lovers of Shakespearian fable.

Mrs. Moffatt dabbed at her eyes but Miss Marcher was unmoved. Had he not known she was capable of great sorrow and heartfelt sympathy, he might have believed her as cold as Allan Giles had claimed. At the end of the first act, Mrs. Moffatt expressed a wish to exercise her bones and her young companions followed to the mezzanine.

Before they had descended the five steps from the box, Cathryn stopped but her companions continued. Following the direction of her gaze, Rupert studied the blue-eyed, once blond object of her interest. A slow, pensive and puzzled, expression supplanted the tension Rupert had sensed during the first part of the evening.

After a moment's hesitation, she walked down the remaining steps, extending her hands toward the man, who caught them, smiling as he examined her and bent his head to kiss her cheek, breathing her name.

Focusing his trained hearing on their conversation, Rupert excused his intrusion as protective.

"I dared not hope of ever seeing you again, Cathryn."

"Are you well?"

"I am. Are you?"

"Very well."

"When you moved back to your village, I worried you would be too lonely."

"I have not been lonely, Jericho. I am fortunate to have friends and occupation enough."

"I still dream and wake. Come," he murmured, "there is someone I want you to meet."

"I do not want to meet any of your family, Jericho, nor your friends."

"But I have told them so much about you. Amelia knows you are here."

"Well, I wonder." Mrs. Moffatt leaned near her observant companion. "Hadn't you better get yourself over there, Rupert Smith?"

He frowned in the matron's direction but released her hand from the crook of his arm and approached the pair from behind Cathryn, to get a good look at the man, judging him easily five or more years older than himself. A veteran. Judging from his cheerful countenance, a man who had few regrets.

"We wondered what had happened to you," he remarked, laying his hand at the small of her back, extending the other to the man he instinctively considered a rival. "Rupert Smith, sir."

"Jericho Colson, sir. I am pleased to make your acquaintance, Mr. Smith. I have not seen Miss Marcher since a year before the recent conflict ended."

Rupert understood by the look in the man's eyes and his gut churned. His jaw clenched. "While Miss Marcher was up to Boston," he offered, "you were one of her fortunate patients, of course. I know there are many who feel as you." He smiled. Cathryn stiffened at his side but he closed his arm around her, drawing her closer to him.

"You did not serve our country in the war, sir?"

"I did, sir, until Cahaba claimed my presence."

Jericho responded with a curt nod, lifted Cathryn's hand to his lips. "I will explain to Amelia that you decline to accept responsibility for saving my life. She will understand, being equally charitable." He nodded once more to Rupert and turned away.

"Why did you do that?"

"Did you want to meet this woman?"

"That is not your concern. He will think—."

"What he thinks does not concern me, Miss Marcher."

"What he thinks concerns me, Mr. Smith. I have no wish to cause Mr. Colson any more pain than he has already suffered."

"I see. Shall I take you to him so you may meet this woman and cause her pain she does not deserve?"

"How dare you? I would not do that. I had no wish to do that. I had already told Jericho I would not meet her."

"Then we have no cause to argue, Miss Marcher." With his hand still at her waist, he caught her fingers. "You are lovely," he whispered, kissing away Colson's touch from her hand. "May I say that to you?"

"Why would you want to say such a thing?"

"Because you are. Because I have wanted to say that to you all evening. Because I have thought you are lovely since you made me a cup of coffee and fed me. Because, to be honest, I have thought you are lovely from the moment I saw you."

"And when would that have been?"

Whether mockery or amusement lay behind the question, he answered, "Ten years ago, Miss Marcher, when I was far too arrogant to know my own heart let alone recognize the beauty of an angel."

Despite the sincerity of his answer, the recipient dragged her hand out of his grasp and stepped back from his embrace, welcoming Mrs. Moffatt's swoop into their midst.

"Off we go, children. The next act promises to be even more poignant. I've just heard the most delicious gossip as well."

As soon as they were settled, the matron surged on. "That man to whom you were speaking just a moment ago will most likely be the next governor of this state, Cathryn. He thoroughly distinguished himself in the final months of the war and continues to do so but he apparently has a dark secret."

"Mrs. Moffatt, with all due respect, Mr. Colson is no doubt a man of great personal courage and," Rupert said, "whatever small taint there may have been is of no consequence in light of his subsequent heroism."

"This is no small taint, Mr. Smith."

"I choose to say it is, madam. Please do not share your news in my presence."

Mrs. Moffatt gasped.

He did not need to hear what he already knew. Cathryn did not need to hear what others may embellish for their own entertainment. Although he doubted Mrs. Moffatt knew all the details, he had no doubt others who heard her gossip would connect names and places. As the second act began, Cathryn lowered her chin for a moment. Rupert, tempted to encourage her to lift her head, cheered in silence when she showed her fortitude.

She was not to blame because she had surrendered to the need of a fellow creature of God's making. And, no one other than God could judge or condemn. Sorrow and regret, self-recrimination—reactions with which he was intimate— were private. His declaration had not met with the response he might have wished, but one glance at her assured him that Colson was not the rival he feared. He had, by his rude silencing of his hostess, prevented an injustice but won no skirmish. He had no plan of engagement.

Mrs. Moffatt glared at the performers, with no empathy for the travails of the lovers. Miss Marcher appeared to follow the story of deceit and betrayal with less detachment than the first act. During the shorter interval, neither of his companions was inclined to leave the seclusion of the box. Rupert ignored Mrs. Moffatt's desire for his departure; her wish to spread her tale would have to wait until they returned to their hotel or travelled the next day.

Although tempted to stay in their company until they returned to the Hill, to keep Cathryn to himself until there was no venom in the story to hurt her, Rupert made only the slightest gesture to assure her. If she interpreted the brief contact as he lifted her velvet shawl to her shoulder as the empathy he intended, he would know soon enough.

A man's actions—or a woman's—under extremes of hardship were not the dominion of tattle-tales or wagging tongues. If he could silence…Rupert clenched his fist on the notion of murder and turned his attention to the final act, finding no comfort in the heroine's choice of death over disgrace.

"Oh, my dear, how brave, how honorable," Mrs. Moffatt echoed the consensus of the audience, sweeping her fan at the side of her face and accepting the offer of Rupert's arm. Cathryn declined, preferring to walk behind them to the waiting carriage. Once Mrs. Moffatt was settled, he offered his hand to the younger woman and was gratified that she accepted. He refrained from clasping her fingers or kissing her wrist as he wished, following them to sit with his back to the driver, knowing, as she knew, the moment he left her, Mrs. Moffatt waited to pounce with the delicious gossip and would have no defense against the viciousness of the righteous.

While he scoured through his resources to postpone the inevitable, Mrs. Moffatt said, "Lands, I had no notion of how tiring this day would be. Don't let me spoil your youthful fun. The opera society's gala ball will go on for hours. I will consider it a great shame if you do not take advantage of the opportunity, Cathryn, to allow Mr. Smith to escort you. I am certain he will be delighted, will you not?"

"More than delighted, Mrs. Moffatt, I will be honored."

"There. No arguments, Cathryn. You will go and you will dance."

Six

Perhaps he had misjudged his hostess. Rupert smiled to encourage Miss Marcher's acceptance but she was reluctant. "I am not a proficient dancer, Miss Marcher, but partnering you will be a great privilege. My ability cannot help but improve in your company."

To his surprise, she chose disgrace over death.

"Good. Excellent," Mrs. Moffatt tapped her fan lightly on his knee. "Cathryn, please do not feel you must wake me when you return to the hotel. I will hear all about your adventure when we all three travel home together tomorrow afternoon. And, rest assured, I will not need to wake you when I attend to my business appointments in the morning."

He *had* misjudged Mrs. Moffatt. The contrite smile he bestowed was received with a haughty nod. Cathryn Marcher was consigned, without a chaperone, to his company for as long as he wished. Rupert almost preferred Mrs. Moffatt's gossiping to the expression of resignation on Cathryn's face. Aware she undoubtedly suspected his motives, expected, if not ungentlemanly behavior, at least having to pretend neither of them knew the truth of such gossip, having to lie to prevent being blackmailed.

They were alone in the carriage and only a few blocks from the ballroom venue before Rupert had formed a plan and reconciled the evening to his best and most constrained character. He glanced at her profile but she seemed absorbed in the buildings they passed. Alighting from the carriage, he offered his hand, grateful she did not refuse and took his arm as they entered the gas lit ballroom. Rupert captured two glasses of champagne and touched his to hers before he offered his arm again, leading Cathryn toward the perimeter of seating.

Reels were formed and the orchestra played a lively tune. They sat facing the dancers. Though neither admitted, each searched the room for evidence that Jericho Colson and his wife had also chosen to attend.

"I cannot remember the last ball I attended," he said, "and I did not exceed anyone's expectations. I doubt I will meet yours but it is my intention to make all efforts to do so."

"Thank you, Mr. Smith. There is no necessity for you to tax yourself on my behalf. I am content to observe."

"No moment spent in your company is in the least taxing but I admit, I would sooner be chopping wood for your stove."

"Then we have no reason to stay other than to please Mrs. Moffatt."

"I would say that pleasing Mrs. Moffatt was sufficient reason for staying until we are both satisfied that we cannot be called to task by that lady."

"That may require several hours."

"As I thought," he laughed. He set their empty glasses on the shelf behind their chairs, stood and offered his hand. Cathryn hesitated, gazed into his eyes and accepted the opportunity to dance a waltz with Rupert Smith.

As the music began, and the other couples floated by them, he held up his left hand, cradled her fingers on his palm and set his right hand a fraction below her shoulder blade as she laid her hand on his shoulder. He neither pushed her in a direction she did not wish to go nor pull her where he chose. They waltzed as though they knew one another's capacity for independence and submission and, if she had not succumbed long before, she would have fallen in love with him on their first circuit of the ballroom.

By the second he surpassed all other men and by the third, she could not help her smile. When they returned to their seats, he refreshed their champagne and brought her a small plate of delicacies. Despite all the potential for conversation about the opera they had seen, their hostess, none of the several topics survived her due consideration. The orchestra promised another waltz and Rupert handed their empty glasses and plates to the waiter. Cathryn brushed a few crumbs from her gown.

During their second turn of the ballroom, Rupert said, "You are lovely."

Cathryn glanced at him but his gaze was fixed on a point in the room beyond her.

The thought that she had loved Jericho Colson crossed his mind. Allan Giles's resentment crossed his mind. The thought she was right to be wary of him lodged where he could not avoid it and he glanced to see if it was true, but her gaze was turned away from him. He considered whether two waltzes and a light meal were enough to mollify Mrs. Moffatt but concluded the opportunity to be near Cathryn Marcher and alone with her would not come again soon.

He led her into a reel, followed with a round dance and as many waltzes as were offered until the torment of being near her was equal to the torment of being the cause of her fatigue. He squeezed the fingers resting on his forearm and resisted the urge to bring them to his lips. "I believe Mrs. Moffatt will be content with our effort, Miss Marcher. May I see you to your hotel?"

"Yes, thank you, Mr. Smith. And thank you for this evening."

"Did you enjoy the ball?"

"Yes."

"Then I am happy and can say I enjoyed your company. And therefore, are we all three satisfied." Studying her face for a moment, tempted to lift a strap wisp from her forehead, tempted as before to kiss away her lover's traces and replace them with his own. "Cathryn."

She responded to the liberty he took by searching for the hotel carriage's approach and answered his unspoken question with silence on their short journey.

In the lobby of the hotel, he bowed his head with formal civility over her hand. "Good night, Miss Marcher."

"Good night, Mr. Smith."

The mechanical dial of the elevator reached the sixth floor. When the operator brought it back to the lobby, he requested the fifth. As he slid the key into the lock, the operator closed the cage and the outside doors shut.

Grateful to be alone, Cathryn fanned her face with both hands, waltzed from the elevator through the hallway to the door of Mrs. Moffatt's suite, but continued to the window at the end of the corridor to stare along the streets radiating out from the hotel's carriageway toward the seaport and the stark masts of the whalers that stabbed into the mist. She had danced all evening with Rupert Smith and had not disgraced herself with giggles, not fainted from giddiness. That she was disgraced in more serious ways had little power to reduce her happiness.

The man she loved had met the man who had once loved her. The floor of the opera house had not dropped her into Hades for all eternity. After one awkward moment of embarrassment, Rupert had been sanguine. Jericho had been a gentleman. The evening could have been so much worse.

Dancing the steps to a reel back to the room, she crept in, undressed in the dimness and lay down on the daybed, staring through a chink in the drapery at the night sky.

Mrs. Moffatt extinguished her bedside lamp and the suite was plunged into darkness. Cathryn folded her arms around her body and made an effort to relax into sleep but an hour or more passed before her eyelids closed. The rattling of milk wagons in the street and breakfast trolleys outside the doors of the other rooms woke her two hours later than her usual time. She happily jumped from her bed to be ready if Mrs. Moffatt requested her help.

Dressed in her travelling suit, her gown packed, Cathryn sat at the window awaiting the matron's call. In a few minutes, Mrs. Moffatt opened the adjoining door and gazed at her protégé.

"You were not long at the gala ball."

"Mr. Smith believed we had stayed long enough."

"Did he indeed? I shall have words with that young man at breakfast. Since you are dressed, you may tell him we will meet him in the dining room at nine. Come straight back, Cathryn. I will need your assistance."

"Where will I find Mr. Smith?"

"Below us. Room five-sixteen."

"Oh." For a moment, she stared at the carpeted floor, wondering if he might have heard that giddy girl dancing in the corridor.

"There is no time to lose, Cathryn. We will only have a few hours in the shops, you know."

"I need only go to two shops, Mrs. Moffatt."

"You may do as you please, Cathryn, if we have time."

"Yes, Mrs. Moffatt."

"Now, tell Rupert to meet us as I said."

Cathryn took the staircase to the floor below, stood for a moment at the door before raising her hand to knock. Stepping back immediately, she quelled the giddy, giggling girl racing to leap out. He was not fully attired. Beyond his trousers and boots, his shirt was buttoned to the middle of his chest and his damp hair clung in curls around his face.

"Good morning, Miss Marcher."

"Good morning, Mr. Smith. Mrs. Moffatt has requested that you meet her in the dining room in thirty minutes."

"My pleasure."

She nodded and turned on her heel, tempted to run for the safety of the stairway.

"You will be joining us, I hope."

"Yes," she said over her shoulder and darted out of sight. On the second step, she took a long breath. If she had been that giddy girl, she might have leaned close enough to take a deep whiff of his shaving soap. That girl might have walked right up to him and inhaled his scent and giggled wildly. Cathryn refused to be that girl ever again.

Despite Jericho's public restraint, only the least attentive child could not have sensed there existed an intimacy between them. She had blushed at the sight of him. Jericho's expression of surprise and…there was no other word for it…passion said so much more. He still harbored some ardor with regard to her, though her care for him had always been secondary to her love for Rupert Smith.

Regret is a fool's excuse.

That Rupert had seen and understood the tension of that moment, that unexpected and unsought meeting, had been as plain to her as what he thought of the giggling, giddy girl, what he *already* thought of her. Breakfast for her was a silent affair.

Mrs. Moffatt was loquacious and inquisitive. Rupert was equally talkative, answering all the older woman's questions about the ball and the guests. Through the meal, Cathryn grew more surprised as he named so many of the people in attendance—people she knew well enough to have greeted and had not noticed. Had she been so absorbed in her effort to keep her heart from exploding? What must they all think of her…that they didn't already think?

Because Mrs. Moffatt had ordered full breakfasts for all, Cathryn force-fed herself beyond comfort but neither of her companions took notice. At the end of the meal, Mr. Smith and Mrs. Moffatt prepared to return to their rooms.

Her services as lady's maid unrequired, Cathryn suggested she begin her own shopping. "So that I do not impede your morning's efforts."

"None of that silliness, Cathryn. There will be more than sufficient time once all our luggage is settled. If you have finished your packing, wait here for Rupert and I."

"Yes, Ma'am."

Mrs. Moffatt scowled for a moment but took Rupert's arm to walk back to the elevator.

Cathryn sat by the window in the lobby, her small carpetbag on the floor beside her. When the porter brought Mrs. Moffatt's cases, Rupert set his portmanteau beside their baggage and Mrs. Moffatt led her young companions through all the best shops but seemed to have no clear intention of making a purchase.

"There, I am thoroughly satisfied. I have all I need for the coming season and know where and what to order for my children. We may now return home, my dears."

Cathryn bowed her head for a moment, a flare of color staining her cheeks and her chin stiffened.

"Mrs. Moffatt, as you have done all you required and are at haste to return, I hope you will allow me to complete the tasks I have set. I will return later today by what means I am able."

"And how do you propose to accomplish that, Cathryn? There are no coaches to Oslo Hill at this time of day and you must return by tonight or you will be unable to teach the Sunday School."

"I have errands I must complete."

"If I may—."

"No, Rupert, do not interfere. Very well, Cathryn, since you are your headstrong self, I will give you an hour to do as you must. I am weary and cannot accompany you as I would have liked. I know Rupert will not mind doing so."

"I am perfectly capable of shopping without a chaperone, Mrs. Moffatt."

"No doubt, but as I will feel responsible if some mishap occurs, Rupert will help you. Will you not?"

"Gladly."

The irritation in his tone was unmistakable, echoing her own. "Very well," she replied, "But I can take no responsibility for your boredom or misery, Mr. Smith. Is it your wish, Mrs. Moffatt, that we return to the hotel at an appointed hour?"

"That will suit me very well, Cathryn. Take as much time as pleases you, my dear. I am content to entertain myself while you two accomplish these errands." The matron turned away, leaving her companions facing one another, once again left to themselves.

"If I were a suspicious man, I might think she had meant——."

Cathryn had turned on her heel and was several strides away, heading for the revolving entry door. Rupert trotted to catch up but said nothing else. The determined set of her jaw discouraged pleasant banter. For six city blocks, she said nothing but, when she had made a decision, she turned to face him.

"I regret you have been inconvenienced in this way but as I am able to complete these errands without assistance, please return to whatever business you prefer. My errands are private, Mr. Smith, and I do not want or wish for company."

"I will allow you a measure of the freedom you clearly desire, Miss Marcher. I have no wish to be where I am unwanted but I will not neglect my designated task. Complete your errands without interference or thought of me. I will be close at hand, should you require."

"I do not wish to be followed."

"I will maintain a discreet distance. I will not remark into which establishments you proceed."

Is there no chance I can dissuade you?"

"None. I will be nearby but unseen. Go. Enjoy your freedom to be alone."

Cathryn turned away on her journey, certain he would be true to his word and did not look back to see if he followed.

Her first task was the music shop, where she purchased *Italian Songs* and *Folk Tunes of the World* for her singing pupils and, after consideration, the music for *The Emperor Concerto*—to learn when the nights became long and cold.

A few streets on and down a lane that led toward the docks, she entered to the tinkling of a bell and greeted the shop owner with a smile.

"Ah, Mademoiselle Cathryn, how good to see you."

"Thank you, Mrs. Lowell. Do you have any work for me?"

"Several orders. I was very glad to hear that you were visiting as I was about to send the fabric and details of the garments with the courier when he next came through your part of the world. This is an order for the Debutante Cotillion so I must have it back by the end of the next month for all the fittings." Mrs. Lowell pushed a brown paper parcel across the glass counter toward her seamstress. "And this one is for later in the year but if you get it to me at the same time as the other, I will be very grateful."

"I will make every effort to do so." Cathryn put both parcels in the canvas satchel the shop owner also pushed toward her.

"Do you want to take your own order with you, Cathryn?"

"I would but I don't yet have enough money to pay you. I have brought only another installment, I'm afraid."

"With this work, you will surely have more than you need."

"I have other calls on my income, otherwise I would gladly do so."

Mrs. Lowell counted the coins and bills Cathryn put into her hand. "Nearly halfway there, Cathryn. You'll have your corset and petticoat when I next see you, I'm certain."

Cathryn left the dressmaker's shop and headed down the lane and turned to walk along the next street. At the corner, she entered a coffee shop and took a seat at the table by the window, removing her gloves and bonnet. While she waited, she gazed out onto the street, hoping but not expecting to catch a glimpse of Rupert at his vigil. The street was clear of all men but dock workers and sailors. The women were engaged in commerce of all manners and while she enjoyed her hot chocolate drink, she considered Jericho Colson's extraordinary contact with her when she least needed to meet him. There had always been a possibility—they were from the same state and had much in common.

At first, she had considered him a patient, in need of friendship, and would not have allowed any deeper relation but his desperation proved to be the greater force. She had not entirely regretted their encounter but she had never wanted Jericho to be part of her life then or after the war had come to an end. Their agreement had been never to seek one another. Although he had not intentionally sought, she was the one to face the consequences.

His wife, if she knew of the relationship, would have already forgiven him. Cathryn's past was her own. She had no reason or right to know about anyone in Rupert's past, why should he be concerned about hers?

When she was within a few blocks of the hotel, she quickened her pace. Though she was not late, she did not want to seem reluctant. At the next corner, she met her watcher coming from the direction of the docks. He lifted the brim of his wide-brimmed hat and took the satchel from her hand.

"Mission accomplished, Miss Marcher?"

"Yes, thank you."

"Judging by the weight of this, not much will be left for those who follow."

Cathryn felt no need to defend or explain but, when he set the satchel on the ground and caught her elbow, she pulled back.

"Evidence of a secret vice, Miss Marcher," he said, taking his linen handkerchief from his pocket to dab at the corner of her lips. His attention was gentle and good-humored as he inspected her mouth and chin. "Mrs. Moffatt will never guess your secret and I will never tell—lest you discover my vice and use it against me." He smiled and released her, his fingers lingering a moment on her cheek. Offering his arm, he raised the satchel from the pavement.

Cathryn hesitated only until his arm nudged her elbow.

"Now, we must come up with a good tale of our shopping adventure or we will never hear the end of Mrs. Moffatt's disappointment in us."

"I do not have to explain myself to you, Mrs. Moffatt or anyone else, Mr. Smith."

"I am the one who will need to explain—a simple matter, Miss Marcher, as I am a man and cannot be expected to take an interest in the fashion affairs of women. Keep your counsel, Miss Marcher. I have no need to meddle in your concerns."

Jericho Colson, Allan Giles and Rupert Smith were men of a kind. At least, that had been true before that April day in 1861 and the first defeat of the Army of the United States. Whether he was still one of that kind, Allan and Jericho were not. Ambition for a life in public office paled minute by minute, day by day each moment he opened his eyes on the squalor, disease, starvation that came of that ambition.

How Cathryn came to meet Colson, where and when they had met, what their relationship had been, what brought them together, how she came away from that involvement were all questions that silenced Rupert as they approached the hotel.

Mrs. Moffatt awaited them in the lobby, her smile fading with each step nearer he and Cathryn approached. Her driver brought the team of geldings and the covered landau[10] to the front entrance at his employer's beckoning. Once Cathryn's packages and satchel were loaded under the driver's seat beside Rupert's portmanteau, Mrs. Moffatt accepted his assistance to board the vehicle.

"Jacob, see that my parcels do not end their journey scuffed beyond repair," the matron told her driver. "Set them to the side of the footboard."

"I would gladly do that, ma'am, but thata way, the road will claim a victim or two before we get any distance toward the Hill."

"I trust you will ensure no such thing occurs."

"Yes, ma'am," the middle-aged man replied, winking at his employer. "I'll be sure to do that." He shoved the portmanteau nearer the edge of the footboard but left Miss Marcher's belongings untouched.

As the young man offered his hand to Cathryn, Mrs. Moffatt spread the skirt of her travelling suit across the bench seat, busy with her carpet case, pulling out a linen doily mounted in an embroidery hoop and plucking at the needle. Her travelling companion settled on the opposite bench, with her back to the driver, as near the window as she could to leave room for Rupert Smith. She remained crushed against the wall of the landau when, after he had tethered his horse to the back of the vehicle, he chose to join the coachman.

Cathryn braced her shoulders against the padded cushion as the carriage lurched forward into the street. Mrs. Moffatt

---

[10] **Landau** a coachbuilding term for a convertible carriage popular in the mid and later 19th Century.

gasped as the needle pricked her finger but waved away Cathryn's instant concern. Both women glanced through the open window as the landau wove through the traffic to reach the highway. With the sway of the vehicle on the open road, once beyond the jostle of the city streets, Mrs. Moffatt dozed, holding her embroidery in her hands until the work slipped to her lap. Cathryn caught the linen before it dropped to the floor and folded it the sewing case, and soon followed her patroness to a light nap, recovering from her own late night.

Seven

Jacob's endless chatter was a welcome distraction but did not prevent him from thinking. As the driver regaled him with information about the country they passed, Rupert responded with grunts and nods, keeping his thoughts clear as he relived Cathryn's *chance* meeting with Jericho Colson. Although their conversation—what he heard of it— suggested nothing more than friendship, Colson's intense scrutiny and Cathryn's swift withdrawal, when he interrupted them, suggested something else.

Had they made an appointment for the following day? Had Mrs. Moffatt's insistence that Rupert accompany Cathryn on her shopping excursion foiled that rendezvous? He suspected her reluctance for his presence was more than a wish for independence but he had not caught a glimpse of any gentleman lurking in the hopes of a tryst, with the exception of his own. The admission made him smile.

"And that be the first honest response to any word I've said."

Rupert glanced at Jacob, a scowl creasing his forehead.

"Tahn't no cause from discomfort, Captain Smith. I know the signs of a young man smitten with a young woman. Can't say you'd do much better than Miss Cathryn."

Soul of a saint. Heart of an angel.

"What makes you say that?"

"Well, if you ahn't smitten, you oughta be."

"Why is that?"

"She's a fine-lookin' woman, shame to waste."

With that he could agree without making a commitment either way. He glanced back at the landau's passenger compartment. Through the glass partition, there was no danger that either woman had heard the conversation. Both were asleep.

"Ay-yuh. So I thought. Mind you don't cause Mrs. Moffatt any concern for her favorite."

"That much I know."

"Hard to miss," Jacob chuckled, as he pulled up on the reins as the team approached the junction of the road to Oslo Hill.

Dusk had already wrapped its cooler arms around the Hill by the time the landau reached the crest of the road at the church square. Mrs. Moffatt roused from her long rest as the carriage slowed near the drive to her house.

She used her knuckle to rap on the glass and her hand to wave Jacob on down the street. "Take my guests home," she called, and dismissed Cathryn's protest with a sniff. "I will not have you walking all that way in the dark with all your packages. Rupert will ensure you arrive safely." She settled back, folding her arms across her chest, challenging Cathryn to argue.

When the carriage stopped at the front of her property, the sun had sunk behind the tops of the trees in the woodlands, casting softened shadows over the grass but the cabin was in deep gloom with no welcoming glow from the wood stove. Cathryn sighed, drawing the edges of her shawl closer around her neck, shrugging to gather to her what warmth lingered in the confines of the landau. As soon as Jacob brought the carriage to a halt, Rupert jumped down and yanked the door open.

"There's no fire in your stove, Miss Marcher."

"What a pity," Mrs. Moffatt answered. "You will need to chop wood for her."

"There is plenty of wood," Cathryn murmured, accepting his offered hand and stretching her foot out to find the step.

Without thinking, Rupert grasped her ankle to guide her.

Mrs. Moffatt tsked and waved her protégé into the night.

"I am capable of looking after myself."

"Nonsense. Rupert is a gentleman. A perfect gentleman. Be certain Cathryn has had no intruders, of any kind, Rupert."

Sternly admonished to behave, Rupert agreed and closed the carriage door with a soft click, tipping his wide-brimmed hat to the matron before he lifted Cathryn's packages and satchel from the footboard and dropped his portmanteau to the ground, untethered his horse, leading the animal up to the front porch.

Jacob tipped his whip in farewell to the pair and guided the carriage horses to turn back toward the village.

Cathryn took the canvas satchel from Rupert and strode to the back porch of her cabin. Rupert followed with the rest of the luggage but stood at the edge of the porch until she lit a small lamp on the table and extended an invitation with a nod. She turned her back on him to put her purchases in a small cupboard in the hallway between the kitchen and front room.

"You can put my satchel down, Mr. Smith. It isn't so heavy that I am incapable of carrying it to my room."

"I would gladly," but he didn't complete the offer. He set the satchel on the floor. While she took the satchel further along the passageway, Rupert opened the wood stove door and built a pile of kindling and struck a lucifer-match[11]. The

---

[11] **Lucifer-match** – precursor to the 'parlor match' of 1862, invented by Charles W. Smith which replaced beeswax (which had replaced sulfur) with paraffin, which was in turn replaced in the 1870s by the 'drunkard's match' impregnated with fire-retardant chemicals that would not burn the user when struck.

flare illuminated his face and the room for a moment before he set the kindling alight.

One of her purchases had not surprised him. Sheet music from a music shop for a music teacher was not out of character but a purchase from a dressmaker for a woman who had always been known for her skill as a seamstress piqued his interest. Did her meeting with Jericho Colson prompt a desire for a store-bought garment?

"May I offer you coffee, Mr. Smith? And a slice of cake?"

"I am tempted, Miss Marcher, but Mrs. Moffatt would never forgive me if I were less than the gentleman she believes me to be."

"Are you not?"

"All men have their limits, Miss Marcher. I do not want to be tempted beyond mine."

"Good night then, Mr. Smith. I am sorry that Mrs. Moffatt imposed upon you for my sake. I assure you both I can take care of myself."

"I am certain of that, Miss Marcher, but it is no less a pleasure to offer my meager services to assist you."

"Your journey home will not be so pleasant," she said. "Allow me, at least, to make your homecoming worth the walk." She wrapped one of her cakes in muslin and closed the tin lid, holding it out to him.

Rupert stared at the offering. "You do not need to repay me."

"Then accept this as it is intended, Mr. Smith. From a friend."

"That I can do, and thank you, as long as you undertake to do the same." He stepped toward the back door, hesitating with his hand on the knob. "Will you be in church tomorrow, Miss Marcher?"

"I will."

He inclined his head, took the tin and left her in her cabin, wishing he had held her as he had as they danced. As he walked his horse through the woods, the back route to the south end of the village, selling his parents' home was no longer his first priority.

"I'm in trouble, Sarge."

Morton flipped onto his back, stretched and yawned though he'd been awake since his commanding officer stamped his muddy boots on the scraper.

"What makes you think so, Rupe?"

"That woman is falling in love with me."

"How is that trouble? I mean, you were smitten with her since I can't remember how long ago."

"I have to find a way to make her hate me."

"Why on God's green earth would you want to do that?"

"She deserves better."

"No argument there," Morton mumbled, turning his shoulder away and thumping his pillow. "Every woman does, or thinks she does. Makes certain every man is sure of it. Get some sleep, Rupe."

"Once I find this Evie and sell this house, we're gone from here."

"Counting the days. Church in the morning, remember."

The children arrived in family groups, clustering around their teacher as she made a futile search of her basket and set aside what she had planned for the morning. The sky was as blue as her mother's treasured lapis lazuli earrings and the wind was a caress in the tops of the trees. Cathryn set her work basket on the low step at the church hall door.

"We'll wait for the rest of the children before we begin our school."

"But Miss Marcher," Megan Giles complained, staring from one to another of the boys' faces, "we can't stay out here. There's no piano and we will have no refreshments."

"On the contrary, Megan, we have all we need."

More of the village children trotted across the wide lawn in front of the church, excited by the oddity of an outdoor school. The boys ran and the girls stood shoulder to shoulder to admire and disapprove. Cathryn dug into the basket and handed the eldest boy a wooden box.

"Fill this with the fruits of the forest," she said, sending the boys into the woods. Another dip into her basket produced a Mason jar. "Fill this with the nectar of the brook," she told the eldest girl, encouraging the others to follow. Megan stayed beside her. "Why do you wait?"

"I wanted to tell you a secret."

"Is it your secret, Megan, or do you tell another's?"

"It is mine, Miss Marcher,"

"Then I will listen. Speak as you wish."

"I sang for Mr. Smith and I wasn't the least frightened."

"You need never be frightened to sing, Megan. It is a God-given joy. Was Mr. Smith entertained?"

"Yes, Miss. He wanted to hear another song but Father was too busy and wanted to speak with Mr. Smith. That was the second time I have sung for him. He thinks I have a pretty voice."

"As you do."

"He said he would most like to hear me and be able to listen with all his attention but he couldn't do that unless someone else played for me."

"Who played for you then? Your mother plays very well."

"Mr. Smith played for me and mother said—."

"Mr. Smith plays the piano?"

"Yes, Miss. Mother has sent me to ask you to come this afternoon, so that Mr. Smith can hear me properly."

"This afternoon."

"Yes, Miss."

"Did your mother give you a specific time?"

"No, Miss. But she will speak to you after the service."

The boys hadn't returned from the woods and the girls were staring at her from a short distance but Cathryn hadn't noticed. She was staring straight ahead of her at a man dressed in canvas trousers and a plaid woodsman's jacket, unlike any she had seen before, and a wide brim hat. He wore a white shirt, a narrow black tie and rode toward her along the track from the road.

"My goodness," she murmured when he lifted his hat by the crown to greet her. No matter how strange his attire, Rupert Smith turned her whole insides to the most appalling state of giddy.

"Miss Marcher."

"Mr. Smith."

She had spoken with hardly a twitter in her tone but her heart beat so fast, blood was rushing to her head and as soon away from her brain that a mortifying faint was a possibility.

"I trust that expression is not one of disapproval, Miss Marcher."

"No—I mean— of course not, sir. Why would you think that of me? I would not have—I am not so rude."

"I didn't accuse you," he chuckled, swung his leg over his horse's haunches and dropped the reins to the ground before he strolled toward her. "Why are you not in the church hall?"

"The door is locked."

"You forgot your key, I presume."

"No, sir. I did not. The pastor leaves the door open after the early morning Bible Study class."

"Now, it is the pastor's error and not a forgotten key?"

"I have never had a key," she answered, stiffening her spine. "I have never needed a key."

"You cannot always depend on others."

Megan Giles stared at him but Rupert kept his gaze locked on Cathryn's face.

"I rarely depend on others, Mr. Smith."

"No, it is more likely you encourage them to depend on you." He waved the Giles girl away but she stayed close to her teacher. "That is the way of many fair flowers. The better to ensnare their prey. Shall I break the door down for you?"

"That will not be necessary," Cathryn replied. "I have made appropriate adjustments to my Sunday school plans for today, to compensate for my lack of foresight." She plunged her hand into her basket for a moment. "I do not mean to be rude, sir, but I have a class to teach."

"You may be as rude to me as you wish, Miss Marcher, as long as you are honest."

"I endeavor to be so, Mr. Smith, without causing injury."

"Is it my jacket or my hat that most offends you?"

"Please, Mr. Smith. That is unfair. I do not wish to comment on your mode of dress. That is of no concern to me."

"Make it your concern, Cathryn," he murmured close to her ear. "Make me your concern."

"You are not my concern." She clutched at Megan's hand and turned her back, searching the edge of the woods for the return of the other boys and girls.

"I will be, Miss Marcher."

"Do you threaten me, Mr. Smith?"

"No, Miss Marcher. I promise you." He stood at her shoulder, gazing at the curve of her cheek before following the direction of her gaze. "I admire you, Miss Marcher. And I will continue to admire you until you admire me."

"And if that never comes about?"

"That will be my misfortune, but like so many others who have succumbed to your wiles, I am hopeful in any case."

A boy's shout cut through the Sunday morning silence and Rupert ran toward the sound. Cathryn followed close behind. Several of the boys ran toward the U.S. Army veteran with as many chasing them, lobbing handfuls of forested fruits at their backs.

"Halt!"

The boys' responses were immediate, as the man dressed like a Western gunman straddled their path. Aurelius Cook confiscated the empty box and hid it behind his back. Rupert motioned the chased boys forward, fixing the chasers in their places with a stern glare. Before he allowed the victims to go on to their teacher, he examined each in turn. When he turned his attention to the chasers, he beckoned them one at a time until he and Mary Cook's younger brother were face to face.

"Miss Marcher gave you a job to do."

"Yes, sir."

"Have you completed the task to your satisfaction?"

"No, sir."

"How do you expect Miss Marcher will respond to that?"

The thirteen-year-old shrugged, dragging his foot backward. "I expect she'll be disappointed."

"I expect she will know you cannot be trusted. What are you going to do about that?"

"Them other boys didn't listen to me so I walloped them."

"All the same, the job was yours. How you did it was up to you."

"That was a big job, sir."

"You can handle it."

"That's not fair, sir."

"Nothing ever is." Rupert glanced over his shoulder. "But sometimes you get lucky, if you work hard enough."

Cathryn scrubbed the faces and hands of the boys at the pump outside the church kitchen. The boys' themselves could be washed but the stains on their clothes made more work for their mothers. As carefully as she worded her apology, no words made up for her poor judgment.

Though his intervention had put an end to the riotous behavior, she did not owe any apology to George Rupert Smith. Straightening as he returned from the woodlands, she folded her arms across her waist. "I should have——."

"They are boys, Miss Marcher. There is very little you can do to change or prevent what they are bound to do."

"They are children, Mr. Smith. I am responsible for them."

"They are not going to become men, if they find someone always willing to take the blame for their misbehavior."

"Nevertheless, I will apologize to their parents."

"These boys will do so and I will be here to ensure that they do. You will not take responsibility for their wrongdoing."

Cathryn had opened her mouth to protest when Aurelius appeared laden with a wooden box overflowing with fruit. He presented his work to her with a bow.

"I'm sorry I took so long, Miss. It was harder than I thought."

Cathryn pressed her fingers to her lips. "You have done a wonderful job, Aurelius. I am so proud of you."

Rupert winked at the boy.

"If you have another box, Miss, I've found a place that's brimming."

Several of the boys offered to go with him but Cathryn said, "Aurelius has gathered more than enough and, as soon as we are able, he will have the first taste and the biggest serving of the pudding."

How she could make a pudding while they stood in the sunshine, no one had found out by the time Nancy Giles made an early appearance. Rupert disappeared with all the boys to the back of the building. Though the Sunday class had not gone according to any plan she had made, lessons had been learned, not least by her. She had no opportunity to redeem herself in the boys' eyes, nor in those of Rupert Smith.

Unwilling for the girls to hear what Megan's mother was about to ask or say, Cathryn asked Megan to take charge and walked a distance to stand with Nancy under the sugar maple on the church lawn.

"I am flattered that you think well of my skill enough to ask, but——."

"I won't accept any excuses, Cathryn. This means so much to Megan. She talks of nothing else but performing for Mr. Smith. He was so kind, so gentle with her, such a boost to her confidence—you know how shy she is, how she dotes on you and retreats so from every chance to call attention to her talent. She will be going away to school in Lewiston before long. She will have this, at the least, to bolster her. I know you won't deny her an opportunity to discover an inner strength."

"Under those circumstances, how can I refuse, Nancy? But this is awkward for me."

"Can't you put your personal aversion to Rupert aside for once, for Megan's sake?"

Aversion? Was she the only one who recognized her giddy, overwhelmed response to him for what it truly was? Or her crimson face whenever she was required to speak to or in his presence? Or did everyone interpret her discomfort and restraint in whichever way best suited their requirements at the time? Did Rupert believe she disliked him and find some perverse sport in tormenting her with his presence?

"For Megan's sake, I cannot refuse, Nancy. I will come this afternoon to accompany her. At what time do you require my attendance?"

Nancy tapped her finger to her cheek for a moment. "We will have our Sunday dinner at two, so I do not imagine your services will be required until three at the earliest."

"I will come at half-past three," Cathryn said, "to give you ample time to enjoy the company of Mr. Smith."

"With Susan there, I doubt either I or Mr. Giles will have much of his company."

"I see," Cathryn replied, glancing away to examine the texture of the maple's bark.

"She is quite bewitched by Rupert. He has charmed her off her high horse, you know."

"He can be charming, when he chooses."

"Allan is beside himself with delight. Nothing would suit him better than to see Rupert wed and settled here again. They are such good friends and Susan is a good match for him—they are both so high brow."

"Yes."

"And, of course, they will be the wealthiest couple and the toast of Oslo Hill for years to come, you know, with their properties joined."

Of course.

"My gracious, everyone in the village is carried away with such excitement—a wedding next Spring, right here and such finery. You know Susan."

Cathryn found a nod her only safe reply when the woman Nancy discussed appeared at the foot of the church walk.

"Remember, three:thirty," Nancy called back as she dashed to meet her widowed friend.

Cathryn returned to her pupils at the same moment Mr. Jorgens, out of breath, appeared with the key to the hall. His smile expressed his apology but otherwise he ignored the situation and the boys dirty clothing when Rupert herded them into the hall.

Though their parents' silent glances in Cathryn's direction called for an explanation, if not an apology, there was no time before Cathryn was called upon to climb to the organ loft. Rupert's promise to force confessions from the miscreants was forgotten.

Susan Miller grasped the man's arm as soon as he came within reach at the door of the vestibule. His lavish attention on the widow and her grand Sunday attire proved Nancy's point. Cathryn concentrated on the service and her musical contribution to it. Despite her intentions, her trained ear disapproved their duets. Their voices, though individually good, did not harmonize or blend. Their pitch was exact but somehow, they did not ring true. The clash was unnoticeable to other listeners whose knowing smiles and nodding heads approved uncritically.

Hopeful idiot. What did that signify? They were or soon would be declaring their intentions. Her own voice faltered but she sang to the end of the verse before restraining her participation to playing the organ. A church service was not the proper place to swoon over the inconsistencies of her heart. She bowed her head to recover her composure and admonished her heart that all her resources would be needed to provide adequate support for Megan's challenge. Under no circumstances, could she let her pupil down.

Eight

As the congregation left the church, some of the boys' mothers glared at her but Cathryn complied with Rupert's dictate and volunteered no apology or explanation. She accepted that some retribution was bound to come but she had an ordeal of another kind.

The walk to her cabin took a quarter of an hour. The return to Allan Giles's house was twenty minutes. Not wishing to be either late or early, she set the mantel clock from her parents' home on top of the square piano. For the following two hours, she practiced the songs Megan was proficient to sing, prepared her own solitary Sunday dinner and, at three in the afternoon, gave Miss Cathryn Evelyn Marcher a severe reprimand for allowing the giddy girl to surface and refuse Cathryn a peaceful walk back to the center of the village.

As soon as the Giles house came into view, her legs wobbled and her hands shook. Her fingers lost feeling and her satchel of music seemed determined to fly from her grasp.

This is nothing more than a job. I will be paid for my time. I am not a guest.

Thus bolstered by the definition of her role, Cathryn took the steps to the veranda and pulled the bell cord. The housekeeper opened the door. Rupert's voice from the parlor drifted above the soft laughter of the two women.

Cathryn entered the drawing room and stood with her back to the doorway as the housekeeper closed her in.

Certainly not a guest. The paid entertainment. Less.

Cathryn set her music on the parlor grand, removed her bonnet and gloves. After she had taken off her coat, she warmed her hands, standing to the side of the instrument awaiting the pleasure of her paymasters. Hours seemed to pass before Megan peaked around the door.

"Mother says we need to practice, but very quietly, so we don't disappoint Mr. Smith with any mistakes."

"I have practiced enough and you need only to warm your voice."

Cathryn played scales for the child and reminded her of her breathing and posture. Within moments, Allan entered the room, open-eyed and narrowed brow.

"What are you doing here, Cathryn?"

She turned on the piano stool as Rupert and the two ladies entered behind the master of the house, who, in no time turned on his wife with a scowl so fierce, his guests remained silent.

Nancy Giles snubbed her husband's anger and strode toward Cathryn with her hands extended. "So good of you to surprise us like this, Cathryn. I'm delighted. Now, Rupert, you can hear my daughter at her very best."

"How very strange of you," Susan said, gazing at the piano teacher with her head cocked. "I've never known you to intrude on a private event."

"Megan asked me to accompany her singing for Mr. Smith," Cathryn replied. Nancy would not admit her part but she could not allow Rupert Smith to believe she was so rude or so bold. *He will believe as he chooses.*

Megan had moved closer to her and Rupert studied her. His expression was as narrow as Allan's but less fierce, more perplexed than angry, until Susan laid her hand on his arm. Though he turned his head toward her, he continued to watch Cathryn.

"Well, since she's here now, I suppose we may as well hear this pretty child, Rupert, though it seems an extreme effort to have come all this way when both Nancy and I are quite competent to accompany Megan for you."

"Miss Marcher is Megan's teacher and mentor, Mrs. Miller," Rupert said, without looking at her. "There is no one in the child's eyes, or mine, as I have made the attempt and failed, more competent than Miss Marcher. I am grateful you have accepted Megan's invitation," he said to her, with a bow, catching a glimpse of Allan's clenched jaw as he led Susan to a chair. When he took another, closer to the piano, Susan's eyes narrowed and her gaze turned with ferocity on Cathryn.

"What will you sing, Miss Giles?" Rupert asked, leaning toward the child, a smile on his face that broadened when the girl leaned against her teacher. With bowed heads, they murmured together and decided the program of entertainment for Mr. Smith—the only person in the room who cared what they did, the only person in the room whose opinion mattered to either accompanist or soloist.

Megan sang three songs and was about to sing a fourth when her father suggested that Miss Marcher had worked hard enough. Rupert had kept his eyes on Cathryn—her hands on the keyboard, her eyes following the music, her mouth as she sang in silence so that her pupil could watch and remember the words. When Allan spoke, Cathryn dropped her hands to her lap. Her posture, as straight as a lightning rod, sagged slightly. She was annoyed at the interruption of what was for her a pleasure and for her pupil a moment of triumph.

"If I'm not troubling you too much, Miss Marcher, may I hear you play *Kindernacht* for Megan? My poor attempt didn't do this young lady justice."

Cathryn glanced at the master of the house but didn't meet his eyes before she raised her long fingers to find the notes as Megan opened the music book to the page. Though she didn't take her eyes from the copy, Cathryn sensed Rupert's stare but she refused to flinch or falter.

"Very pretty, Megan," Susan cooed, gliding from her chair to stand by Rupert. "Do you sing any American songs, or does Miss Marcher only teach European ones?"

"I can sing 'Yankee Doodle', Mrs. Miller."

"Oh, Megan, my dear, I don't believe that's quite what a young lady should sing. Did Miss Marcher teach you that too?"

"Everyone knows that song, Susan," Cathryn said, angry that her friends treated her as though she was not in the room but she blamed their behavior on Rupert Smith—his presence and influence tainted their manners.

"In that case, perhaps you could play it for Megan to sing."

"Certainly. Sing along if you like," Cathryn urged the guests. She and Megan sang the first verse together but when Rupert joined in the chorus, Cathryn stopped for a moment but went on after one line.

Susan gazed at him and smiled when he met her eyes. Cathryn sang the second verse with very little help from Megan and abandoned any intention of a third verse when Susan slid her fingers over Rupert's coat-sleeve and touched his bare wrist. The look they exchanged made even the well-known chorus difficult for the giddy girl now gritting her teeth.

Megan sang alone for a few bars but Rupert sang with her and continued to the third verse as a solo for eight bars when Allan joined him and Susan hummed. One final chorus and Cathryn dropped her hands to her lap.

"That must be—."

"Oh no. Now that we've started, I demand an opportunity to entertain Mr. Smith as well. You will play for me, won't you, Cathryn?"

"What will you sing, Mrs. Miller?"

"Something sweet. You know the one."

Cathryn began the introduction to a war-time love song, a melancholy tune and story that all the girls had sung at every opportunity. When Susan began the verse, looking directly at Rupert, Cathryn stared at the wall above the music. His gaze fixed on the side of her face, burning through her cheek and making her eyes smart. *He thinks I'm jealous. She's off key.*

Cathryn changed key to compliment Susan's voice but it only served to confuse the singer and Cathryn reverted to the original, apologizing under her breath. At the end of the song, Susan's voice faded and Cathryn slid to the end of the piano bench. At the same time, Allan clapped and praised his Sunday guest.

Mr. Smith presented Susan with a smile in appreciation for her serenade but as soon as the widow moved toward him with her hands outstretched, he rose from the chair and turned to his host.

"Thank you for allowing your lovely, talented daughter to sing for me this afternoon. Mrs. Miller, also, I am grateful."

He lifted his hat from the rack at the door when he followed Cathryn to the entry hall and held her short coat while she put it on.

"Allan, Mrs. Giles, thank you for your hospitality and Miss Megan, I am in your debt. Good afternoon, Mrs. Miller."

Cathryn spoke to her young pupil, reassuring her and agreeing with Nancy when and where the next lesson would be as Mr. Smith left the house. Susan Miller huffed at the piano teacher's offer of the same, staring after Rupert Smith as he strolled along the front path to the gate.

"Rupert is having some difficulties at the moment," Allan commented to his guest.

"It cannot be easy for him to be in that house alone," his wife added, "after all his solitude during the war and living so far from his friends."

"There is no excuse for rudeness," Susan replied, "especially when we have been so close these past weeks."

"I'm sure he didn't mean any—."

"He was certainly charmed by Megan and Cathryn," Nancy interrupted her husband. "He hardly took his eyes off...them." The hesitation brought a scowl from her husband but Susan turned her own scowl on the teacher.

"You are such a fool, Cathryn Marcher."

"I doubt Mr. Smith had any other interest than in my ability to accompany his favorite songbirds."

"Of course not," Allan assured Mrs. Miller.

"Good afternoon, Nancy," Cathryn said as she closed the door and marched to the gate, slamming it so that the fence trembled. She reached the corner of the main street and turned toward her home.

"I see you have made a hasty retreat as well," Rupert said as he caught up to her.

"I made no retreat, Mr. Smith," Cathryn said after a few steps and her heart had regained a more even tempo, "my duty for Megan was at an end."

"Why were you not at dinner, Miss Marcher? Was that to avoid meeting me again so soon?"

"No, Mr. Smith. I was not invited to dinner. I had been engaged to accompany Megan, to entertain you."

"I see."

They walked along the pavement for several blocks as the sun descended toward the treetops. Rupert raised his wide brimmed hat to several villagers returning home from after dinner strolls.

"Was there something else, Mr. Smith?"

"No, Miss Marcher."

At the junction of the main street and the road to the cabin, Cathryn bid him a good evening but he continued to walk beside her in the twilight.

"Take my arm, Miss Marcher," he commanded when she ignored his silent offer.

"I have walked this road at all times of day and night and in all weathers, Mr. Smith. I have no need of assistance."

"All the same, Miss Marcher, I am a gentleman and my mother would be ashamed if I did not behave as one—or as near to one as my years in uncivilized circumstances will allow. Please. Allow me to show you the courtesy your friends do not."

Cathryn stood still as he spoke, watching his averted face, wondering if, as Nancy said, he was seeking companionship, wherever and from whomever it was offered. *If so, why leave the company of friends? Where has he been all these years?*

"Forgive me, if I seem rude, Mr. Smith," she answered in a soft voice. "I am accustomed to doing as I please and for myself, except when I am required by others to show better manners."

"I do not criticize you. I offer my service, to make your journey home a safer one."

"Thank you."

Had the giggly girl spoken without giving away her state? Cathryn raised her hand and he clasped it, drawing her fingers through the crook of his arm to be kissed before he patted her hand into place and held it there as they resumed the walk.

They were in twilight by the time her cabin came into view without having said another word. She was grateful she had not been required to make any intelligent observations. Incapable of conversation, her heart stung and thrashed around in her chest. On her small porch, he held her hand in place and stared away from her.

"Miss Marcher."

"Yes?"

"May I see you again?"

A brief, searing wave crashed inside her. "I am always about. I expect we will meet." She had managed two sentences. She believed she had not faltered nor revealed the sense of hope and disquiet that stung her eyes. She was thankful for the darkening sky and lack of light shining from her cabin.

"I expect we will," Rupert replied as he removed her hand and took a step back with a slight bow.

Somehow, Cathryn moved toward her front door and lifted her hand to the handle of the screen door. When she pulled, the stubborn door refused to admit her. She yanked harder, the sting in her eyes threatening to become a spring.

"Allow me." Rupert wrapped his fingers around the handle and eased the door free from the warped jamb. "That will need fixing before winter."

"Thank you, Mr. Smith."

"Good night."

She stepped into the front room and pulled the screen door closed, surprised to see him facing her, unmoving with his western hat in his hands.

"Good night, Mr. Smith," she murmured, trusting her voice no louder than *pianissimo*, as she closed the inner door.

"I believe it is customary for courting couples to use less formality, Cathryn. I would like you to call me by my name—the name my friends call me. Rupert."

Courting. There was no need for Cathryn to wonder what expression she presented, even in the darkness. Her eyes were wide and her mouth had dropped open.

"Good night...Rupert." The sound emerged from her as though she had been winded. Before he said any other word, she pressed the door into place but did not move from it until she heard him step off the porch and the crackle of gravel under his boot heels as he reached the road. Three strides away toward the village, he whistled

"Yankee Doodle" and made a racket until, as Cathryn judged from the blessed silence at last, he had reached the junction of the main street.

For the whole of the seven minutes, she remained at the door, her forehead pressed against the wooden frame, stupefied into giddy, thoughtless girlish giggling that came out of her in frantic hiccups.

Susan Miller calls him 'Rupert'. Cathryn's powers of deduction brought her to the conclusion he was courting Susan. "Oh, pishah, Evie. He's teasing you," she scolded aloud, "and now is no time to waste on that sort of shenanigans."

The remainder of the evening, by the light of her oil lamps, she began the work Mrs. Lowell had entrusted to her. The gown for the Cotillion was light work. The fabric was easily worked so by the time one lamp sputtered, Cathryn was confident the silk gown would be complete and on its return journey to the dressmaker in time for fittings before the event.

Though her eyes were weary when she prepared for bed and her body was fatigued, her head did not release her for so long that she was still asleep when she should have awakened naturally to make her biscuits and coffee for breakfast. The whispering at the warped frame of her screen door became part of a dream from which she had no reason to wake.

A full hour passed beyond five:am on Monday morning before the rhythmic thump at the back of the cabin became as incessant as her own heartbeat but was a counterpoint to her body. Cathryn kept no timepiece in her bedroom but the amount of light between the chink of her curtains announced she was too late for biscuits. She blamed the escapade to Portland, the late nights, the journey back, her fright—in short, she blamed Rupert Smith.

"What is that noise?" she asked the room, grabbing one of her father's work shirts and a pair of boot-socks before trotting into the cold kitchen. "Darn it."

The fire in the stove was out. "What's come over you, Evie?" she whispered. Heartbeat. Thump. Heartbeat. Thump. "What in tarn—what are you doing here?"

There he was in shirt sleeves, his braces hanging around his hips, the axe poised above his shoulder.

Thump. Her heartbeat was quickening and its tempo pushed blood like hot coals to her cheeks.

Thump.

"Mr. Smith."

"Rupert," he reminded her as the axe plummeted to split another log.

"Why are you here?"

"What does it look like to you, Cathryn?" He set a section of a tree trunk on its side and plunged the axe into it. The two halves fell off the block. He split each half into quarters and eighths, tossing them onto a pile.

"There's enough in that pile to burn 'til Arbor Day," Cathryn said, pushing through the back door and wrapping her arms around her chest.

"Good. Let me know when there's enough to last 'til next Christmas."

After a moment, she stepped to the edge of the porch as he wiped his brow on his forearm. "Rupert."

He looked at her as the axe split through another log. "What is it, Cathryn?"

"I don't know what you're doing or trying to prove but it isn't necessary. I can chop my own firewood."

"I know. I've seen you do it." He swung again.

"Why, then, are you doing this?"

"Needs doing." Thump. "Go back in the kitchen, Cathryn. I'm about done and I could sure use a cup of your fine coffee." Thump.

She filled her arms with kindling and a few logs, built a stack in the stove and set it alight. When she had the kettle on, she went to her room to dress. There was ample time to bake biscuits since he had done the biggest chore she had set herself that morning. While she made the dough, rolled it out and cut squares, the strike of the axe reverberated in the center of her being. The biscuits baked and the coffee perked.

Rupert honed and cleaned the axe, wiped the blade down with an oily cloth and stowed it in the box on the porch. He bent over the pump and washed the sweat from his face and neck, dried his hands on his handkerchief, gazing across to the woods as the sun climbed through the branches.

He was not the almost-grown man she had been all aflutter about when she was still a schoolgirl. Although she couldn't put her finger on how he was different, she liked him as much though she had no more reason for it than she had ten years ago. "I guess you can't tell your heart what's sensible if it's got a mind of its own."

She set the biscuits, wrapped in a napkin, on a plate on the table.

"You had best come in and have some breakfast, Rupert." She could get used to saying his name even if it was going to hurt so much more to hear Susan Miller call him back to her. And there was that sting in her eyes when he stood inside the back door that she could only control by swinging away to pour his coffee. She set the cup by his plate and got busy with sweet butter, jam and stewed peaches from the cold store beneath the pantry.

Where his shirt was still damp from his exertion on her behalf, it clung to his shoulders and down his spine. She might have caught enough breath between the pantry and the larder not to faint but she had never been so light-headed.

Wouldn't Susan laugh if I end up in a heap on the floor at his feet.

Never once in all the years she carried severed limbs to the incinerator or soothed rotting flesh with useless infusions had she faltered. Through all that, she kept herself strong and fearless for Rupert's sake—what she did for those men, she prayed another woman did for Rupert. And here he was in her home with no need other than a hot cup of coffee and she was weaker than a newborn and as terrified as a rabbit.

What are you thinking, Evie?

She passed her hand over her brow and settled her score with the timid giggler enough to carry the jam and sweet butter to the table. When he thanked her, she blushed, returned to the pantry as though he had growled.

"Is my presence so painful for you that you cannot be in the same room with me?"

"I don't understand why you are here," Cathryn replied, turning toward him but unable to look at his face. "I don't know what you want, what I'm supposed to do."

"I have already answered that, Cathryn. I have asked to see you. I have declared my intention to court you. In your own way, you have granted me the privilege of your company."

"But why? What about Susan? I should think she will expect you to be more in her company than mine."

"I am not courting the widow, Mrs. Miller, Cathryn."

"Tell that to her friends, to the whole of Oslo Hill and half of the county." *He's mocking me.* Her voice, even in her own head, had risen, turned strident.

"I have no reason to tell them. I have told you. I would sooner sit in a tree with a hungry pole cat than be any closer to Mrs. Miller than I am, right now, to you."

"That's not the impression you gave her or anyone else yesterday."

"I am not responsible for anyone's impression. If you believe I would rather be with her, why—tell me why you think I'm here."

"I told you, I don't know."

"Don't know or refuse to know?"

"Don't."

"Then you give me no choice," Rupert said, taking the three strides that separated them. "You're the prettiest damned girl I ever set eyes on. If not for you, I'd never have set foot back in this town. I've thought about you every day I wasn't just trying to keep alive for the best part of ten years. If not for you, Cathryn Marcher, I'd have gladly died in that prison camp than live another day like an animal."

"That can't be true. None of that is true."

"Is it Jericho, Cathryn?" He bowed his head to see her face. "Do you still love him?"

"No." With no more sound than a breath, she said, "I never loved him."

"Never?"

"Never." She turned away with a sob, too late to hold back that terrible confession.

Rupert stood close behind her but refrained from touching her, taking a breath to catch the scent of her hair and skin, feel her warmth. "Can you love me? Can you ever love me?"

She covered her face. *He's fooling. Don't let him fool you, Evie.* But it was too late. He already knew. He'd guessed and she couldn't stop the words. "I've always loved you."

As soon as she spoke the words she knew she'd never be able to deny them. They hung over her like a shroud and the pantry was thick with their pall. "There. Now you know."

She dragged her hands away from her face and clutched the edge of the slate slab, waiting for him to laugh or go or say something but he stood behind her in silence. Breaking the spell of the appalling truth was up to her. She moved to the side and past him, back to the kitchen.

"Your coffee is getting cold."

For the next few minutes, he stood in the pantry doorway as she filled his cup, brush crumbs for the table, put the biscuits he hadn't eaten in a tin, drew water from the pump in the backyard, set a kettle on the stove.

He'll go soon. He has what he came for. They'll have a good laugh about this next Sunday. She needn't think about it or worry again that she had let it slip. The terrible truth was gone, out of her control. Over and done. Resignation, not anger, that she had been right and there was no need to hold any hope filled her with relief.

Nine

Rupert lowered his gaze. Cathryn rushed from one task to another then stood aside as he returned to the table, drank the fresh coffee, ate the last biscuit, put all the dishes in the sink. "I'll make certain that door jamb's planed smooth before I stack up the wood."

Though people were sure to see him, Cathryn didn't stop him from going onto the front porch. He ran his hand over the wood, checking for rough patches, sanding them down, testing them again with his open palm. He blew away the sawdust with a whistling breath, peered hard at his work and raised his hand in greeting to the chicken farmer taking his eggs into town.

"Powerful nice mornin', Rupert," Noam called, searching the windows for sign of his tenant.

"Ay-yuh," the younger man replied.

"Cathryn gone to town?"

"Didn't say, Noam. Weren't around when I turned up."

"Maybe I'll catch her on her way back."

"Any message if you don't."

"She'll know. Good day to you, Rupert. Glad to see Cathryn's letting someone help her for a change."

Rupert nodded his farewell and returned his attention to the final touches to his work. When Noam Snyder's cart turned onto the main road, Rupert slid into the front room where Cathryn stood out of sight in the narrow passage leading back to the kitchen.

"No sense in getting him all riled up for no good reason."

"Thank you."

"So what's his message?"

"Nothing important."

Rupert locked the screen door and pushed the other closed after him. "I'll stack up the wood pile before I go."

"There's no need for you to do that. It's not a big job, Rupert."

"You have better things to do."

She moved backwards to the kitchen and out of his way as he came towards her. The doors to the two small rooms on opposite sides of the passageway were open but he didn't look into either. Once he was in the kitchen, he left the house and filled his arms with firewood to stack on her back porch.

"I'll put the green wood at the back."

"You've been very kind." She stood at the back door, her arms folded.

He glanced up and grinned for a moment, finished his job and pulled up his braces. "Least I could do, Cathryn. I'll be gone for a few days. Didn't want you to be cold or stuck out of your house when I'm not around."

"Where are you going?"

"I have some business to get done up to Augusta."

"How long?"

"Not long enough for you to miss me. I'll be calling on you for more of your coffee and biscuits before you even notice." He hooked his plaid jacket over his shoulder and planted his hat on his head. "Don't let that fire in the stove go out like you did last night."

"How did you know that?"

"No smoke. No fire," he said, nodding toward the tin flue running up the side of the cabin. "I don't want to come back to find you frozen solid."

"I won't."

"See you don't."

"Yes, sir, I'll see you when you get back."

"That you will, Cathryn Marcher. That you most surely will."

He took the trail through the woods and was a long while out of her sight before she stopped watching where she had last seen him.

A few days was longer than she expected when she woke near five:am two days in a row to make coffee and biscuits only to drink the coffee herself and store the biscuits in tins. Noam Snyder called by on the Friday morning and told her she was making every mouth on the road water with the aroma of her biscuits and jam. He still expected the rent money but Cathryn brought the total down some when she handed him the three tins and a pot of her blueberry jam.

As much as she disliked the task, she wrote out a bill for Nancy Giles and walked across town to hand it to her before mid-day.

"Well, I never," Nancy said as she unfolded the paper. "I'd never have asked if I thought for a minute you'd take this attitude, Cathryn."

"I understood you wanted me to accompany Megan as an entertainment for Mr. Smith."

"Well, yes, but as a favor—to a friend. I thought you'd welcome the chance to impress him."

"Impressing Mr. Smith doesn't pay my rent, Nancy."

"Hmm, well, that's not what I've heard. Half the town saw him walking you home. And don't think Susan doesn't know you're after her beau."

"That is not true. Can you pay me now or should I wait for Allan to get home?"

"This will have to come out of my housekeeping allowance, you know."

Cathryn stepped over the threshold, sick at the thought of taking money—she was not a beggar but asking her friends to pay her made her feel she was.

"Don't you dare tell Allan. He's mad enough to spit already." Nancy had no conscience about using her to flail her husband but Cathryn was not to profit by it. With the money in her purse, Cathryn walked home again and turned the remainder of her rent over to Noam while he had his dinner.

"Seen Rupert Smith lately?"

"No. Is he back?"

"Back from where?"

"Wherever he's been."

"How'd you know he was gone?"

"I'm not a Pinkerton, Noam. Everyone talks about Mr. Smith. He's hard *not* to miss."

"Hmm, I suppose. Just you watch you don't get caught up in what everyone is talking about."

"Why would anyone talk about me in the same breath as Mr. Smith?"

"Same as they talk about any unattached females with a man like him, you being a spinster and Mrs. Miller a widow. Ahn't no two ways about it, he's playing you against her, otherwise what was he doing at your place before the roosters were a'crowing?"

Why should anyone believe Rupert was courting her when she didn't believe it herself?

"Same as any gentleman neighbor I suspect, Noam. Probably feels some obliged since his mother was poorly."

"Glad to see you're taking this sensible."

"When you're passing, please leave my rent receipt as usual, Noam. I'll be by this coming Thursday as usual for the girls' lessons."

She didn't so much as walk back to her cabin as swoop on her broomstick to the back door, grabbing an armload of wood and slamming the door behind her.

"Is that how the front door got warped so bad?"

All the wood fell to the floor as she clasped her hands to her chest in fright. Rupert crouched at her feet to collect the split wood and tumble it into the basket by the stove. "I'm a half a day early for biscuits but I was hoping for some of your coffee," he said when she still hadn't spoken. The moment she tore her bonnet off and slammed the door of her bedroom and commenced the banging of drawers, he whistled a bit and said, "Guess the answer to that is pretty clear."

Despite all the noise she made, Cathryn heard him open the creaky door of the stove's firebox, pump water and set the kettle on the hot plate. She sank to the edge of the bed with her mother's shawl still crushed in her hands. She smoothed it flat and folded it back into the drawer, quelling the giddiness. *See sense, Evie. Everyone else can.*

When he tapped on the door, she flattened her skirt and stood, breathing deep.

"Water's boiling." His boot heels thumped on the bare floorboards back to the kitchen. When she opened the door, she saw his legs stretched out away from the table and his arm resting on the back of the chair. He didn't take his gaze off her face when she refused to look at him, couldn't look at him, flat out willed herself not to look at him. She dumped coffee beans in the hand grinder, turned the crank until she lost count, set the coffee to brew for a few minutes while she set out slices of her sour cherry cake.

The whole time, his gaze followed her around like a beacon searching the sea. After she had poured his coffee, calmed her nerves enough to carry it without shaking, she put the cup and plate of cakes in front of him and backed away.

"I must have given you some cause but I can't think what I've done except be eager to see you." He sank his teeth into a slice of cake, taking almost half of it in one bite, washed it down with a swallow of coffee. In a few moments, he'd finished off what she offered and pushed the plate away. "Since you're not in a talking mood, I'll be going."

Although his comment felt like a hard and fast kick, Cathryn drew herself together on a slow breath and stood her ground. He stepped onto the back porch and settled his hat on his head.

"Much obliged for the coffee, Miss Marcher."

"Rupert." She stood in the doorway, behind the screen, slipped the hook into the bracket. When he turned to face her, she said, "Please don't come back."

Before he answered, before her own shame knocked her down, she closed the inner kitchen door with a soft click and set the bolt lock. She covered her ears to shut out the sound of his footsteps when he left the porch and occupied herself with tidying the kitchen, willing herself to refrain from looking out the window above the sink and abandoning any thought of an evening meal for the seclusion of her front room and the music she had purchased in Portland.

Even that forced her back to Rupert Smith. After unhappy attempts to come to grips with the *adagio*, she closed the lid over the keys, spreading her hands and stretching her arms along the smooth wood. *Why has this happened to me? What have I ever done to deserve this? Self-pity does not finish a lady's ball gown.*

With a resolve born of necessity, Cathryn walked into the other small room along the passageway. She unfolded the brown paper from around the brocade fabric and held the half-constructed dress to her body before she sat down at the sewing machine to add the sleeves. When the light faded and the oil lamps gave off too little light for her to work without causing damage, she returned to the kitchen to prepare the stove for the night, working by the light of the embers.

The owls swooping through the branches was a rustle that signaled death for anything that ventured into the darkness. Cathryn washed by the light of a candle in her bedroom and crawled into the middle of the wide bed. Unlike previous nights, she fell asleep, concentrating only on the sounds of the trees scraping against the window, as rhythmic as her breathing.

When she woke at her usual hour, as on previous mornings, the yard was silent but for the creaks of the old cabin as the air warmed. Though she had no reason, she baked biscuits and made coffee. When they had cooled, she wrapped them in muslin and stored them, drank the coffee as she ate her slice of toast and planned her day. She had grass to cut and weeds to hoe, pumpkins to raise and beans to grind.

Dressed in her father's work shirt and canvas pants, stamped into her mother's work boots and tied her hair back with a strip of sacking. In the front yard, at the side of the road, she piled the few rain-blasted leaves at the edge of the lawn. Her landlord drove by with his milk cart. She waved but neither spoke.

The fresh, bright glow in the sky promised a fine day and the breeze was no more than a sigh that brushed her cheek whenever she turned her face into it. She left her boots on the porch when she went for the rake to drag the leaves into burlap sacks, and stayed barefoot to rake the grass cuttings into the same sacks for mulch. The twittering chipmunks above her accompanied *The Emperor* concerto floating in her head but was no more successful than her effort to play the notes on the old piano. *I wonder if Rupert noticed his mother's piano? He'll want to know how I came by it. I'll tell Noam to get some of his boys to take it back where it belongs so he won't think I had stolen it.*

"Blazes and tarnation, Evie," she moaned, "what are you going to do without the Singer?" She sat down on the damp lawn with the rake across her knees as the concerto died to nothing more than a wisp of sound, winding its way through her thoughts.

Why did he come back? Why didn't he stay missing and none of this would have happened. I'll have to write to him, make a list of all his father gave me when his mother died. Better if I ask Allan to do it so it's all clear, legal, above board. He won't know to connect any of these things to Evie. No one knows about her. And she's gone, now he's back. I can never tell him now I didn't straight out when he asked. Oh, Lord. What if he finds out I lied? Not lied exactly. But how could I tell him that without having to tell him what happened, why they used that name? Oh, you are more than a fool, Evie Marcher. No one's going to believe you now. Might as well pack up, move to Portland. Boston. No one in Boston knows a thing about you. Tarnation!

She jumped up from the ground and raked through the damp grass. Determined to get into town and everything done and over with, Cathryn ran into the house to change. All the yard work and the sewing had to wait. Slapping her bonnet on her untidy hair, she made sure the front door was locked and was locking the back with a key—no more leaving the cabin open for any stranger—.

"What are you doing here?" she demanded of the pair of black boots sticking out from behind the wood pile. "I thought I asked you not to come back."

"You did." He pushed to his feet and stretched his back.

"Then why are you here?"

"You didn't say anything about staying, Cathryn, and if that's the only way I can see you, that's what I'll do."

"You can't have stayed here all night You'd have frozen to death."

"Sleeping on your back porch was near enough to a grand hotel compared to some places I've slept."

"I don't believe you."

"Almost killed me when you made those biscuits. I thought for a minute you were going to take pity on me and let me in for some of your coffee but it wasn't to be. When you're riled, you stay riled for a good long time, Cathryn Marcher."

"That doesn't prove you were here all night, Mr. Smith. I make biscuits near every morning."

"You don't rattle pots, pound away on that piano or stamp that treadle board half the night."

"That doesn't prove anything." She turned the key in the lock and dropped it into her bag. "I'm going into town. I don't want you to be here when I get back." She turned away and swung back. "And I don't want any of your tricks, Mr. Smith. When I say 'here,' I mean anywhere on my property. Is that clear?"

"Clear as day and your pretty brown eyes, Cathryn, but as this isn't your property—."

"I pay my rent and while I do, it's as good as owning it." She gasped. "Someone will see you walk back to town. You can go through the woods."

"Not today. You've ordered me off so I'll have to go along the road. Otherwise, I can't be sure when I'll be on or off your property 'til I get all the way back to my own property."

"Why are you making this difficult? Why are you so stubborn?"

"How else is a man supposed to court his girl when she has taken against him for no just cause he can see? Last time I was here, you said you loved me. I can't think of anything I've done in the hours between then and now to make you change your mind."

"I'm no fool giddy girl, Mr. Smith. I know when someone is making fun of me."

"I don't doubt that for a wink of your sparkling eye, but I do doubt you have any inkling when someone truly loves you."

Cathryn turned her head away, staring at the neglected vegetable patch, recognizing all the signs of rot and spoil. Another day of decay and she couldn't think of making or selling any of her pumpkin pies. She hadn't saved herself for him, why should she save herself from him? If she had nothing else, she'd have that and they'd all be satisfied. They'd all know what she got up to in Boston.

Pulling her bonnet off and untying the strip of cloth, shaking her hair loose over her shoulders and moving close enough, closer than she had ever been to a man she loved with all her heart and soul, close enough to feel the heat of his body and his breath on her face, so close all he had to do was bow his head and brush her parted lips and he would know what he wanted to know, could tell Susan and Nancy and Mrs. Moffatt, Aurelius Cook's father and Noam Snyder exactly what they had always thought—because she loved Rupert Smith more than she cared what any one of them thought they knew about her, because she loved him and mourned for him and longed for every lonely moment she was apart from him to be swept away even if that meant he was proved right and could walk away from her, never look back or wonder what their life together might have been—just one moment of loving him as she had always loved him and would go on loving him because she couldn't do anything else.

She pressed her lips against his unshaven jaw and her brow against his temple. The coarser waves of his hair caught in her blonde curls as she tilted her chin upwards to offer her mouth. She leaned her shoulder against his chest, turned her body into his, sighed his name, raised her hand to his cheek. He turned his head into the caress. His lips pressed on the heel of her palm and his arm encircled her waist, his hand locked around hers.

"Rupert." *He will know how much I love him. At least he will know that.* She kissed his jaw, the corner of his hard mouth, straining every muscle of her body to reach him, until his hands clamped on her shoulders and he pushed her away, held her at arms' length. She strained to see his face but he kept his gaze averted.

He swept up her bonnet from the bare boards of the porch and shoved it into her arms. "If I had come here for that, no damned flimsy screen door could have kept me out. Go do what you have to do in town, Miss Marcher. Be assured I won't be here when you return."

Running and stumbling through the woods like a mad woman got her as far as the clump of lilac she'd hidden in as a little girl, afraid to go home for the licking her father promised when she refused to help her mother with the washing because she wanted to play the piano for a few minutes more.

The ground in the center of the clump was soft and black with mold but she didn't care when she dropped to her knees and broke her heart with sobs, caring not a whit who might hear her, who might talk, who knew that George Rupert Smith had all he wanted and nothing of what she wanted to give him.

She hadn't given him the satisfaction of tears. Her dignity was intact. He didn't have to know that, when she twisted her hair into a knot and crammed the bonnet on her head, tied the ribbons under her chin, she was about as close as she ever come to dying of shame. In no mood or condition to go to Allan Giles's house, Cathryn stayed in the woods, wandering toward the river and the mill, as far as Noam's until she made a decision about what she had to do.

At dusk, she crossed the fields and through the rows of hen houses, dodging the roosters and knocked on the Snyders' kitchen door. Noam was out with the hands but Lila Snyder let her in, gave her a glass of water while the two girls pestered her for a lesson.

"I can't pay him," Cathryn told her landlady, "but do you think he'd accept extra lessons for your girls until he thinks I've paid him back?"

"Well, I don't know, Cathryn. You know how he can be. There isn't a fairer man than Noam but he does expect his due. You go on home now and I'll talk him round."

Walking along the road in the dark, dawdling until she was too close to avoid being seen and assured by the cold silence all around her that Rupert was true to his word. She had her wish. She was alone and just as miserable as she was when he pushed her away. She didn't have to trouble wondering what he thought of her—exactly what he did when he saw her with Jericho. And she'd given him all the proof he'd wanted, throwing herself at him.

Can't be any worse. She unlocked the backdoor, latched the screen and banked the fire for the night. For as long as she could work, she stayed in her sewing room, stomping on the treadle, using what few hours she had left of the machine before her landlord brought a crew of his farm hands over to pack it into his wagon along with the Gilbert piano and all the sheets of music George Smith had sent to her. Noam was the only one who knew the broken old man had wanted her to have it. He had helped her then to take it to the cabin. Just a few days later, George Smith died.

"Oh, why is it never enough?" There was no answer in the dark cabin but the sound of the sewing needle sliding up and down.

Enduring the Sunday school and church, alone in the organ loft, refusing to acknowledge the imperfectly blended voices of the widow and the prodigal veteran, Cathryn returned to her cabin to make the fruit pudding she had promised young Master Cook.

Monday afternoon, Cathryn waited at the front door of her cabin, behind the screen, for her young guest. When he ran to within sight of the cabin then slowed to a stroll, smoothing his clothing, his Sunday School teacher stepped onto the porch, holding her shawl around her shoulders.

The small table, set with linen cloth, crockery and tinplate stood to the side.

"Thank you for accepting my invitation, Master Cook."

"Thank you for inviting me, Miss Marcher."

"I always keep my promises, sir." She made a slight curtsy and offered him a seat at the table as he joined her on the porch. "Make yourself at home. Do you prefer coffee or lemonade?"

The boy thought a moment, twisting his mouth up at the corner. "Coffee, Miss, thank you."

Once he was settled at the table, Cathryn went into the house and returned with a tray. She poured him a cup of coffee and cut a slice of the fruit pudding. "Be my guest, Master Cook, whatever you don't eat you can take home with you."

"This is nice of you, Miss."

"Nonsense. I promised. You worked very hard and you are a gentleman."

"That's what Mr. Smith said."

"Did he?"

"Yes, Miss. He said, sometimes, if a feller works hard enough, even when life 'tahn't fair, a feller can get lucky."

"Mr. Smith is a philosopher as well. Please taste the pudding and drink your coffee, sir."

"Are you having any? 'Twouldn't be right if you didn't, Miss."

"I'm delighted to join you."

The thirteen-year-old consumed more than half the pudding and after some thought, decided he was taking the dish home, even if he ate the rest on the journey, so he didn't seem too much of a glutton. He was near to stuffed to the gills when he sat back and took a deep breath.

"You've done very well, Master Cook. I doubt even Mr. Smith could have matched that performance."

"I think he could, Miss. He could eat that and a pie— even a pumpkin pie."

"That will be tested when the church has its Summer Fete."

The young man offered to do some of her chores in return for her hospitality but Rupert Smith had weeded her squash patch and set her pumpkins on tripods of sticks while she wandered the woods and talked Lila Snyder into sending Noam with the piano back to its rightful owner. She was still working on a plan to pay for the sewing machine—a tool she had to have to earn a living.

Her guest left with a basket of biscuits, jam and the remainder of the pudding as the sun dropped into the mountains behind the sawmill. Cathryn smiled to herself as she cleared the table and carried it back to its place in her sewing room.

Running her hand over the spine of the machine she hoped Rupert Smith was willing to sell, she calculated she'd have the Cotillion ball gown ready to take back to Mrs. Lowell before the Summer Fete, if she was able to keep Margaret Smith's treasured Singer before she'd paid for it—in the same way Mrs. Smith had purchased from the manufacturer. It was now Cathryn's treasured machine and essential to her livelihood.

Torn between work and pleasure, Cathryn chose to make the most of her last few hours of being the owner of a square grand piano made especially for Peggy Smith by her husband's abolitionist[12] friend, Timothy Gilbert. She lit the two candles at either end of the keyboard and spread the sheet music ready, poised her fingers and began again to master Beethoven's piano concerto.

She had struggled through the *adagio* to the *rondo* when the knock on the screen door stilled her fingers. She paused

---

[12] **Timothy Gilbert** maintained an active station on the Underground Railroad and at the passage of the Fugitive Slave Law, announced in the papers that his door would remain open to runaway slaves.

long enough to be sure she hadn't been mistaken. The mantel clock ticked onto the quarter hour before eight in the evening. The only light on the porch came from the candles beside her and whoever called had seen her at the instrument. She rose and opened the door before her visitor knocked again.

"Good evening, Cathryn. May I come in?"

She stood for a moment, in silence. When she lifted the hook out of the latch, she stepped back and walked to the back of the cabin when Jericho Colson drew the curtain over the front window and followed her.

Had she thought her situation couldn't be any worse? She filled the kettle with enough water to make coffee, lit the hanging oil lamp and folded her arms around her body, dragging her shawl close to her neck.

"Why are you here?" she asked of the man filling the doorway.

"After our meeting in Portland, I haven't had an hour's peace."

"So you come here, to my home? You found me. How?"

"Mrs. Moffatt is well-known in Portland society—a single question, a simple answer."

"I asked you not to do this. We agreed. For the sake of your family—your wife and daughters."

"Amelia knows and cares not a whit, Cathryn. I promised, you are right but I have not broken my word to you. Nor have you reason to doubt me."

"Meeting in Portland was unfortunate," she said, "I never intended or envisioned such an occurrence."

"But we have met again," Jericho replied, taking a step toward her, extending his hand, "my dearest. There is nothing now that impedes our friendship." He held his hand palm upwards, waiting.

"There is an impediment."

"I know you do not mean that wastrel who interrupted our conversation."

"Mr. Smith is another matter."

"I know he is not important to you," Colson said.

For a moment Cathryn held her retort and her confession. One man had that knowledge and he was the only man who would ever know. She did not need further humiliation. She did not want another clandestine visitor.

"I prefer you to leave my home, sir. The hour is late and your presence is inappropriate. *And* unwelcome."

"How else may I see you, Cathryn?"

"The church service begins at eleven, as with most denominations in this county. I do not wish to be rude, but I must prepare my lesson for my Sunday School class and the music for the service."

"As you wish, my dear," he said with a smile. "I understand your requirement for propriety in this hamlet. I concur. We will find ample opportunity to renew our friendship while I attend to matters of business at the college. Until Sunday, my darling." Though he glanced at the steaming kettle, he made no comment regarding the promise of a more hospitable welcome and left her house as he had come.

Cathryn locked the screen door and gritted her teeth at the drawn the curtain. His intrusion, unexpected as much as unwelcome and unwarranted, had robbed her of any sense of peace or contentment that practicing music had given her. With each step she took to return to the kitchen, her sense of injustice grew. What right did he have to presume she welcomed a renewal of their friendship? What right did Allan Giles have to presume she was content to endure his insults because she was poor? And what right gave Rupert cause for such arrogance preceding such acts of kindness?

Ten

While she sipped the coffee she made for herself in the hours after Jericho's departure, she stared into the darkness of the squash patch, the light of the moon reflecting on the deep green of her young crop and the white strips of cotton tying up the string bean stalks. *Wastrel?* She had never known a man so industrious, so instinctively correct in his presumptions—as though he knew her mind. But *his* mind was a mystery—closed at least to her.

Perhaps he was ashamed of his arrogant dismissal, his rejection of her offer and, in guilt, made amends. Any fool could have seen her pumpkins required attention. *Don't read into him what you wish to be, Evie. See what is.*

When she retired to her bedroom, she was tempted to read Jericho Colson's letters, to remember what had been. He wanted her but he, like Allan, came to her in secret. She knew the reason and closed her eyes in rage. A man can be a villain, a notorious womanizer, a rogue of the worst sort but a woman, however it come about for whatever her reasons or intentions, is fallen and never forgiven.

Cathryn's choices were clear to her as she stared into the beams above her. Remain alone and live as she pleased—her preferred choice as long as she was left in peace to stay where she had always felt at home. Leave to find another life where her past would still be a subject of speculation and investigation and she would feel even more an outcast. For all their drawbacks, both were infinitely better than the preferences of the two wedded men who pursued her, intent to make her their mistress—a choice that, in five or so years would see her destitute and as alone as either of the other choices but more degraded and hopeless.

And so, when she awoke in the early Tuesday morning hours to make her coffee and warm her biscuits, Cathryn Evelyn Marcher's answer was *Never* to Jericho and Allan—as well as any other who came forward with any less desirable offer than marriage—well-knowing that could not be.

At her usual time, she locked her cabin and began her journey to the church in the center of the town but had not left her front porch when Rupert Smith appeared at the bottom of her path from the road, plaid jacket, western boots, and hat in his hands.

"Good morning, Cathryn."

"I have made myself as clear as possible without being uncivil, Mr. Smith," she said as she reached the road, standing a foot away, erect and proud when he looked her over, from bonnet to walking boots.

"I am not on your property, Cathryn, as you have dictated. However, since we are courting, I have come to walk with you on the public road to the church to give piano lessons to the village urchins. Unless you tell me, in all honesty, that I may not walk with you in public on common ground, that is what I intend to do."

How is it he remembers these appointments? "Thanks to you and many others like you, Mr. Smith, this is a free country and I cannot deny you the freedom for which so many have given their lives."

"Will you accept the offer of my arm, Cathryn?"

"As kind as your offer and as grateful as I am for your contribution to my chores, Mr. Smith, I prefer to rely on my own strength."

Rupert smiled and settled his wide-brimmed hat on his head, waited for her to join him on the road and walked beside her, keeping the arm closest to her, ready behind his back at the first sign of her slightest need.

"I am truly grateful for your help with my vegetables."

"If not for my stubborn impulse, you would have had ample time to see to them."

"What stubborn impulse was this?"

"There are so many, Cathryn," he laughed. "I should have gone home Friday night." When she didn't disagree, he continued, "Instead, I was clever, at your expense. I regret I did not think further than my own selfish wish to spend as many hours with you as you grant. Cathryn?"

"Yes, Mr. Smith?"

"Will you grant me the pleasure of your company? If I behave as a gentleman and not some rough cow hand?"

"Is that what you call lurking on my back porch and scaring the wits out of me?" Before he answered, she asked, "Is that the work you've been doing, Rupert?"

"For a few years. That and anything else that came along."

"Why didn't you come home?"

"Home wasn't an option, not for a long time."

"Why not?"

"And when it was, there didn't seem to be any reason, with my parents gone, nothing but the house and memories I couldn't, didn't want to face. Disappointments I wasn't ready to accept."

"You seem very sure of what you would find."

"I wasn't," he replied. "I presumed, from past knowledge, what future awaited me."

"What finally brought you home, if you were so certain?"

"A good friend, who knows me better than I know myself."

"Did this friend ask you to come home?"

"No, he told me to go home."

Cathryn glanced at him in surprise, her own presumptions having taken her toward another kind of friend.

"But it was a letter from another friend that had held me sound to this place and made it impossible for me to have any future until I came home."

"Was that Allan?" she asked, hoping he would not say Susan.

"No, Cathryn. That was you."

This time, when she glanced at him, she stopped walking. "How can that be? I only wrote once, to tell you of your parents' deaths."

"You wrote twice and I have kept your first letter with me." He removed the leather wallet from his jacket inside pocket and held it open for her.

The wretched, inappropriate giddy girl sprang into her and she reeled, breathless, blood rushing in every direction. He caught her before she stumbled backwards onto the dusty verge but she was too lightheaded to stand. "Why would you keep such a silly, childish thing?" she demanded when she had recovered. She was sitting on the milk churn platform in front of a neighbor's farm gate.

"This was all I had of you. Why did you never write to me again?"

"How foolish do you think I am, Mr. Smith?" She straightened her back. "Did you reply? No, thank heavens. At least you were kind enough then not to do so. But why now? What have I done in these ten years to deserve your ridicule now?" She stood again without assistance and resumed her journey, leaving him at the milk stand.

"Cathryn!"

She quickened her pace and reached the junction of the main street when he caught up to her.

"How can you believe that? How can you believe I am capable of such insensitivity and still love me?"

She stopped again, staring away from him, mustering all her force of will not to wail, though her throat was ripping with barbs of self-mocking. "Because, because I am that silly, childish, ridiculous romantic girl. Still. I can no more stop loving you than I can stop that river from flowing."

"That's good."

"How is that good except it makes tormenting me so much more rewarding?"

"That's good." He gazed in the same direction she stared. "Cathryn." He studied her profile for a moment. "How could I answer you? How can I answer you now? When that letter arrived, I had no idea if I'd be alive in the next moment. Days, weeks, months of uncertainty and I wanted to—all I wanted, all I could say—was to beg you to wait for me. What kind of cruelty would that have been? Every moment, I saw men blown to damnation. Wherever I looked, I met the eyes of condemned men, all of us waiting our turn to die.

"How could I ask a girl to wait for what I saw in other men's hearts and knew that same evil grew in me? When I was wounded, I prayed to die. The surgeon in the prison camp marked me for amputation—to save what was left of me but I refused. I wanted to return to you a whole man but I was less whole than any of the men who lost limbs. I couldn't come back to you like that and I was glad I hadn't written, hadn't tied you to a dead man." He remained silent a moment. "In what way could my answer have been of any use to you?" he asked, laying his hand on the wallet. "I could not return here half a man, not to you, the warrior maiden."

She began her walk again and he kept pace.

"You are the most forthright, courageous woman I've ever known, Cathryn. You need a whole man, not a broken hulk who'll play sad songs on your heart strings 'til I break you as well. I need a woman who'll stand up to me and with me."

This time, when she stopped walking, she turned to face him and met his gaze.

"You've always been the woman I've wanted and needed. I'm the man for you. Will you marry me, Cathryn Marcher?"

That ridiculous giddy girl leapt up again and almost choked her to death trying to get out and make a fool of her. "Why would you want me to do that?"

"*You* shouldn't want that. I meant to make you despise me, but I have loved you for so long, I couldn't go on hurting you. Proving that will take most, if not all, of our married life."

"What do you want me to say?"

"For now, that you will think about it but you best know I'm telling everyone I meet, from this moment, you and I are engaged."

Cathryn turned to walk the remaining distance to the church. "In that case," she said at the start of the footpath, "I'd best say yes so I don't make a liar of you."

When they reached the door to the hall, Rupert put his hand in his pocket. "I hoped I could bring this and not have to take it home again." He caught her hand and slipped a ring on her finger. "My mother's. She'd have wanted you to have it."

"Thank you, Rupert."

"One more thing." He held up a key before her eyes. "I'd say this was the key to my heart, Cathryn, but you've had that all these years. I had this made for you so you won't be locked out and have to herd rowdy boys again or face disapproving little girls. It won't do either of us much good with all the rowdy boys and forthright girls we'll have ourselves."

"Are you sure about this? I won't blame you if you change your mind," she said, looking into his blue eyes. "You know I'm not—."

"I know all I need to know, Cathryn. You'll need to know a deal more about me. The main one being I love you." She stepped closer. "Maybe that I'm not in trouble with the law...now." When her eyes widened, he laughed. "I'm not changing my mind, Miss Marcher, and neither are you." He glanced at the children turning onto the footpath. "I'll be waiting for you, right here."

"What makes you think I want you to do that?"

"Regardless, I will be here. Up to you if you let me walk you home." He stepped back and bowed, squared his hat and walked past the children gathered for their group lesson, heading for the town.

Cathryn unlocked the hall door and dropped the key into her basket. Megan Giles marched straight toward her.

"What did Mr. Smith ask you? Does he want me to sing again?"

Cathryn patted the little girl's head and smiled. "You'll have to learn a new song, I think."

"I already am, Miss. Mrs. Miller says Mr. Smith wants me to sing a duet with her. She's teaching me."

"What song is she teaching you?"

"*For the love my heart doth prize.*"

"An Italian song," Cathryn commented, "sung in English." She turned her attention to the young man beside her who volunteered without a word between them to set up the chairs in a semi-circle around the old piano. A smaller boy peaked in Cathryn's basket.

"Mr. Smith will be sorry he didn't stay for these biscuits," he crooned, placing the tin on the table.

Miss Megan Giles swung her layers of skirts and pantaloons as she said, "Mr. Smith won't miss any of that. He is having morning coffee with my father at Mrs. Miller's house and she made a blueberry shortcake with whipped cream."

Mrs. Moffatt commandeered her at the end of the lesson, herding her protégé up the stairs into the pastor's office and requesting her help to arrange the music for the Sunday service.

"I will not bother to ask because I will not accept no for an answer. You will be coming with me for your dinner today."

"That is very kind of you."

"I hear a 'but' in that statement, however, I cannot possibly allow you to have an excuse."

"Is there a special reason for your invitation?"

"Of course. I do nothing without good reason. Walk with me and I will explain."

Cathryn offered her arm to the older woman and was glad of the occupation. Allan Giles stood on the lawn, in conversation with Jericho Colson. Mrs. Moffatt observed the two men as she and Cathryn descended the steps from the church.

"It is unusual to have so many handsome men in sight but I would not trust any of them."

"I was under the impression you were fond of at least one in the village," Cathryn said as they passed the twosome at a distance.

"My dear, a woman can trust only two things. Herself and her property. I admit to a certain warmth for Rupert Smith but that has more to do with his poor mother—how she suffered when he was taken prisoner. I have never seen such grief destroy a woman so thoroughly."

Cathryn nodded, her own grief for the woman who had been a second mother to her threatening to unravel all the bindings she employed to control the hysterical girl. She twisted the ring Rupert had put on her finger a few hours before, wondering why he had not kept his promise. *Such a fool you are, Evie. You truly are.*

"You'll thank me, Cathryn, when you know what I've done."

"I am always grateful to you, Mrs. Moffatt."

"Do you remember the incident at the opera house, when Rupert was so impertinent?"

Cathryn remembered too well and had been grateful for his rudeness. "I'm sure he didn't intend any offense, Mrs. Moffatt."

"Nevertheless, he prevented me from speaking my mind—for your benefit."

The hysterical girl panicked. "How—? I mean—."

"I had received some distressing information concerning Mr. Colson, information that could very well reach the Hill and hurt you."

"Mrs. Moffatt, I know you are a friend and I have always relied upon your faith in me—."

"Hush now, my dear. I mean you no harm at all but there are those who do, especially now that Rupert Smith has returned. What do you suppose could hurt you concerning Mr. Colson?"

"I cannot see how this has any connection to Mr. Smith," Cathryn murmured. "He has been away for so many years."

"Nonsense. He has made his intentions perfectly clear, Cathryn. A woman would have to be utterly deluded not to realize he has set his cap to wed and to wed very well indeed."

"Susan Miller."

"Yes, yes. I know all about that. All the same, my concern is for you. Such a trusting, innocent child. I have no wish to see you trampled in the dust. Therefore, I had thought for some days before I came to this conclusion."

"Thank you, Mrs. Moffatt, but I very much regret I don't know what has brought on this concern."

They had reached Mrs. Moffatt's residence at the end of Adams Street. "All these comings and goings at your home, of course."

"There are no suspicious circumstances."

"I am your most staunch supporter, Cathryn Marcher, but this cannot continue." The older woman lifted her skirts and climbed to the veranda where she studied her guest for some moments. "Until this is all behind us, you will come to live here. Everything is arranged. Noam Snyder will move your belongings—."

"No, Mrs. Moffatt. I am grateful for your concern but I have done nothing of which I am ashamed. I know of no reason why I am not safe in my own home and no one has encroached in any way that threatens my reputation."

"Cathryn, I know you want to believe that but with Rupert lurking at all hours and now Mr. Colson appearing at your door in the dead of night."

"Mr. Colson visited me at dusk for no more than five minutes. I asked him to leave."

"But not Rupert."

"Mr. Smith has helped me with some of the heavier yard work for which I am greatly indebted to him."

"And how are you repaying this debt? I am only asking what is being asked by certain circles."

Cathryn gasped a breath and turned away on her heel.

"I have no wish, ever, to harm you, my dear, but others do. Come into the house, Cathryn. It is unseemly to conduct this interview in full view of all the town."

No one had passed in the minutes they had talked in Mrs. Moffatt's front garden and no one but her family ever came as far up the hill on Adams Street. Though the slope was gentle, Moffatt House was the only residence and stood as though at the end of a long drive, surrounded on both sides by wide lawns and white birch into the distance. If Cathryn had been younger, she would have delighted in trotting away between the slender trunks to play among the fairies.

"I cannot begin to express my gratitude for your care and friendship. I know you mean to show only kindness but I must live my life according to my beliefs and abilities. I have no intention to offend or harm. I am a grown woman. I owe no one but those who have provided me with work and shelter. If others wish me harm, I must rely on my own virtues to defend me."

"I see, my dear. I can only commend you and continue to worry." The matron extended her hands. "Come in, Cathryn, to have your supper with me. I promise I will not hound you any further."

Jessie, the woman who worked as Mrs. Moffatt's housekeeper and cook, met the two women at the bottom of the hallway stairs with cups of fruit punch and retreated to the kitchen to finish preparations for the meal.

Mrs. Moffatt invited Cathryn into the back parlor where the open window admitted a cooling breeze through the room and up into the bedrooms through the grates in the floor boards. Cathryn removed her bonnet and short coat, hanging them on a hook on the back of the door. She flexed her hands for a moment before sitting down at the piano. Mrs. Moffatt dug into her workbasket, found a piece of embroidery that attracted her fancy and settled to listen to her guest's practice piece, a customary scene for them when the occasion allowed.

No spurts of conversation interrupted their activities for the remainder of the afternoon until Jessie Small came to announce the meal was to be served in a quarter hour.

"We'll have our meal in the dining room, Cathryn. Please help Jessie set the table for us and another guest."

"Yes, of course." Before she left the room, footsteps echoed on the front porch but she didn't linger to see to whom Mrs. Moffatt opened the door and greeted with a scolding. Cathryn found all she needed for the table from familiarity. Muffled voices from the back parlor, through the door Mrs. Moffatt had closed, were a low hum accompanying their work. Jessie set the serving dishes in the copper chafing stands on the sideboard while Cathryn folded the linen napkins.

When her task was done, she joined Jessie in the kitchen, rather than disturb her hostess or attempt to discover who the other guest might be. Her reluctance to investigate did not prevent her from speculating which man of Mrs. Moffatt's acquaintance owned the heavy tread on the porch. His voice was too deep and inaudible to be recognized but was distinguishable from his hostess, especially when she laughed with girlish abandon.

"She does enjoy the company of handsome men," Jessie remarked, setting the roast on the sideboard to rest while she made the gravy.

"Who is here?"

"If he is a recent arrival to Oslo Hill, he will have an invitation to dine with Mrs. Moffatt."

"I wonder if Mr. Colson is her guest," Cathryn mused, peering at the kitchen door as if she could see into the parlor.

"Could be. Fine looking man. He called to pay his respects yesterday afternoon."

Cathryn took a step back. "I'll see if there's plenty of fuel for the stove."

"No need—." Before Jessie said another word, Cathryn darted onto the back porch, down the steps heading to the woods.

Jessie carried the gravy boat to the table and knocked on the parlor door. "Dinner is ready to be served, Mrs. Moffatt."

Her employer, and the male guest, emerged and crossed into the dining room. Jessie brought the roast and set it before the gentleman for carving.

"Please ask Cathryn to join us, we're waiting."

"I would, Mrs. Moffatt, but she's taken a walk to the woods for fuel before I could tell her the box is full up."

"Did she know I was here?"

"Nonsense," Mrs. Moffatt chuckled, "she'd have no reason after what you've told me. Jessie, call her back, will you, please?"

"She did skedaddle like a rabbit, Mrs. Moffatt. She's half way home by now if she kept going."

"Well, I'll be. What have you done to make her so skittish?"

"Which way did she go, Mrs. Small?"

"Up toward Morgan's Pond."

"Well, you'd best go after her, young man, or all this will come to nothing."

Eleven

Cathryn reached the pond as Jessie had predicted but went no further, catching a glimpse of her face in the moment of panic. The pond surface sparkled with gold and scarlet petals riffling in the breeze from the north.

No matter who had been invited to join them for dinner with Mrs. Moffatt, Cathryn was expected to accept the dictates of her hostess as she had been expected to perform for Rupert Smith and to accept that he could ask Susan to teach Cathryn's pupil a song which was inappropriate for both her voice and her age.

She raised her hand to examine the ring Rupert had placed there. He expected her to accept his wish and she had, with no more than a moment's hesitation or thought.

At the sound of approaching footsteps, she dropped her hands behind her back, turning to face whatever came. After one sharp breath, she strode toward her pursuer.

"Was there some word in what I said that was unclear? Is there some reason you are compelled to ignore my wishes?"

"I have none other than your wishes in my heart, Cathryn."

"Then turn on your heel and go back the way you came, Jericho. I have no wish to see you. I told you this plainly enough when we parted in Boston, when you left."

He opened his arms, holding his hand out to her. "I know you said what you had to say then. I know you wanted to believe you did not love me. I understand why."

"I did not and do not love you, Jericho. How often must I tell you?"

"I cannot believe that, not after what we meant to each other. My wife has given her blessing—she knows my feeling, she desires only my discretion. There is no other barrier to our happiness."

"There is, Jericho. I am engaged to Mr. Smith. He has asked me to marry him and I have accepted."

"You cannot feel even a tenth for him you have and do still feel for me. I will not allow you to sacrifice yourself to his meaningless intentions."

"I am not. I love him. I have always loved him."

"He's a blackguard, Cathryn. He has wasted his life on outlandish schemes. He is a criminal of the lowest sort."

"You need not tell me, Jericho. I have known him all my life."

"Then you know he spent three of the last five years in prison."

"He told me," she said.

"Did he tell you his crime?"

"We have no secrets, Jericho. I have loved Rupert as long as I have known him. I know what is in his heart."

"And he knows what is in yours, I presume."

"Yes."

"Then why have you kept your love for me a secret from him?"

"I have not done so. I have never needed to mention you—he knew what had happened between us."

"There. I have proof you love me and will always love me."

"No. I have made clear to Rupert that I never loved you."

"The man you claim to love has seen for himself by your manner that you love me."

"He saw only your feeling for me."

"I could have no feeling for you without your prior need of me."

Cathryn studied her pursuer for a moment before she judged that no argument would dispel the delusions he held. "I have nothing more to say, Jericho, other than I wish you well." She turned and strode away, picking up her skirts to run when he chased after her. Though he called her name, she had reached the houses on the main street before she slowed to a walk across the Smith's backyard.

She stomped up the porch steps and pounded on the screen door. "Where were you?"

Her fiancé looked like the man Jericho accused him of being. His dark hair hung forward and his eyes were shadowed.

"Where have you been, Rupert?"

He pushed the screen door open and she went into the back kitchen, as neat and orderly as the day of his father's funeral, exactly as she had left it. She continued to the kitchen and plunked into a chair by the table, across from where he had spread the newspaper to read. His cup of coffee was steaming.

"To what do I owe this ... honor?"

"There is no reason for you to be sarcastic. I asked a civil question. Where were you after my group lesson?"

"I didn't notice you waited for me."

"Why should I wait? You said you would be there, at the door. You weren't."

"Where have you been, Cathryn? Where is your coat?" He stared at her stained hem and muddied boots. "You have leaves in your hair."

"I wouldn't if you had kept your word. I'd have my coat and my bonnet if you hadn't gone to have coffee with Mrs. Miller."

"How could I ever have forgotten that a man's life isn't his own business in this town?"

She raised her hands from her lap. "Not two minutes—in fact, you knew where you would be before you even showed up at my house—."

"Don't take that ring off, Cathryn." He slapped his hand flat on the table.

"Why should I keep it? You didn't mean anything by it. Just another of your cruel tricks—."

"I meant everything by it, Cathryn. Everything." He dropped to one knee by her chair. "I knew this would happen," he said, clasping her hands together so she couldn't work the ring free. "I knew if I came back here, you'd be the one to break me. Tie me to this place so I'd never be free."

"You can have your freedom, Rupert Smith. I wouldn't dream of tying you to this place or any place else." She yanked her hands back but he held her fast, keeping his gaze locked on hers.

"It's too late for that, Cathryn. It was too late when you wrote me that first letter." He plucked leaves from her hair and tossed them into the firebox. "You didn't answer my question," he said with two furrows forming between his eyebrows. "How did you get in this state?"

"Why weren't you waiting for me?" She couldn't prevent the angry tears at the corners of her eyes from blurring her vision so she saw only a shimmer of his face. "Rupert."

With one hand, he pulled a chair closer, not letting go of her fingers. "I was there, Cathryn," he said in a low voice. He sat in the chair, drying her tears with his thumb. "I had coffee at Mrs. Miller's with Allan. Joshua Miller had made a business loan with my parents. Allan thought it would be advisable to discuss with Joshua's widow on friendly terms to begin. The matter hadn't come up before I left. Mrs. Miller invited me to return for dinner after church but I told her I was otherwise engaged. When I got to the church hall, you were singing with the children, *Onward Christian Soldiers*, so I stood by the door and listened until Mrs. Moffatt shewed me away and whisked you off. Is that where you've been, Cathryn?"

"She insisted. I can never say no to her." *Or anyone else in this town.*

"Why did you leave without your coat or bonnet. It's a cool day for a walk in the woods."

"I left. Before dinner. She had a guest." Each admission was punctuated by a silence until Cathryn took a deep breath. "Mrs. Moffatt invited someone. Without telling me."

"Who?"

"Jericho Colson." *How have I become this rabbit? When did I lose my courage, give up the fight?*

"Why would she do that?" He released her hands and sat back in his chair, still fixing his gaze on her face.

"Rupert?"

"Why didn't you stay, Cathryn?"

Her questioning expression hardened and she withdrew. "I shouldn't have come here." But when she shifted on the chair to stand, Rupert caught her hands.

"Why did you?"

She broke his grip and looked away from his suspicion and jealousy.

"I don't know."

"Don't know or won't tell me?"

"What do you want me to tell you?"

"The truth, Cathryn."

"How will you know what the truth is?"

"I know what I want to believe but unless you tell me, I'm lost in a dream."

"What dream? What do you want to believe, Rupert?"

"I want to believe you left because you don't want him. I want to believe you came here because you want me. Did you? Do you?"

"I left Mrs. Moffatt's house because she assumed I would not object to her meddling in my life. I have already told you I never loved Jericho." His eager expression made her smile. "As for why I came here, I did. I ran from Jericho and here I was. I have always come here, Rupert, whenever I've been frightened or confused or lonely. When my parents died, I went up to Boston to be near you, so, if you needed me, I could be with you. After your parents died, I came here, to be near you. Somehow. Where have you been, Rupert?"

"Are you going to marry me, Cathryn?" He lifted both her hands clasping them together to kiss each.

"Yes, Rupert, I am." She freed one hand to brush his hair back from his forehead.

"That's good. That's all I need to know." He sat back and released her other hand.

"Do you have any coffee?"

He leapt from the chair to put the kettle on the big range at the other end of the long kitchen.

"I haven't had any dinner," she remembered aloud.

"There's not much here," he apologized. "My skills are basic."

"I'm sorry. I didn't mean to ask, I mean——." The giddy girl was fumbling all around like a spinning top. "I should go."

"Not 'til you've had some dinner. I'm no cook but I can be a damned good host, Miss Marcher, given the right circumstances. You sit right there and watch."

"If you insist, Mr. Smith," she giggled and blushed immediately, so hot she couldn't breathe. He dove into the back kitchen and came back with his arms loaded with mason jars and loaves.

"It won't be anything close to what you're used to," he explained as he pulled out an iron skillet, cut a pat of butter and beat eggs with milk, "but you won't go hungry."

"Where did you learn to cook?" she scoffed with a laugh.

"Another of the jobs I did for a while."

"After you got out of prison?"

Rupert remained still for a moment, looked at her over his shoulder and said, "Yes."

"In Wyoming?"

"In Kansas."

"I don't even know how far away either of those places are. If I saw them on a map, I couldn't say which was which."

He set a place for her at the kitchen table with a linen cloth and his mother's china. "Eat your dinner, Cathryn and I'll show you." While she ate, he spread a map beside her and pointed to all the places he'd travelled after the war and when he'd been released from the prison camp but gave her no details of what he'd done in any of the places until he reached Kansas. "This is where I got into trouble and spent some time in prison. When I'd served my time, I met up with a friend from the Army and we got ourselves out to Wyoming, ranching mostly."

"What's that? Is that being a cow hand?"

"Yes."

"What does a cow hand do?"

"Ride the range all day long, eat dust and sleep in the dirt."

"Doesn't sound like work I'd want."

"It's honest," he said and started to fold the map.

"Wait. Where were you in Wyoming?"

He pointed to a corner in the southeast. "I was working for a syndicate of ranchers. With Morton Pierce."

"Where is he?"

"Up in Franklin County, waiting for me to decide when to leave here, go back out west."

"When will you go?"

"Once I've sold this place. We're planning to buy into the syndicate, already bought some land and a couple hundred head of Texas Longhorns, driven up the Goodnight Loving Trail[13]."

Cathryn finished the eggs but the last few swallows stuck in her throat. "What's that?"

"Couple of adventurous men forged a trail for cattle driving. Sold the cattle and went back for more."

"What's it like there? Apart from the dust and the dirt?"

"One of the prettiest places I've ever seen, Cathryn."

This is his future. The question she had to ask remained locked in her heart. She peered at the map, holding her cup of coffee in both hands, calculating the journey and wondering at the distance before she sipped the cooled drink.

"When I first went across the plains in spring, I thought Morton was soft in the head," Rupert confessed. "You can feel the heat coming up from the ground and pushing down on your shoulders as though you're in an oven. And there's hundreds of miles of open land with nothing to recommend it but air. Then you drop down a slope to a creek so fresh and green you can't help but think you've been blessed just to see it."

"How long does the journey take?"

"The government and some business men have built the Union Pacific Railway now. Cuts the journey down to days instead of months."

"How long did you take to reach Wyoming?" she pressed.

"A few weeks…a month."

"That's a long way."

---

[13] **Goodnight Loving Trail** Goodnight and Loving were two businessmen/cowboys who forged a cattle drive trail between Texas and Wyoming to bring beef cattle (Texas Longhorns) to the range lands of the eastern Wyoming plains. Other trails were used to drive cattle to the rail stations to eastern slaughter markets such as Chicago and Kansas City.

"The trip doesn't seem a long way when there is so much to see—so much beauty."

She drank her coffee and considered the map. "I thought up to Boston was the other side of the world when I first went there."

"You were only a girl then."

"I was eighteen."

He closed his eyes for a long moment. An expression she thought was physical pain seared through his eyes when he opened them. "A girl," he repeated, folding the map along its well-worn creases. He set it at the other end of the table and pushed his chair away. "I'd better get you home or someone in this town will want my hide."

Cathryn glanced out through the window, reluctant to go in case Jericho was waiting for her or Mrs. Moffatt had taken offense at her departure. *Such a rabbit.* Afraid to stay in case Rupert thought she was a loose woman and wanting to stay where she'd always been welcome, always felt safe. And the giddy girl could be who she was, happy and childish and so carefree, so full of life and her dreams.

When she turned to meet his gaze again, her eyes were already filled with tears but he'd risen to stand over her, ready to be rid of her, the tarnished spinster. "No one will think the less of you."

"I will. Right now, I can't afford any false steps."

How she managed to hide the shock his admission caused her was a mystery but she stamped the hopeful girl into the muddy dirt from her boots as she walked toward the back door.

"You can't go like that, Cathryn."

"What do you mean? I wasn't going to walk on the road so you don't have to worry about tarnishing your good name."

"It's too windy without a coat."

"I'm not going back to Mrs. Moffatt's for that or any other reason, not tonight anyway."

"Wait here."

He skipped two and three stairs at a time up to the bedrooms and trotted down again with a coat and bonnet in his arms.

"Where'd you find those?"

"In the spare room. They look like they'll fit you. My mother had more coats and hats than I remember."

"She liked to go for walks," Cathryn said without thinking, absorbed by memories of the day Rupert's mother left the house and walked all the way to Market Street and bought the fur-trimmed coat and hat to match. Cathryn ran her fingers over the deep fur and purple wool. "She loved this coat."

Rupert held it for her and when she pulled the collar toward her neck, her hands grazed his fingers. She raised her gaze but he was staring over her head and she stared, for a long moment, at his mouth, tempted to tilt her chin, strain so slightly forward. Instead, she lowered her gaze to button the front of the coat.

Rupert held the hat out to her. He shrugged into his plaid jacket and slapped his hat on his head, cocked to the side, trapping his hair swept back from his brow. At the door, he offered his arm and walked her to the end of his front path to the street.

"Through town or through the woods, Cathryn?"

"The woods."

He took a few steps in that direction then continued along the road. She shrugged inwardly and walked beside him through the town, once again meeting neighbors and pupils as they went about their evening business. Rupert held his arm close, trapping her arm against his ribs, occasionally tensing his fingers so that the muscles of his forearm stiffened under her hand but he remained silent until they were on the road to her cabin. "May I hold your hand, Cathryn?"

She made only a slight movement of her fingers in the crook of his elbow and he clasped her hand in a firm grip without breaking the stride of his journey, holding her hand at his side. Within a few strides they reached the corner of her front yard—too soon. She made no move away from him nor to pull her hand from his grip.

"Cathryn." His voice was less than a whisper, a sigh on the evening breeze. He removed his hat and the gusts swept through his dark waves, clearing his face of all obstruction. "May I kiss you?"

She resisted looking along the quiet street. She resisted the cold fear that made the giddy girl want to bolt away. She even resisted the impulse to moisten her lips and close her eyes. She raised her chin a fraction. His body swayed on the force of her compliance. Nothing moved. The wind came to an abrupt halt as though holding its breath.

Rupert dragged air into his lungs, tilted his head, casting a shadow over her face as his lips touched hers, waiting in perfect motionless restraint until she trembled. And he was gone, lifting his head away to look over her shoulder at the small, unlit cabin.

"You've let your fire die."

"I haven't," she protested with less voice than his accusation demanded. "I haven't," she repeated, searching through the pockets of his mother's coat. "I don't have my key. All the doors are locked.

"Are you sure?" he asked, searching her face.

"Of course. I've locked the doors since—."

He half-smiled, "Since you found me in your house."

"Yes."

"Looks like you'll have to sleep on the porch unless you let me on your property to get the door open."

"How can you do that?"

"Surprising what a man learns in prison."

"Thank you, Rupert," Cathryn sighed, safely in her front room. "Would you like some coffee and cake?"

"No. Better for me to stay out here."

"Why?"

"Because that way you're safe."

"What do you mean?"

"All I want right now is to find out what's under all those layers of good manners."

"Oh."

"But that isn't going to happen until you marry me. And right now, that's not likely." He stepped back, combed his fingers through his hair, and dropped the western hat on his head. "Good evening, Miss Marcher." He disappeared in the deepening dusk.

Closing the door one slow breath at a time until no trace of him remained but the taste of his kiss, fading fast, on her dry lips, she had nothing in her thoughts. She refused to think about any word he said or why. The fire in the stove was low, smoldering but with a little tinder, it flamed enough to add firewood for the night. The house was still dark when she set the kettle on the range and sat at the table until the water came to a boil.

She lit the oil lamp over the table and drank her coffee, secure that the doors were lock once more against everyone except a man who had learned surprising things in prison, a man who kissed her as though kissing her was the last thing he wanted to do and followed that with downright rudeness—as if he'd been dared to kiss, but still wanted to take advantage of, someone he wasn't ever likely to marry.

Why would I want to marry a man who'd been in prison? Why would I want to marry a man who was going to herd cattle for the rest of his life, way out west? That may suit the likes of Susan Miller.

The thought of the Hamlins' snooty daughter in the wild lands brought a much needed laugh.

Cathryn carried a candle into the front room and poured her heart into practicing a section of the Beethoven, over and over until she made no false strikes on the keys of Margaret Smith's square grand and the sound flew around the low-ceilinged room, filling her head with sweet music. As soon as she stopped, the only sounds were the reverberation of the strings and a whisper of the wind in the shingled roof.

She folded the music and used the last hours of the evening to work on the Cotillion ball gown and wonder who the young woman was and to what grand ballroom she would wear such a fine garment. The gown she had worn on the evening she danced with George Rupert Smith was folded away in her mother's trunk along with all the dresses she had refashioned as a younger woman, before Boston and long before her fateful encounter with Colonel Jericho Colson.

She had known exactly what she was doing and she held no ill-feeling toward him. She had not been a naïve child, believing lies. She had been lonely and so sad that being with another person was life-saving, vibrant and affirming. That she had allowed Jericho to believe, even in his illness, that she returned his love was an act of kindness and she blamed herself for his state of mind but their parting was his choice to return to his wife—in a strengthened state of mind.

She had made leaving her as easy for him despite his profession of guilt but with no less honesty. She had given him comfort as a nurse and as a compassionate friend. His wife's indifference could not have been foretold nor his renewed interest in Cathryn. *I am not that woman.* The Cotillion ball gown shimmered in the lamplight and she shook it free of wrinkles before draping it on the dressmaker's dummy to assess her work. She held pins between her lips as she studied the lines of the dress.

The young woman for whom it was being made was the same height but slender. Although Cathryn was not as stout as Mrs. Moffatt, she was substantial—sturdy, as a woman who is used to chopping her own firewood and paying her own rent had to be. As a nurse, she had lifted inert men from their beds to change their dressings or soiled sheets.

As a friend and nursemaid, she had shepherded Rupert's mother home from her escapades—the memory brought a smile and tears at the same time. Evie could understand a mother's grief. If not for her own, she might have shunned the poor woman as others so often did.

"Evie, I'm sure Rupert said he was coming home on the mail coach," Mrs. Smith sobbed one March night, while the wind screamed around them.

"I don't doubt it, Mrs. Smith, but the coach doesn't come at midnight."

They fought their way back from the town against the wind and against each other. In every house they passed, the following morning, the conversation was the same. "Peggy Smith got out again last night. Hardly a stitch on her."

And they all looked at Cathryn asking why she, with all her experience couldn't do anything to prevent their lives from being disrupted, their children frightened, their property from damage. "It's a blessing," they said when Rupert's mother caught pneumonia that spring and died, believing her son was sitting by her, holding her silky hand and singing her favorite hymn.

Cathryn never now sang *St. Denio* when Mr. Jorgens listed it; she could never sing more than a few words without losing her voice in tears.

And now, she prayed that Rupert did not discover Evie or learn how his absence decimated his mother's heart and drove despair into his father's soul.

She extinguished the lamp and returned it to its place on the pantry shelf, banked the fire and closed the door of her bedroom, dismissing her sudden fear that a man who had been in prison could unlock her front door at any time. She shivered for a long time, unable to resist the wish that he made good on his threat, if only so she could steal some of the warmth of his body.

Twelve

Loving Rupert wasn't going to keep her warm but wanting him in useless dreams was no better. *He will be gone soon,* she comforted herself. *He will go and I will be here—maybe I won't. Maybe I'll take the work Mrs. Lowell offered. I'll live in Portland. I'll be independent. I'll go. I'll go.*

The decision was sudden but she knew it was what she had to do. Once it was made, her eyes closed and she slept through the night until her natural waking time arrived and along with it the rasp of a saw to the rhythm of whistled tune she knew. Cathryn dressed in her work clothes, tying her uncombed hair behind her ears.

She couldn't see him from any of the windows in the kitchen as she warmed the biscuits and heated water for coffee.

The sun was sliding along the horizon, lingering low as if to avoid workday chores. Noam Snyder's milk cart rattled along the road and she trotted out to meet him.

"Cooling down some."

She agreed and took the tin he held out to her. "When will you be collecting Peggy Smith's piano?"

"Been thinking about it. Can't be for a while."

"Why not?"

"Ahn't no sense with Rupert packing up all he don't want ready for the auction end of July. Might as well tell Lewis to bring his men 'round here for it."

"I suppose," she murmured.

The rasping had stopped. At the thump of metal against metal, Noam turned his attention toward the backyard.

"You got someone helping you?"

Cathryn nodded and shrugged.

"I told yah I'd get around to them jobs before fall. Just make sure that man knows what he's doing, any damage and yah'll have to pay for the repairs." Though his statement was a threat he'd make good on, he nodded in the direction of the hammering. "No surprise what a man'll do for a cup of good coffee."

"Ay-yuh," she breathed when he shook the reins over the cart horse's back.

"Ahn't bothering with that pianah any time soon, Cathryn." The cart lurched forward. She gazed after her landlord for a time then crossed the lawn to the side of the cabin where a ladder leaned against the gutter. Setting the milk tin on the storm cellar door, she climbed up high enough to see a leg in a western boot straddling the hitch.

"Well, ahn't you something?"

The fright knocked her against the ladder rungs when she screamed. Rupert straightened his back to look down at her.

"I thought you said she weren't skittish, Rupe. Pretty nervous if you ask me."

"Who are you?" Cathryn asked the auburn-haired man holding the ladder steady and staring up at her from kind brown eyes, his sun-darkened face wrinkling with a smile. "Name's Morton, Miss Marcher. Friends call me all kinds of names but I answer to Mort specially when pretty girls say it."

"You scared me half to death."

"From what Rupe has told me about you, that'll take some doing."

She glared up at Rupert through fire-charged slits but received a smile in return. She grabbed the struts of the ladder as it tilted backward. She was perpendicular to the ground with her arms around the legs when Mort said, "Come on down here, Miss Marcher. I don't bite and I'm mighty eager to try these biscuits I heard tell of."

"Let me go."

The ladder jerked back. She screamed again.

"Mort. Leave her be."

"Yes, sir," the big man laughed. "Whatsoever you say, Rupe. Ahn't about to do no harm to you, Miss."

The ladder titled forward degree by degree until it rested against the eaves. Cathryn closed her eyes for a moment and huffed before climbing down again between Morton Pierce's out-stretched arms then glared down at him until, with a whole face grin, he stepped back to let her reach the ground.

"I see what you mean, Rupe," he called up. "One fine, damned pretty girl you got here."

"Mr. Smith, come down off my roof this very minute. I want a word with you."

"Guess I've caused you a mite of trouble, Rupe."

"When don't you?" Rupert laughed, sliding down to the ladder. "He doesn't mean to cause offense, Cathryn, just says what he thinks, straight out."

"What are you doing here?"

He dropped to the ground in front of her, dusting his hands on the back of his pants. "Saw a problem with the roof hitch."

"Mr. Snyder isn't happy about you interfering with his property."

"I thought this was your property."

"You're splitting hairs. I don't need you to fix my roof. Or chop my firewood or mend my axe."

"That's good. I don't want to do any of that."

"Then what are you doing here, Mr. Smith?"

"Didn't I tell you she was a warrior, Mort?"

"Yes, you sure did, Rupe."

"And I thought you were on some Franklin County farm," Cathryn growled back at Morton.

"I had some family business myself, Miss. Came along back here to help Rupe out with his once mine was done."

"So, Cathryn, how about some of your coffee for my friend here? Those biscuits should be hot enough by now."

Cathryn looked from one to the other. "I'm not feeding cow hands who leave jobs half-done." She pushed between them as they laughed and retreated to the sanctuary of the kitchen, poured a cup of coffee with a dollop of cream from the milk tin.

"Sure can sashay," Morton Pierce commented.

"Keep your eyes on your own business," Rupert hissed as he climbed up the ladder.

Morton threw his head back with a laugh so carefree Cathryn smiled despite her irritation. The hammering and rasping continued for another hour while she made more biscuits and had a fresh pot of coffee ready when her help knocked on the back door. Morton peered through the window but Rupert had turned his back until the lock sprang open and the hook on the screen door was lifted.

"Do you want to inspect the job, Miss Marcher, or are you happy to accept Mort's word that I've finished?"

She glanced at Rupert's big friend. Mort nodded, rubbing his hands together and taking a deep breath as he strained to see around her to the table.

"You prefer staying outside, I know, Mr. Smith. What about you, Morton?"

"I don't mind sitting at the table, Miss." He stepped forward.

Rupert slapped his hand on the doorframe, blocking the entrance. "He's staying outside."

"This is a free country, Mr. Smith. Mr. Pierce would prefer to sit at my table and I have invited him to do so. Unless you're prepared to knock me down, step out of the way and let my guest pass."

"He's not coming in."

Morton laid his hand on his friend's shoulder. "Thank you kindly, Miss, for the welcome, but I'll stay here with Rupe."

"I understand, Morton, though it's a pity he won't let you at least come out of the sun to have your breakfast. I've heated some water for you to wash up but I guess you'll have to be satisfied with the pump as well." She pushed the door shut without looking into Rupert's eyes again.

While she prepared a tray, slamming crockery down and splashing coffee over plates, Morton said, "Funny way you have of courting Miss Marcher. I won't be surprised if she takes a gun to run you off."

"Better if she does," Rupert snarled back and pumped water into his friend's hands.

Cathryn set the tray on the rainwater barrel and locked the door. When she returned to the kitchen, dressed and washed, her hair brushed and pinned into a knot at the back of her neck, her face still glistening from a scrubbing, ready for her first pupil, the backyard was empty and silent. She brought the tray in and retired to her sewing room.

Noam's cart rattled up the road but he didn't stop to inspect the work. Her Wednesday morning pupil, as late as usual, failed to arrive at the appointed hour and Cathryn used the spare moments to pin the hem on the ball gown and begin the tacking. She was on her hands and knees at the back of the dressmaker's dummy when whistling and Morton's booming laugh broke the silence. With a relieved sigh, she returned to her task, stabbing her palm with a needle when Rupert growled.

"Hand me that blasted saw, Mort, or I'll come down and take your arm off with it."

If I had a gun in this house, I wouldn't just run him off. I'd shoot him. "I thought you were gone," she said, standing cross-armed on the front porch. "What are you doing in that tree, Mr. Smith?"

"Cutting it back some."

"I hope you have Noam Snyder's permission."

"Don't need it," he grunted, inching along the branch.

"He might have something contrary to say about that." She straightened her arms and frowned at Morton, who stood side on to her, hanging his head.

"He might have but he didn't when I talked to him about it half an hour ago." Rupert measured his distance from the trunk and set the saw, starting his first cut. Around his waist, a wide belt with a rope attached tied him to the stout trunk above his head and looped around Morton's waist. The big man braced his legs to take the lumberjack's weight if Rupert lost his footing.

"That will cut you in half, Morton."

"Don't you worry none about me, Miss. Rupe's a feather compared to most of the men I've spotted."

Cathryn huffed for a moment before striding down the path. "Is this another one of the jobs you've done in Wyoming, Mr. Smith? If so, I'll have you know this tree isn't just an ordinary tree to be hacked at. This is an ancient oak, grown from an acorn planted here over a hundred years ago."

"No need to tell me, Cathryn. My great-grandfather was the truant schoolboy who kicked that cone into Millie Snyder's yard."

"I might have known," she murmured and returned to the house, glaring at the clock. "Doesn't anybody think I have better things to do than wait for them?" She sat on the bench with her back to the piano, twisting her fingers together and wondering why she was still wearing Peggy Smith's ring. *Damned silly, foolish girl, I guess.* Resigned to her character and that Susan Miller had changed her mind about a singing lesson so she wasn't going to have the money she needed to pay Noam for her weekly order of milk and eggs, she dragged back to the ball gown.

Over the next few hours, the sound of eerie rasping and shouts of "Timber!" whenever a branch was amputated, accompanied Cathryn's work as she crawled on the floor. Their voices, laughter and easy friendship for two such different men, how easily she took to Morton Pierce, how often she wanted to shoot Rupert Smith—all crowded into her thoughts. The tacking was done and she had gotten up to begin the lace work when Morton crossed in front of the window and knocked on the back door.

She swung the door wide and unhooked the screen door but he stepped back.

"We're about done, Miss."

"You'll be wanting some dinner."

"Rupe didn't mention it."

"I've made soup. You're welcome to a meal after your hard work, Morton."

"Much obliged, Miss Marcher. I won't turn you down. Can't speak for my grumpy friend, though."

"Mr. Smith will eat if it suits him," she replied, turning on her heel, leaving the screen unlatched while she set three place settings at the table. In a moment, Morton scraped his boots, knocked lightly and said, "Rupe'll be along now, Miss."

"Come in."

"I'll—uh—wait for him, if it's all the same to you. Don't want to rile him unnecessarily when he's playing innkeeper. Never know when he'll put his boot in my back."

Tempted to ask too many questions about a man she shouldn't even be talking to, Cathryn clamped her mouth shut and warmed the bowls in the top oven. The aroma of sweet yeast rolls filled the kitchen. Morton took an appreciative deep breath, pressing closer to the door until his surly friend set his foot with a thud on the top step.

"Your sweetheart's made some fine dinner, Rupe. You going in or staying out here."

No answer came but the door swung back on its hinges wide enough for a tall, broad-shouldered man to enter. Cathryn kept her back to him, catching her breath when he kept coming across to the stove.

"You can wash in the sink," she said without turning. "There's hot water in the jug." She was relieved to hear a second pair of boots on the wooden floor and the screen door banging shut.

"Sit down when you're ready."

The water in the kettle steamed through the lid and the aroma of the summer squash soup and sweet rolls earned a contented whistle from Morton and a low groan from his friend. When she turned with two bowls in her hands, Rupert sat at the table in the seat beside his friend, leaving the seat opposite him empty. Though she could easily talk to Morton, she had to endure Rupert's scrutiny—if he looked at her at all. Even when she had two bowls of hot soup to manage, she couldn't help looking at him.

He nodded when the bowl appeared in front of him but didn't glance at her or meet her gaze, once she had settled in the chair opposite him. Morton murmured a *Grace* and his companions said, "Amen," in unison. Rupert's eyes remained closed for a few moments longer—as though he was praying for strength to endure.

"Mrs. Miller gave a good reason for not attending her lesson, I presume," he commented, ripping a roll apart and dipping one half in his soup.

Morton had taken a second roll, eating it in the same way.

"She didn't say."

"Didn't give a reason or didn't tell you she wasn't coming?"

That explains his being here all day. "Both," Cathryn said, allowing her anger to put a snap in her voice.

"Rude little button, she is," Morton said.

"She...has commitments...business and Joshua's estate," Cathryn said in Susan's defense, embarrassed by her anger.

"Rude."

Cathryn stole a glance at Rupert but he was tearing another roll when he repeated his friend's comment.

"She can't always——."

"You get your fee, don't you?"

"Not always," she said, embarrassment for her disloyalty to her lifelong friend burning her cheeks.

"You're not much of a hard-nosed businesswoman, are you?"

"My arrangements with my students are none of your concern, Mr. Smith."

"What's Mrs. Miller studying, Cathryn?" he asked in a gentler tone.

"I'm sure she will be happy to tell you, Mr. Smith." She rose from her chair.

"I'm asking you."

Morton straightened his big frame to stand when Cathryn brought a pie out of the warming oven. His delight made up for the tone of Rupert's voice. She grinned back at him as she cut slices for both men, leaving less than half in the pan.

"What you teach isn't confidential, is it?"

"I am not at liberty to speak for her, Mr. Smith."

He had already eaten his slice of apple pie and threw his napkin on the table. "I'm not asking for state secrets, Cathryn. I just want to know why she comes here."

"All you have to do is ask her. She'll be more than happy to answer any question you have, since——." She pushed back from the table and jumped to her feet.

Morton caught the chair before it hit the floor and took a shelf of crockery with it. "Any more sparks and this whole place'll go up in flames," he said, narrowing his glare at Rupert. "We've got that whole pile of wood to cut up for Miss Marcher, Rupe. Best we get it hauled to her backyard."

"It's a damned simple question."

"And she ahn't got any damned reason to answer. Now get back to work that ahn't going to get you in trouble." Morton turned to their hostess. "He doesn't know when to quit. Like that time he near took John Falmer's head off——."

"You wanted to get back to work," Rupert growled, "let's go." He slammed out onto the porch.

"You got company, Miss," the big man said, nodding toward the front door. "Thank you for the meal, Miss."

Cathryn recognized the profile of her visitor and ran to the front door, yanking it open before Susan knocked.

"I know I'm late." Strident and impatient, Susan Miller pushed past her singing teacher, tugging her white gloves from her small hands.

"Come in, Susan. I've just finished lunch."

"What's going on here?" Susan waved her hand in the direction of the lopped branches strewn across the lawn.

Cathryn gasped when she looked up to see her once magnificent oak tree cut back a third of its grandeur. "Noam will——."

From the back of the cabin came the racket of wheelbarrows and rakes. "Come in. We can get started with your lesson."

"I wanted to talk to Noam anyway."

"He's not here, a couple of——." She was about to say *cowhands*. "Men, helping out."

"You were always the Charity Miss." Susan removed her peaked bonnet and tossed it on the sofa. "How are you paying them? I haven't brought any money with me."

"Susan, we agreed——."

"I was too busy. Rupert has asked—he's very demanding."

Morton turned the corner of the cabin. "Stand here," Cathryn ordered, turning her student to face the piano, away from the window.

Susan huffed, unbuttoning her walking jacket while Cathryn began the warmup scales before she sat down, as loud as she could on the instrument, mentally expressing her apologies to the piano. Above the music, she gave instruction, "Breathe. Control your diaphragm. Open your mouth. Don't strangle the note."

"I cannot open my mouth any wider."

"You can. You must. Otherwise you are cutting the life out of the music."

"It looks very rude. You may not care about that, I know, but ladies—on my!"

"What?"

"Is that Rupert Smith?" Susan gasped, her mouth dropping open. "It is. What is he doing here ... like that?"

Cathryn folded her hands in her lap. She didn't need to look to imagine what Susan saw—she hadn't been blinded since the first time he showed up to chop her firewood. Golden skin. Broad shoulders, loose shirt clinging to solid muscles from neck to waist, braces draped around slender hips. Thighs that—. *That's enough of that, Evie.*

"Just how are you paying *him*?"

"Pardon?"

"You heard me. I know you had to beg Nancy for money to pay your rent. Were you going to beg me for money to pay him or have you struck another of your bargains, bartering with *my* beau?"

Cathryn slid to the end of the bench and rose to her full height, taller by several inches than her student. "I think this lesson is over."

"Oh no, you owe me the full thirty minutes and more for this trick."

"I have not tricked you, Susan, in anyway." She folded her arms, conscious that Peggy Smith's ring was in view and drummed her fingers. The stone caught sunlight from the window but, though Susan glanced at her teacher's hand, she said nothing.

"I want to go over this song before I perform at the charity fund-raising concert at my club."

Cathryn held out her hand as Susan shoved the music toward her. "Is this the song you're singing with Megan?"

"No. I am singing this duet with Rupert and you will accompany us." Susan stepped forward. "After what you've done, I deserve that much."

"I have done nothing to you."

"Of course not, Cathryn. There is nothing you can do to me. I feel sorry for you. So humiliating to be reduced to selling...anything to pay your rent and such I cannot imagine how you do it."

"To what are your referring, Susan?"

"You and Rupert, here in this little cabin, alone."

"We aren't alone," Cathryn declared, resuming her seat at the piano. "Morton is here. They have both been here since sun-up. I was so exhausted, I slept past breakfast. After all they've been up to, I'm sure they'll be in need of rest. As you know, so demanding." She played the piece through, ignoring the lyrics. "This is a difficult piece, Susan, but not beyond your ability."

When Susan made no response, Cathryn glanced at her pupil. The widow had turned half away and watched the two men working in the front yard.

"I'm not happy with your selection for Megan. She's not ready for that level of vocal maturity."

"I don't care about that," Susan said. "I only asked her because Rupert is fond of the creature. And she wanted to please him."

"Are you going to tell her?"

"You're the one who objects. You can tell her."

"Susan, that's—."

"Unfair? I think you're unfair. Oh, why should I worry? All I want from you is a promise to help me with this concert."

"Of course, I will."

For the remainder of her lesson, Susan sang through the six verses and choruses of the romantic song accompanied by her teacher and the screech of the wheelbarrow each time Cathryn's laborers loaded it.

"I want another lesson this week and three next week. And don't worry, Cathryn, I'll pay your fee so you won't have to stoop so low for a while."

"I don't consider my arrangement with Rupert Smith or Morton Pierce stooping."

"What else can you call it?"

"A privilege."

"Cathryn! I—I have always been your friend. Your best friend, but this is beyond friendship." At the top step of the porch, she glanced back and tossed her head as Rupert came around the corner of the cabin. "Why, Rupert Smith, what are you doing here? If I'd known I'd have been out here to say hello."

"I don't see how you could miss Mort and me with all the noise we made. We certainly knew you were here."

"Why didn't *you* say hello?"

"Not here to disrupt Miss Marcher's business.

"What are you here for, then?"

"Work."

"She pays you? I didn't realize you needed money or that she could afford laborers."

"Don't need money. Cathryn makes the best damned coffee and biscuits in Oxford County. Ahn't that right, Mort?"

"Don't forget the apple pie, Rupe. Say, ahn't it about time for another coffee?" Morton flexed his shoulders and grinned at Susan Miller. "You're a mighty grand little button, ma'am. Tell me you ahn't spoken for and make me a happy man."

"Rupert, who is this person?"

"Mort, see if Miss Marcher needs any help while I walk Mrs. Miller to the road."

"You could walk me home, Rupert," Susan said, taking his arm. "We could practice our duet for the charity concert." She leaned heavily on his arm, peering up at him. "And I can make you coffee."

"Didn't sound like you were practicing."

"Did you like my interpretation?"

"More like Cathryn's but it was about as good as I expected. Be the talk of the county for days."

She lifted her chin, pursing her lips. After a glance back at the cabin, she said, "They make a handsome couple. I'm happy for her, of course, but I wonder if she's been honest with him."

"About?"

"Boston, of course. Are they courting?"

"They should be."

"I think so too," Susan whispered, pressing her palms against his chest. "After all, you and I…"

Thirteen

"Rupe won't kiss her," Morton said for Cathryn's benefit as they stood on the porch together.

"Why do you say that, Morton?" she asked, turning toward him.

"Same reason I ahn't going to kiss you."

"What reasons is that?"

"I ahn't no rustler. Man puts his brand on his heifer, got tah respect that."

"He has a unique way of showing his cowboy[14] skills," Cathryn replied, retreating to her front room when the couple at the road kissed one another.

"That ahn't kissin'," Morton assured her, shutting the door. "That's being waylaid by a wicked little vixen. His way ahn't no funnier than yours," he laughed and strode after her into the kitchen.

"More pie, Morton, or do you want some of my sour cherry cake?

"There's not enough cake for both of us, Cathryn," Rupert said, hitching up his braces. "He'll have pie."

"It's not for you to decide, Mr. Smith." While she filled the kettle, she kept her back to him.

---

[14] **Cowboy** – a direct translation from Spanish of *vaquero* used from about 1849 and generally replaced 'cowherd'; buckaroo is an Anglicization of *vaquero*.

He took a long breath. "I'm having all the cake, Cathryn. And the damned pie."

"Are you now? It's *my* cake and *my* pie, Mr. Smith. And my decision."

When the backscreen door bounced back open and slammed shut again, Cathryn stared at Morton.

"Now *that* was funny," the big man chuckled.

"Seems Mr. Smith had left the cake *and* the pie for you."

"Just coffee for me, Miss Marcher. I know what's good for me."

Cathryn sat down at the table with the last piece of cake and a cup of coffee. "Where did you meet Rupert?"

"The day we both signed up. We've been friends since. Lucky we served in the same unit or we'd never have survived the war."

"Why do you say that?"

"Contrary natures. On our own, we'd have gotten ourselves killed. Probably the same reason you two're fighting so hard not to love each other."

She cut into the cake and put the piece into her mouth, grimaced at the stale consistency but cherries were too expensive to waste. "Who was John Falmer?"

Morton looked at her for a moment, relaxing back in his chair and hooking his thumbs in his braces. "I told Rupe you were listening but he's not ready to believe it. Falmer's the reason Rupe spent three years in a Kansas jail.

"I see," she said, finishing the cake and pulling her coffee cup closer with both hands.

"Do you want to hear the story?"

"No, Morton, I don't."

"Any particular reason for that?"

"Yes, but you don't need to know that either."

"That's all right with me as long as you give Rupe a fighting chance to show you want kind of man he is."

"He wouldn't have liked this cake much."

"That man would like mud if you had anything to do with it."

Cathryn shook her head, giving her guest a doubtful smile, and took the dishes to the sink. "Are you going to be doing any more work, Morton?"

"Not today, Miss Marcher. Time I was going to see what he's got up to."

"I don't want you to think I'm ungrateful for all the help you've given me today. Both of you."

"My privilege. I'll be in town for a good while and Rupe's not going anywhere."

"Not to Wyoming?"

"Not for a few months—gotta get moving west before long, though. Winter on the plains is certain death, even for a man like Rupe."

"You like him."

"As far as I and a few others are concerned, Rupert Smith is the only man as close to being able to walk on water as any of us sinners are evah likely to know."

The sun was all but gone behind the Oxford Sawmill and Lumber Yard when Cathryn stopped watching the path through the woods that had hidden Morton Pierce from view fifteen seconds after he spoke. She locked all her doors and windows, shut all the curtains and hid in her closet-like sewing room to finish the gown in time for Mrs. Lowell's delivery man to collect at the end of the week.

While she worked, she considered the dresses she had inherited from her mother she could adjust to suit the occasion of the charity concert now that she had no excuse to stay away. The only suitable gown was the same gown she had worn to the opera in Portland. She had worn it earlier in the year as well and at every event in the previous year. Though she was in good company among many women in the village to have one ball gown, she was the only one with the skill to make another but who could not afford to do so.

Shrugging away the momentary wallow, at the whistle of the kettle, she jumped in confusion to run to the kitchen.

"No need for me to ask how you got in, Mr. Smith."

"You called me Rupert yesterday."

"This is today, to*night*. Why are you here this time?"

He glanced at the table and leaned toward her. "I brought your clothes."

"What do you mean?"

"The clothing you left at Mrs. Moffatt's house. Had the devil's own time getting them back but once I talked to Mrs. Small, I had better luck. That woman thinks the world of you—can't say I blame her. She's fond of me as well, otherwise, I'd have come empty-handed."

"I'll give you your mother's coat."

"Don't. I want you to have it. She'd be happy for you to have all her things." Before she turned away, he caught her hand. "I know I shouldn't be here, Cathryn. I know I shouldn't scare you like this."

"Then why are you? Why do you?"

"I don't seem to be able to manage any other way."

The only light in the room came from the open grate of the stove. She surrendered to the warmth and the persistent pull of his hand drawing her to him.

"You said you have always loved me, Cathryn."

He wore a suit, silk waistcoat, polished boots, clean and shining, though he had loosened the brocade cravat and removed the gold tie pin. Awakening to the fact he'd come from a formal event, she resisted his hold, working her hand free but he caught the other.

"That was a long time ago. When you were a girl. I'm not the man you knew then." He stepped closer. "I need to know if you can love the man I am, the man I've become. You've promised to marry me but you can't do that in all honesty if you don't know me."

"How can I know you? Or you know me, for that matter, when we can't be more than thirty seconds in the same room? You're gone at the first sign of trouble."

"I have a good reason for that."

"Then you'd better tell me."

He grinned at her in the red glow, raising his hand to her cheek. "I've never known anyone who can rile me like you do. I don't know the reason but I can't think when you do. All I want to do is hold you, then you say something that makes me realize you're a woman."

"I'd be a pretty sad creature if I wasn't, if I was still a giggly girl at my age after what I've seen."

"That's what I'm talking about. I've been thinking about you as you were the last time I saw you, thinking you'd be the same, hadn't grown up—even though I was sure you'd be a wife and mother by now, I couldn't imagine how you'd change, especially around me. You never spoke then, not to me. I'd hear you explain how something had to be done and think you were a firebrand, a warrior for good, telling all your friends what they had to do to make the world a better place."

"I was naïve."

"You were idealistic and brave—so was I. But I wasn't going to get stuck here with a war coming. I was going to fight for my country, for what was right and come back and make things right for folks here."

"But you're not anymore. You're going west to make things better for yourself and worse for anyone who gets in your way."

Rupert's laugh echoed against her stone-faced silence. Cathryn took a long breath, stiffening every muscle and vertebrae one at a time from her hips to the base of her neck. Her long breath had filled her lungs with a scent, she recognized lingering in the fine wool of his suit, on his skin. "Leave my house," she growled. "How dare you come here, demanding that I love you?"

"Not demanding, Cathryn."

"Get out of my house."

"Not until I've done what I came here to do."

"What could that be?" She lurched backward, realized she had backed into a corner and reached behind her for any weapon.

"Have a slice of the cake you offered and a cup of coffee."

"The cake is gone. Finished."

"Pie?"

"Morton had the pie—what he didn't eat, I scattered for the chickens."

"Just coffee." He stepped back and stretched into a chair at the table, reaching up to his neck to untie the cravat and unbutton the neck of his pin-striped shirt. "I know you have biscuits."

"I am not making coffee or giving you biscuits, Rupert Smith. You are leaving my house and you are not returning." She tugged at the pressure of Peggy's ring.

"You will not remove that ring, Cathryn."

"I will."

"That's what you'll say when we stand before the preacher. You won't take off that ring because you have never and will never do anything you don't down deep, want to do."

She slapped her hands on the table top. "Get out."

"Seeing as how you're not in a hospitable mood, I'll make the coffee. You can send me the bill tomorrow." He draped his suit coat over the back of the chair and rolled up his sleeves.

"Why won't you just go?"

"I told you and I'm taking a leaf from your book, Cathryn Marcher. From this day and moment, I'm not doing anything I don't, way down deep, want to do."

Despite the childish futility of the gesture, she strode to the backdoor and flung it open.

"You don't want to be doing that tonight, Cathryn. Make sure you latch the screen door and lock the other when you close it."

For all manner of reasons that she didn't bother to think about, she did as he suggested, taking from the tone of his voice a calm assurance she would more regret the refusal to do so. Rupert chose a tin from her pantry, the butter dish and a pot of jam. Nudging her into a chair he took the seat at the head of her table and filled her cup and his own.

"I hear you're not allowing Megan to sing a duet with Mrs. Miller."

"The song isn't suitable for Megan's voice."

"The words aren't suitable for her age, either."

"No, they are not."

"Why do you suppose Mrs. Miller suggested it?"

"I prefer not to speculate on Susan's thinking. She has no contact with children."

"Ignorance?"

"I doubt she would appreciate that term, Mr. Smith."

"Rude. Ignorant. Devious."

"I wonder what you say about me when you speak to her."

"I don't talk about you with her."

Cathryn clasped her cup in her hands and raised it to her mouth, to prevent the self-deprecating girl from speaking. He ate another two biscuits before he sighed, leaning back in the chair. "Any damned fool——." Cathryn jerked her head in the direction of the front door when the screen creaked.

"It's locked," Rupert said, "I checked when I came in."

She didn't ask any question, glancing at the clock above the stove. *Almost nine.*

Rupert covered her wrist with his hand. "Stay here. I'll take care of it."

"I don't——."

"Cathryn, I know what I'm doing. There's more coffee in the pot." He pushed away from the table, strode through the dark house and ripped open the door onto the front porch.

"What are *you* doing here?"

"I could ask the same of you, Mr. Colson. This is no decent time of evening to call on a lady."

"I want to speak to Cathryn."

"Then I suggest you come back tomorrow—in daylight."

"You have no call speaking to me in that tone. Do you know who I am?"

"Well enough. Doesn't change the facts."

"What facts are those, Mr. Smith?"

"Cathryn Marcher does not open her home to late night callers."

"And just what are you doing here?"

"I arrived at a decent hour and we've been discussing a few arrangements for our wedding. Any objections, Colson, if I get back to my fiancée? We were just coming to picking the date." Rupert stepped back, shut and locked the door. When he turned back to the kitchen, Cathryn stood in the passageway.

"Did you know?"

"Wild guess." He walked forward until he was standing in front of her. "I like the idea of the first Saturday in August. Unless you have a better idea."

"Did you come here tonight to embarrass me? You come here with demands that I accept you as you are but you have no intention of offering me the same respect. You have insulted a man I respect and expect I will be grateful for your interference in a part of my life that is not your concern. You make a mockery of your proposal of marriage and I do not wish to continue as part of your amusement."

"Is that all?"

"No. How can you think I will be content that you come here at any outrageous hour that strikes your whim but especially after you have spent the evening in the polite and proper society of one of my friends? Am I so pathetic in your estimation that you believe you can keep company with Susan and amuse yourself with me as though I am less—." That wretched weak girl flew up in her face. "Please go. I don't want to see you again."

She was not going to cry. She was not going to beg him to give her the same respect he demanded.

"Is that the kind of man you believe me to be, Cathryn?"

"Aren't you? From the moment you learned about Jericho Colson, you have been tormenting me. What have I done to deserve this?"

"Nothing. You're right, everything you've said about me is true. I am the man you believe me to be. Everything I have done has been a ploy, a game to wear you down so I could take advantage of you as he has. You have beaten me, Cathryn. I will not trouble you again."

He was gone before she had taken a full breath and left her standing, still in darkness, in the passageway. She felt for the wall but crumpling to the floor offered more comfort. She didn't cry. Her jaw locked too tightly shut that her teeth hurt. Her hands clenched and her fingers dug into her palms. She filled her lungs with dragging breaths, relieving the pain in her forehead with each gasp until she located the source of anger, focusing on that rather than her frustration with him.

As soon as she identified her villain, Cathryn rose from her pathetic helplessness and latched the screen door to her back porch, locked the door and for good measure, used a chair to form a braced barricade to keep lock-pickers out. She did the same with a chair in the front room. Securing her freedom from intrusion—at least against less determined criminals, Cathryn lit her oil lamps and prepared her supper of day-old soup and stale biscuits.

As she put the dishes in the sink, Rupert Smith walked from the woods in shirtsleeves and his coat slung over his shoulder. He looked at her through the window but made no gesture other than to step onto the porch and knock. She crossed the room to the door, faced him through the light organza curtain. He knocked again.

"Why have you come back?"

"I've thought about what you said."

"Everything?"

"One in particular," he answered. "May I come in?"

"I see no purpose in that, Mr. Smith. You will only turn around and go out a few moments later."

"That's what I was thinking about. Will you let me in, Cathryn?"

"I'll be dumbfounded if you're here more than five minutes."

"I'll stay. Until you kick me out."

"I think you need to follow your own advice, Mr. Smith, and come back tomorrow."

"Will you let me talk to you then? Without doors between us?"

"You're the one putting doors between us," Cathryn said.

"And you're the one building barricades."

"I wouldn't have to build barricades if you didn't break in."

"I won't again. I swear."

"I'll be the judge of that, Mr. Smith."

"What time tomorrow?"

"Depends if you want breakfast or not."

"I'll want breakfast. You can put money on that, Cathryn Marcher."

He grinned. She smiled in return. "Good night, Cathryn."

"Good night, Rupert."

As soon as he stepped back, she doused the light in the kitchen oil lamp and carried the smaller lamp to her bedroom.

The night was as silent as a snowfall and she woke at the first sound of dawn. Expecting to hear the rasping and thumping of tools, she threw off the blanket and slid her feet into thick boot socks. Wrapped in a shawl over her everyday work clothes, she trotted to the kitchen to make fresh biscuits and the expected coffee. Humming Peggy's favorite hymn tune, *St. Denio*, occasionally singing the words she knew, "Yet still I am with thee, My promise shall stand… The helpless, the hopeless, I hear their sad prayer…".

Cathryn stopped. No sound of tools filled the gaps in her singing or the birdsong. With both hands, she spread the organza curtain above the sink. The backyard looked the same as it had when Morton departed. At the front window, she looked out onto scattered branches, twigs and broken stems, disorder that her landlord would see in a short time and call her to task about.

"Just as well I didn't put money on his wanting breakfast," she complained, stamping into her work boots and shoving her arms into her father's work shirt. Dragging, grunting and cursing, she moved the debris behind the cabin. She had no choice, when Noam's cart appeared at the front walk, but to meet him to collect her delivery of eggs and milk.

"No help today?"

"Did you know Mr. Smith was cutting the tree?"

"Been meaning to do that and a few other jobs. Didn't want it done now, too early, but he cut the branches proper, no stripped bark on the trunk."

"Is that good?"

"Better done at the end of the fall when the saps not running, but that tree ahn't been trimmed in too long. Lots of dead wood in there." He nodded toward the twisted branches she hadn't dragged to the back and lifted the reins. "Mind you don't hurt yourself with this yardwork."

"I won't." She dragged the last of the debris away and raked the leaves and twigs from the lawn. In an hour, she was eating breakfast without coffee, not sure she was relieved that Rupert hadn't come for breakfast.

She put all that had happened the evening before to the side and made ready for the day of sewing, teaching Noam and Lila's two children and finishing at Megan's house. By the time she walked up the steps, she had decided what she would say to the child to soften the blow of not performing for Rupert. Still, the child sang with her throat in a vice, straining to reach notes that were the middle of her range.

"I think it best if we shorten your lesson today."

"It's true," Megan wept. "You don't think I can sing this or any song Mr. Smith likes."

"Who told you that? Where did you get that idea?"

"Mrs. Miller said you won't allow me to sing for Mr. Smith because I'm not good enough."

"The song isn't right for you."

"But Mr. Smith likes it."

"Mr. Smith is not your teacher. He doesn't know your voice or range but I know he would not choose a song like this for you to sing."

"Why not?"

"It is too old for you and, if he likes it, he would ask Mrs. Miller to sing it, alone."

"But *I* want to sing for him."

"I will help you pick a song he will like—one that is right for you."

"Mrs. Miller says you have very narrow notions of music."

"Needless to say, Miss Giles, as long as I am your teacher, I know what is best for your age, voice and level of skill. Even if I am not your teacher, I will know better than Mrs. Miller."

The lesson was a fight for supremacy until Megan's voice broke on a note she usually sang with ease. The little girl glared at her teacher and Cathryn glared back at her until Megan blushed and hung her head.

"You have strained your vocal chords with this caterwauling to please Mrs. Miller. From now on, you will either listen to my counsel, or I will refuse to teach you."

"But Miss—. I'm sorry, Miss Marcher. I so wanted to sing for Mr. Smith—now I will not."

"I will find a song, I promise and you will have an opportunity to sing to your heart's content. I give you my word and I will play for you. Now, let's see if we can begin to repair the damage."

Cathryn left the Giles residence in mid-afternoon with her fee in an envelope, and walked the three blocks along the main street to the Miller house.

"I'd like to know where you get the gumption to come here," Susan said as she walked away from the door.

"You told me you wanted three lessons this week. If so, they will have to be when I can offer the time."

Susan turned in the hallway and folded her arms across her chest. "You are mighty sure of yourself these days, Cathryn."

"You came to me. If you want to sing this duet with Mr. Smith without mishap, you will need all the help you can get from me—as you know."

"I can sing that song with my eyes closed."

"That is exactly what it will sound like."

"You are just jealous because he didn't ask you to sing with him. He has the most wonderful voice. I go weak when he stands by me and the way he looks at me. Dear!"

Cathryn untied the ribbons of her bonnet and set the music on the piano.

"This is not a convenient time for me, Cathryn."

"This is the only time I have to spare. If you cannot do this, I will go but I will have to ask you to pay the usual fee plus for yesterday's lesson."

"Jealousy does not enhance your charms—such as they are."

"Mr. Smith encouraged me to be more business-like," Cathryn said, sitting at the piano and running through scales to warm her fingers.

"That advice has done you no favors," Susan replied and launched into the warm-up exercise Cathryn played for her.

"Except for the top note, that was very good, Susan. Keep your mouth open. Relax."

At the end of the lesson, Cathryn presented her pupil with a written bill, signed she had received the full payment amount and walked onto the front drive, tying her bonnet.

"One certainly discovers one's friends' true nature when money is involved," Susan sneered.

Cathryn turned. "One certainly does, Mrs. Miller."

The door slammed shut as Cathryn walked down the drive and onto the street. She shrugged as she turned onto her road and walked with a lighter step at the end of the day than she had when Rupert had not kept yet another promise. *Why do I persist in my faith?*

Neither dithering nor loving a man unworthy of her love were in her nature. Jericho Colson had earned her sympathy and compassion but he could not win her heart in the way that Rupert Smith had from his first appearance when he returned from university and, instead of dedicating his talent and energy to his chosen profession as Allan Giles did by paying another man to take his place in the Union Army, enlisted at the first call of his home state and his country.

Despite the conflicts in her beliefs about war, Cathryn understood without doubt his commitment to what he believed to be right regardless of the cost to him or those who loved him. Without any doubt in her heart, she understood his commitment was supported by his belief in justice and equality. The day he returned after his initial training, to say good-bye to his parents, all of them knowing they may never see one another again, Cathryn had held back though the other girls swarmed around him—tall, handsome and proud in his First Lieutenant's gold stripes and wide-brimmed hat.

During his three days of leave, she was in the Smiths' house, helping in the kitchen so Peggy and George could spend all their waking hours near their son as visitors crushed into the parlor and library to show their appreciation for his patriotic spirit. As she brought coffee to Peggy Smith, Rupert crossed the room toward a young girl and bowed, taking her hand onto his arm to present her to his parents. Later, Susan told Nancy, "She's no one, the sister of one of the soldiers in his unit, from a backwoods farm."

Cathryn stood in the crowd with her parents in front of the town hall when Rupert's unit was on parade in the square on the day they marched to war—the last day anyone had seen him. Though there were boys her age she didn't recognize them but made a point of looking at each as they marched past. The young girl stood across the square, her gaze fixed on one of the boys, sobbing aloud. The boy kept his gaze straight ahead, his gun on his shoulder, marching in formation with his follow soldiers, tears glinting on his cheeks.

Cathryn was not among the girls who flirted with the soldiers and blew kisses on their wafting lace handkerchiefs. She wasn't the only one to witness the expression in Lt. George Rupert Smith's eyes when he met his parents' gaze and acknowledged what they knew. Years would pass before he returned, if he did. She was not among the gaggle of giddy giggling girls who called his attention to them as he passed.

She memorized the boy-soldiers' faces and lifted her head when Rupert saluted the local officials and turned his gaze to the front. As he did, she met his gaze but did not return the slight smile he gave her. Her heart was too sore, too broken not to express her sorrow for the future she could not help but foresee for him and all the folks around them on that bright July day when the Union Army had endured a second defeat at Bull Run.

Messages had already arrived. Men were dying and towns were decimated by cannon fire. In Lt. Smith's face, Cathryn saw a man who could neither deny nor escape his character and for that, his suffering was written. And for that, as she now admitted ten years later, his friends would believe he could walk on water.

Cathryn never saw the girl again and wondered if Rupert knew what had happened to the young soldier.

Though she was within a few steps of her cabin, Cathryn turned back and took another road, walking with her eyes on the horizon as she turned again into the church cemetery. She tidied her parents' grave assuring them of her well-being, releasing them from any worry about her poverty, laying her hand on the cold granite to assure herself by its rigidity that they, with their joyous, loving hearts were not locked within the stone. At the Smith's family memorial, she cleared away moldy leaves with her bare hands.

"Hello, Peggy, George," she murmured. "It's Evie. I'm sure you know and have seen for yourselves but I wanted to tell you in my own way. Rupert has come home. He is the man we always believed him to be and was meant to become. You can be as proud of him as it is in your hearts to be. He is struggling with many demons but you needn't fear for him. He knows what is right for him to do and in that he will not falter."

Again, she laid her hand on the stone, in no doubt her words had reached their destination and comfort taken.

Fourteen

She had reached the first step of her front porch when she heard the sounds she had expected that morning. She picked up her skirts and slipped through the side yard, peering around the rough corner to watch two men at work clearing the branches with saws to make a pile of green firewood ready for the next year. Neither of the men was the man she expected nor even one she knew. She stood in silence, waiting to be seen. When she was, one man straightened his back and nudged the other.

The first man wiped his brow. The second nodded at her and returned to his task. "Rupe couldn't be here, Miss, so he asked us to finish the job."

"Where is—. Is Mr. Pierce also unable to be here?"

"That's right, Miss. You have no cause to worry. We know what's needed."

"Is Mr. Smith's business elsewhere likely to keep him a long while?"

"Well, that depends on whose opinion you ask for. A damned long time if you ask Rupe. Not long enough for others."

Cathryn wasn't in the mood for speculation and wasn't surprised when he said, "My guess is as you'd be one of those who'd be in the damned long time camp like the rest of us here."

"And who are you?"

"All friends of the Captain, Miss Cathryn."

"Where is he? Your Captain."

"He'll be another few hours. But he'd want us to get on with the work."

She guessed the two standing in her backyard were among the friends who thought Rupert Smith had a special relationship with water. She offered a smiling apology for disturbing them before she disappeared into her kitchen, reappearing half an hour later with coffee and biscuits.

"Rupe mentioned your coffee," the speaker for the two grinned at her.

"Where are you from?"

"Guess it's easy to tell we ahn't from around here by the way we talk. Name's Arne. Tom Arne and this here is Malcolm, my brother."

Malcolm Arne nodded once and returned to his work, setting his cup on the rail fence between her yard and the Snyders' field.

"Are you from Oxford County?"

"Mighty funny, Miss, 'cause that's where we grew up, had a farm but it weren't in Yankee country."

Cathryn studied the two men a moment.

"Don't you go getting scared of us. We're peaceable. Done sworn off rebel ways for a while now. Mal and I come from Oxford County, Mississippi."

"Did you meet Captain Smith after the war?"

"Durin', Miss. We were at Cahaba."

"Cahaba?"

"Best let Rupe tell that story if'n he's got a mind to. Anyways, that's where we all met up."

"A battle?"

"No, ma'am. Mal and me was mighty impressed by that Yankee—a real gentleman, not like some as call themselves by that title. He weren't General Lee or nothing as grand as President Davis but, even when we caught him and his men burning up the railway and making them Sherman

Neckties[15]. Fought like devils, ended when they ran out of bullets and were throwing rocks and dirt." He laughed, shaking his head a moment, met her gaze with a grin. "We had orders to kill the black soldiers on sight, but Captain Smith and Mort stood in the way. Mal and me didn't have no heart to kill the contraband[16] so we let the blacks go, took the others to prison. Pity 'cause we could tell he was quality."

"I've always thought so," Cathryn mused. "There will be hot water for you to wash up when I've made supper for you."

"Ahn't no call on you to do that, Miss, but we'll be mighty grateful."

"That's the least I can do, gentlemen." Though she was bursting with questions, Cathryn bit her lips together the whole time she prepared a meal, forgetting her plans to finish her work for Mrs. Lowell in her eagerness to return their kindness.

She fed Tom and Malcolm at her kitchen table, allowing them to eat in peace while she bustled back and forth with plates and cups. The sun was below the roof of the Oxford Sawmill when they offered to wash the dishes and clean the stove. Tom set the firebox ready for the night and both men took their leave.

The few hours Tom had promised had stretched to four and were fast on their way to five before Cathryn thought of

---

[15] **Sherman Neckties** during General Sherman's march through Georgia in the summer of 1864, he instructed his officers to destroy the railways by burning the ties and twisting the red-hot rails so that they could not be used again, sometimes wrapping them around tree trunks.

[16] **Contraband** Free African-Americans and escaped slaves joined the Union Army and, after the Emancipation Proclamation, escaped slaves followed the Army encampments, became known as 'contraband'; some African Americans served in the Confederate Army—many as conscripts, some as volunteers.

the work she should have been doing. By then, her eyes were tired, her hands trembled as she gathered the garment and there was not enough light to work on the delicate fabric. Promising to work with diligence the following day, she prepared to go to bed and was asleep in moments.

No sound woke her the next morning but her routine opened her eyes as the sun crept up from behind the woods. By the time the first rays struck the panes of her bedroom window, she was at work in the sewing room, undisturbed until the steeple clock chimed ten.

About to make her morning coffee, a knock on her front door drew her from the kitchen toward the dark-clothed figure of a stout man at her front door.

"Miss Cathryn Marcher?" When she answered, he continued, "The sheriff of this township has received a complaint. I am here to ask a few questions."

"About me?"

"Concerning you."

"What sort of complaint? From whom?"

"I have questions for you, Miss Marcher. May I come in?"

Cathryn stepped aside without hesitation, only thinking better of it when the man closed the door. She led him through to the kitchen, offering him a chair at the table. He chose the seat opposite her and took a notebook from his breast pocket, flipping through several pages.

"Have you seen any strangers in the area in recent days?"

"Strangers to my neighbors or to me?"

"Men who have not been here before, whom your neighbors might not know."

"In that case, yes."

"How many such men?"

She thought a moment and said, "Four."

"Known to you?"

"Two, yes—no, only one. The second was introduced to me by a long acquaintance, a resident of this village."

"The other two were also strangers to you. Not just your neighbors?"

"They introduced themselves."

"Are you in the habit of opening your door to men unknown to you?"

"No. These men are close friends of a man I have known since I was a girl—since before the war—he lives in Oslo Hill, Mister—?"

"Constable McLain, Miss. Why would this man send strangers to a spinster as yourself?"

"To finish some yard work he and his friend started—work my landlord wanted done."

"Laborers?"

"Yes, in a manner of speaking. More friends doing favors."

"But you didn't know them?"

"No. What is this about, Constable? What have I done?"

"Have any of these men behaved in a way that gave you cause for concern?"

"None at all."

For a moment, he made notes. "Why was that, Miss Marcher? How were you reassured?"

"My fiancé was here at the time when one man came late at night. My fiancé asked the others to help me in his absence." Since the constable did not ask her to name her visitors, she saw no reason to volunteer information.

Though the situation seemed strange, when the constable closed his notebook, he smiled in such a benign way she had no qualms when he asked, "Do you wish to file a complaint against the man who came late at night?"

"No, Constable. As I said, my fiancé was here at the time. I don't believe there is any purpose in making more of the incident."

After the policeman left her house, walking back into town, Cathryn realized she had not offered him any of her usual hospitality. She stared after him for several minutes, puzzled by the event, the questions and her own use of fiancé—for the first time, aloud.

The interview had stolen precious time from her day and she lost more by fretting while she made a small, solitary meal and sat alone in her kitchen.

"Cathryn."

"Where have you been?" she demanded of the man standing at her kitchen window.

"Are you all right?" he asked, as soon as the door was open and she fought with the screen door latch, looking her over from head to foot.

"Are you going to tell me where you have been?" She folded her arms, refusing to budge from the doorway.

"I've been out of my mind worrying about you." He caught her arms, pulled her closer to him and searched her face. "Was he here? Did he come here?"

"Who, Rupert? The only people I've seen are your friends, the Arne boys—."

"Thank God Morton got word to them."

"What's wrong? Why didn't you come yesterday for breakfast?"

"I—I couldn't. Something came up before I left the house."

"Something or someone?" Cathryn clamped her lips together and turned away. "Don't tell me. I don't want to know."

"I didn't think you would," he said, lowering his empty arms to his sides as she walked to the other side of the room, putting the stove between them. "Mal and Tom did a good job." He nodded toward the new wood pile on her porch.

"Yes, I was surprised to see them, just about as surprised as I was by the constable from town."

"McLain was here."

"Yes. Was he who you meant? The 'reason' stopping you from coming here? He asked some odd questions, Rupert."

"Doesn't surprise me. He wanted to know why I was here, correct? If I was frightening you? Breaking into your house?"

"Nothing like that," Cathryn replied, turning away again and swinging back to stare at him. "Rupert, what is this? Why was the town constable asking me if I always welcomed strange men into my home?"

"What?"

"You heard me. Of what am I accused?"

He slammed his fist on the table. "He's a toad. A lackey," he hissed. "Come here, Cathryn."

He beckoned, holding his arms open and she stepped into the circle of his embrace, studying his face. "What has happened?"

"I couldn't come for breakfast because I was arrested. I've spent a day and a half in jail."

"But why? What have you done? Who arrested you?"

"Near as I can figure, I'm in the way of someone with a lot of powerful friends."

"What does that have to do with me?"

He met her searching gaze for a moment, dropping his arms away from her. "I'm in the way."

"Of what?"

"A man's ambition."

"And how does that include me?"

"He wants you."

"That's ridiculous," she said, stepping back.

"When you told me to go away—the night Jericho Colson came by—he was still watching. He saw me storm out, saw how you reacted, setting chairs against the doors and refused to let me in when I came back. He made a complaint to the constabulary in town. He told them I was disturbing you, his fiancée."

"Oh."

"Mort persuaded McLain to come here to talk to you. I guess he was satisfied when you told him *I'm* your fiancé, not Colson."

"I didn't tell him that."

He drew back, staring at her, his brow creased.

"I didn't tell him the name of my fiancé. I just said my fiancé was here when Jericho came. I didn't mention Jericho's name either. He didn't ask that, only insinuated I had gentlemen visitors—too many for a decent woman." She ended on a sob.

"I can guess who gave him that notion," Rupert said, lifting her chin on his crooked finger. "Cathryn, don't worry. I'll make certain this doesn't happen again, I promise."

"But why is it happening to me now?"

"It is my fault."

"How? What did you do?"

"I couldn't let him think he could have you, that he could walk back into your life—not without a challenge."

"You are talking such nonsense, Rupert."

"I know why you think that, but you are for once wrong. Jericho Colson will never be a part of your life again. He won't get anywhere near you."

"You're talking as if I should be afraid of him. I've never been afraid of him or anyone."

"And I'm going to ensure you go on feeling that way." He clasped her fingers and raised them to his lips. "Mal and Tom have been watching the cabin since yesterday—as soon as Mort got word to them. Colson was bound to try something to force you back to him—that's why McLain asked you about visitors."

"To soil my reputation?" He nodded. "As you know, I am already ruined," she hissed. "What does my reputation matter? To you or anyone?"

"It matters to me, Cathryn Marcher, because I want you to be my wife and no one is going to make you feel—I love you, Cathryn, I want to marry you. Nothing else matters. If you'll have me."

"How many times are you going to ask me and how many times will it take for you to believe me? Is it because you hope I'll change my mind?"

"I feel I'm dreaming," he murmured. "I've thought of you, of marrying you, of wanting you all these years, even when I went to prison and knew the possibility was beyond remote, I kept that hope. I'm here, just holding your hand and that is too much to believe is real."

"Rupert, why don't you kiss me?" she asked, instantly regretting when he dropped her hand and leaned back, his eyes wide.

"I have kissed you."

"I just thought," she whispered, "if you did, you'd know—believe—that I love you."

"I know that. You don't have to prove anything to me, Cathryn. It's me. I have to prove myself to you."

"Prove what to me, Rupert?"

"I've sworn I won't ask for anything from you until we are married. I won't break that vow, on my honor."

"Do you think I'm soiled?"

"No, I think…I *know* what Colson did. I read it in his eyes. He's the kind of man who believes he owns a woman—I knew that but I still challenged him. If I hadn't been so blatant, he'd never have known. His predator instincts were sparked at the opera. He doesn't like the idea that he's lost you, that you could love someone else, especially a man like me."

"What is a man like you?"

"Wild, uncivilized, an outcast, unwelcome in polite society except as entertainment, a wastrel—."

"You are the only person who sees you like that. No one else, not even me."

"You should. Of all people, you should."

She did not want to hear anymore harsh words about the man she loved even from his own mouth, his own beautiful, strong mouth.

"Why are you looking at me like that?" he demanded.

"I'm sorry. I didn't mean to stare."

"Anymore of that and you'll know—."

Her lower lip trembled. Her eyes brimmed over with tears.

"Don't." He pushed away, lunged for the door.

"Rupert, please. Don't go."

His fist gripped the door knob so hard, the frame rattled.

Cathryn covered her face with both hands and let her sob escape because she was going to be alone again, for how long she had no way of knowing—hours or years as before. Because her tears refused to be stopped and her sorrow could not be contained by any sense of propriety; because she had loved him for so long without any hope and hope was snatched away from her at every moment she caught sight of its bright dazzle; because everyone she loved deserted her when she most needed their love in return; because she couldn't be strong every moment or unselfish at every turn. She sank into a chair, dropped her head on her arms and grieved for Evie, that timid, gangly girl, bereft and frightened.

"Don't cry," Rupert commanded.

She held her breath for only a moment to hear his rough tone and sobbed louder.

"Are you trying to—. Cathryn, please stop. Don't cry anymore, my darling," he pleaded, his voice softer.

She made an effort to stop but her throat ached from the terrible restraint and she covered her head with her arms.

"Cathryn. Angel."

She pulled away from him, pushing to her feet when he laid his hand on her shoulder, lurched to the wall, fought against his embrace, gasping when he kissed her neck and his arms tightened around her. He turned her to face him, stilled her sobs and protests with kisses until her arms locked around his neck.

"Push me away, Cathryn," he begged against her lips. "Make me go."

"I can't. I won't. I love you. I've always loved you. So much. Don't leave me, Rupert."

"I must, I promised you," he whispered against her throat. "Make me go. Don't let me do this."

She kissed his mouth again, groaning when he yanked her against him and clenched his arms so tight she lost her breath. He pulled at the pins holding her hair in a loose knot at the back of her neck, hissing as it tumbled apart and across her shoulders, covering his arms as he crushed her to him and forced her lips to part for him. With each pin that dropped to the kitchen floorboards, he urged her a step backward, into the hallway, dim and obscured from view.

As he lifted her from the floor, he leaned hard against the wall by her bedroom door, taking deep breaths. "I want you. I want—I've wanted you since that spring day I saw you in my parents' house, serving coffee to those snobs. I've fought hard, Cathryn, I've done all I could to protect you. Tell me what you want from me. Tell me. Before I make any more mistakes."

"What mistakes have you made, Rupert?" Her fingers trailed into the rich waves of his uncombed hair and fought with the stubble on his chin. While she caressed him in a haphazard, distracted way she sighed, cocking her head. *He is wearing the clothes he wore when he came here after spending the evening with Susan.* There were traces of her scent and that indefinable odor of fear she had come to recognize in her work at the hospital. Her gaze locked on his eyes, realizing he hadn't been home, hadn't slept, shaved or eaten since she turned him away. "Rupert, why have you stayed away so long?"

Like her other question, this one remained unanswered though he had met her gaze for a moment before burying his face in her hair and holding her harder against him. His jaw set against any confession at the same time as he held her closer. He pressed the back of his head against the wall, closing his eyes and swallowed hard. Moment by moment, he loosened his grip until her toes touched the floor and his breath came easier.

"I don't need to know," she sighed, laying her head on his shoulder, settling her own breathing. "Are you hungry?"

"You should know. You need to know."

"You'll tell me when you're ready. This minute, I'd like to make dinner. I still have soup."

"Biscuits? Coffee?"

"And pie."

Before either moved, he said, "You need to know more about me."

"There will be plenty of time for that while I'm making your dinner." She set her heels down and stood erect as his arms glided away and he inhaled on a sigh. "Now who can that be?"

With a huff, Cathryn strode to her front door and yanked it open when she saw the two faces peering back at her.

"I'm sorry to intrude, Miss Marcher but I've come, *we've* come, to ask a favor."

"What is it, Mary?" Cathryn stepped back, sweeping her arm to invite Mary Cook and her beau into the front room. Rupert walked forward to greet the young man with a handshake.

"Sir."

Accepting the young man's salute, Rupert asked, "What brings you, Miss Cook?"

The young woman curtsied, her blush enlivening her sweet face as she stepped closer to her young man, swishing her gingham skirt back and forth like a child. "North and me want to get married."

"That's wonderful, Mary," Cathryn cried, embracing the Giles's maid with a laugh. "That's so wonderful."

"We think so too," Mary replied.

"But?" Rupert asked.

"Oh, there's no 'but', really. That's what we want. I came to ask Miss Marcher a favor."

"Well, what is it, Mary? What can I do for you?"

"Can you make my wedding gown?" the girl blurted. "I can't afford to buy one from that dressmaker in Portland but I want to look special, you know, because North's folks will be there."

Cathryn glanced at the intended groom.

"My folks…" he murmured, turned his gaze on his fiancée and cleared his throat.

"They haven't met me is all. North's been here since he left the army, working in the sawmill. His folks live way up the coast. They'll come for the wedding, 'course, but I want to make the best impression I can since they won't have a chance to get to know me afore that day."

"I will very happily make your gown, Mary. When is this wedding to be?"

"Not 'til just afore Independence Day."

"That's not that far away," Cathryn mused. "We'll have to get started."

"I was hoping you'd say that. 'S why we came now." Mary looked up at her intended and pouted so sweetly, Cathryn pressed her fingers to her lips to keep from weeping again, wondering if this happy young bride-to-be had noticed anything amiss between her dressmaker and the other man in the cabin. *She's too happy to see anyone but her beau.* "There's just one thing, Miss Marcher, Captain Smith…we're not making any announcement for a while."

"Why?" Cathryn asked without thinking.

"We don't think Mr. and Mrs. Giles will be happy when they find out I'll be leaving their house. I don't want to lose my job there until we've saved up enough for my dress."

"Don't worry about the dress, Mary. That will be my gift to you."

"Oh no, thank you, Miss Marcher but I can't let you do that. I— We appreciate it but we'd rather get started in the right way. Paying our way and not taking advantage."

"All the same—."

"These two have the right idea, Cathryn. More people in this village should take note," Rupert interrupted, extending his hand to the younger veteran. "Congratulations, Mr.—?"

"North, sir. Just North. I go by North."

Mary pressed her head against the young man's shoulder. He held himself as erect as Rupert always stood. His proud bearing belied his taciturn, almost embarrassed, behavior. Cathryn glanced at her fiancé, aware that he studied North as well.

"Congratulations, North. My friends call me Rupe." He clasped the man's hand, cupping his elbow as he did. "You've done well for yourself with this young woman."

"She's too good for me, sir—Rupe."

"As is my fiancée," he replied, extending his hand toward Cathryn to beckon her closer. "Cathryn, once you've taken the measure of this bride-to-be, perhaps she'll return the favor so Mrs. Lowell can make your wedding gown."

"Oh!" Mary clapped her hands over her mouth, jumping in excitement. "I thought—. Everyone thought—."

Once Cathryn had responded to his invitation, Rupert grinned at the couple, closing his arm around his fiancée's waist and said, "Everyone is wrong."

"Congratulations," North murmured.

"You're not the only man whose luckier than he deserves," Rupert assured the groom-to-be. "Our task now is to make sure these ladies don't regret their decisions. Come with me, North, we'll leave our future brides to their work while I make some dinner for us all."

★★★

Fifteen

"Do you trust I love you, Rupert?" The question was fair, one he could answer with either yes or no and she would understand his answer. She stepped around him and opened the door of her sewing room, straightening her clothes and pushing her hair behind her ears as she sat at the small table. He stayed at the door. *Are we always going to be so careful of each other, so distant.*

"If you knew—."

Cathryn glanced over her shoulder in his direction but not long enough to see him though he took a step toward her. He studied the room, examined the stacks of fabric and the work she now had only a few hours to finish.

"If you knew what I've done, Cathryn—. I don't want to frighten you."

"I have witnessed what war does to men. I know how it affects women too. There is nothing you could have done that is any worse than that—what I have already witnessed and done myself."

"There is nothing in all this world you can have done that has the power to tarnish even a single hair on your head."

"I'm grateful for your kind blind-eye to my transgressions but I am not so foolish as to believe you do not think of them."

"I don't blame you for what Colson did. You were a child—."

"I was not a child, Rupert. I was lonesome and fearful but I knew what I was doing." While she spoke, she threaded a needle and lifted the delicate fabric.

"He took advantage."

"I cannot blame Jericho for that, any more than I could have blamed you in his place."

"I am not like him. I would not have done that to you."

"We are all more like than we want to see. Susan married Joshua Miller because she was frightened of being alone, of being a spinster. I chose to be with Jericho for similar reasons. Susan is alone still but as a recent war widow. I am alone still but—."

"You are not alone, Cathryn."

"I am as long as you cannot trust that I love you. I don't care what you've done. Whatever it is, you had reasons—good or bad."

"I almost killed a man—if I hadn't been stopped, I would have succeeded and been satisfied."

"What stopped you?"

"My friends. Mort, Tom, Mal—it was for them I went for the kill and they kept me from it. They held me back and I owe them what little humanity I have left."

"They are good friends. Are they also the reason you came home?"

Rupert bowed his head for a moment, listening to the clatter of her sewing machine. "That belonged to my mother. I remember how often she complained about her lack of skill. She'd say 'I'll give this damn thing—.'" He was silent for a moment. "You need a better chair, Evie."

She opened her mouth to refute his statement and caught her breath. She had been proved a liar. "This is the chair that came with the machine."

"I know," he replied. "This has been part of my life since my mother bought this machine on a whim."

"I didn't steal them. I asked Noam to take them back to your house…weeks ago but he hasn't come yet."

"If you didn't steal them, Cathryn, why would you return them?"

"They belonged to Peggy. They belong to you."

"How did they get here?"

Cathryn continued working, her foot pumping the treadle in a rhythm that reminded her of the piano piece she had neglected for so long. "Allan told me your parents had left me a few of their possessions and Noam brought them here."

"Such as?"

"This sewing machine. The chair. Your mother's Gilbert piano…"

"I wondered where it had gone," Rupert said, glancing down the passage to the front room where only one chair and a table took space away from Peggy's treasured instrument. "Anything else?"

"No. I wanted to return them. I'm sorry. Noam hasn't brought his cart——."

"That explains why he's been so cussed ornery since I came back."

"What do you mean?"

"I don't want any of this, Cathryn. My parents gave them to you. My mother was always fond of you. She knew before I did what I felt for you. She warned me I'd lose you if I didn't speak before someone else saw you were like no one else in the world."

"She was kinder than she should have been."

"She was right. I did lose you."

Cathryn stilled her hands on the shimmering fabric.

"Why did you choose Jericho?"

"He was there. He was kind. He needed my help and I had no one else." She spoke in a matter-of-fact tone, rose from the chair to drape the gown over the dummy.

"Whose dress is that?"

"I don't know. One of Mrs. Lowell's clients. I think I've made dresses for her before. Same taste and measurements. I have to finish it tonight, I'm already late." She gazed at him for a long moment. "Where is your coat? The last time you were here, you wore a suit."

"I left it—somewhere. In a hurry to get here."

"You can borrow my father's jacket when you leave." She had dismissed him more than once during the course of the day but he seemed immune to her wish to be rid of him. "You might need it when the rain breaks open those clouds."

He glanced at the window, standing his ground when she came toward him and sliding his arm around her as though she had meant to walk into the embrace. He didn't bring her closer or clench his muscles to hold her but met her gaze with a tilt of his head and the smile that always won her smile in return. "Are you ready for coffee and a slice of pie?"

"I am." Before he stepped aside, he lowered his head and pressed his jaw against her cheek. The square bone flexed and she leaned into the pressure for a moment before pushing past him.

He sat at the head of the table, turning to watch her preparations. "One or two of your fine biscuits wouldn't go amiss."

"Between you and your friends, I'll be lucky to have a crumb left for myself by Saturday."

"All the more reason for you to accept my hospitality, at my house."

"Nothing can induce me to—."

"Don't lie to me, Cathryn," he laughed. "You've already confessed you come to my parents' house when you need assurance and comfort. I don't intend for you to feel any different because I'm there. In fact, it's a damned fine idea for you to accept my hospitality now."

"You know that isn't possible."

"Why not? We're engaged. And you'll be safer there."

"I'd have to come here anyway—every day to take care of my garden, work, teach some of my students."

"You go to most of them."

"How do you know that?"

"Cathryn, that's common knowledge. Every single one of your piano and singing pupils is from this village and everyone talks about their lesson or their children's lessons. Sometimes you teach in the church. Other times in their home. Susan Miller told me she comes here half the time— when you aren't teaching Megan on the same day."

"And if I'm at your place, Susan can come there."

"I'd rather you went to her place."

"Why?"

"Not alone. Not while Colson is anywhere near."

"Rupert, I think this is all a tad too dramatic for the Hill."

"Doesn't change the facts, my darling," her fiancé said, reaching out to take the cup she held. "But there is no reason for you to worry. You've got four friends who won't let anything happen to you, no matter what Colson tries."

When she set the plate of biscuits in front of him and sat near, Rupert clasped her fingers. "I'll be here," he murmured, pressing her fingers to his lips.

"Rupert, I don't want this. I want to live as I always have. I've never had to depend on anyone."

"Only because you had no one."

"I'm used to taking care of myself."

"Now, I'm here to do that for you. You won't know I'm here. I won't interfere except when—."

"That's the problem, Rupert. I can take care of myself. I don't need you to protect me or do my yardwork."

"Good. I don't want to do that. I'd much prefer to make love to you and keep you warm at night. We'll be married before long—maybe before Mary and her young man. I have already spoken to Mr. Jorgens and booked the church.

I'd like you to pick the hymns." He patted her hand to the table and pried the first biscuit open.

Cathryn sat back and stared at him while he devoured the last of her biscuits. "The first Saturday in August."

He nodded and drained his cup. "Just two days after Susan's fundraising concert." Again, he nodded. "At which you'll be singing a duet with her."

"And you'll be accompanying."

"So, it is true?"

"For charity. I couldn't say no, under the circumstances. Ensnared before I knew it."

"I see."

"No, I don't think you do, Cathryn. If you're jealous, you have no need to be. If you don't want to accompany us, I'll understand but Mrs. Miller will make more of that than you want or need. Only you can accompany your pupil to make the least of her flaws. She's dependent on you. As mean-spirited and rude as she is, making a fool of her is not in your nature."

"Convenient."

Rupert laughed followed by a hiss and, as soon, he growled, "I'll have to remember you are as thorny as a blackberry bush."

"And as resilient," she replied, pushing away from the table.

He caught her around the waist and gazed up at her. "And as sweet."

"I have work to do."

He stood without letting her go and slid his fingers through her hair to the back of her neck. As he kissed her, he resisted making ardent demands though the kiss was languorous and as passionate as her unresponsive patience allowed. He lifted her chin and smiled into her soft, serious eyes.

"Anything that worries you, my beloved, all you need do is tell me."

"What happened to you last night?"

"When I left here, I walked through the woods. I didn't see McLain waiting for me at the house. Colson had already made a complaint—as I told you. If not for Mort, I'd still be in that cell until the circuit judge came around in January. Mort's handy with the law among a few other things so he told McLain he'd have to interview you, as the alleged victim of the assault Colson accused me of committing. Once you told him what happened, he had to let me go— even though he thinks Colson is your fiancé. I'm glad you decided not to make a complaint," he ended with a grin.

"I should have told him your name."

Rupert pressed his finger to her lips. "McLain isn't that smart but he's no fool. He didn't say in so many words but any fool could see Colson was acting from jealousy not concern. If Colson knows I'm free, he'll come here. I won't leave you alone no matter how sure you are you can take care of yourself. You don't know what he's capable of doing."

"And you do?"

"Yes, Cathryn, I do." He pulled her into a gentle embrace, cupping her cheek. "I'll be in the pumpkin patch if you need me. Mal and Tom will be around and Mort is keeping an eye on Colson. You do your work. I'll take care of all the rest."

Still doubtful Jericho Colson had any strong feelings for her—strong enough to make him dangerous—she did consider the possibility he was jealous of Rupert. Why she couldn't live her life without him when he had chosen to go back to his wife with hardly a look back, she didn't understand. He hadn't loved her any more than she loved him. *Perhaps, he believed I loved him and can't fathom my love for Rupert. Perhaps he believes I want to spare him any guilt, that I don't truly love Rupert.* Cathryn glanced out the window as her future husband bent his back to the hoeing around her pumpkins and pressed her fingers to her lips where he had kissed her.

Jericho's kisses had not caused such tumult in her body as the merest touch—as gentle as a summer breeze—from Rupert Smith's lips. His strong, full mouth so eager for a generous response that she hadn't been able to offer. With Jericho, she had been calm, reserved, ladylike and modest. None of those words described her reaction to Rupert's kisses. More likely to explode in giggles or gasps, to collapse in sighs and moans—disgraceful behavior inappropriate for a spinster. Cathryn hoped she could contain her giddiness until, as he promised, they were husband and wife.

The instant someone knocked on the door, Rupert was beside her.

"Do you know that man?" he asked, peering hard at the partly obscured face on the other side of the screen.

"Mrs. Lowell's delivery man," she gasped, lunging for the door knob.

"Afternoon, Miss. I've come for the parcel."

"I thought you were coming Friday."

"Change of route. I'm sure Mrs. Lowell explained, Miss. All her other seamstresses had their work ready."

Cathryn stared at Rupert, biting her lip. "I'm not sure, Mr. Blanchett, but the work isn't ready. Can you come back tomorrow."

"Sorry, Miss. You're near last on my list. I'll be on my way back to Portland by the end of the day."

"Where are you going next, Mr. Blanchett?" Rupert asked, squeezing Cathryn's shoulder.

"Over to the Falls, then on to Bowdoinham."

When Rupert questioned her with a cocked eyebrow, Cathryn shook her head.

"Tell Mrs. Lowell Miss Marcher will deliver the dress on Friday."

"She won't be pleased."

"She'll be pleased enough when she sees the work."

"Ay-yuh, well, nothing for it," the delivery man said, and trotted back to his small buggy.

"How can I finish and deliver the gown up to Portland by Friday?"

"I'll worry about the delivery." He turned her by her shoulders and with a slight push propelled her to her sewing room.

For the rest of the late afternoon, she stitched and pressed and clipped. By the time the sun went down and her eyes were too tired for more, Rupert and his two brother friends were in the kitchen with a pot of rutabaga soup and crude biscuits piled high.

"Ahn't a patch on yours, Miss," Tom laughed, stuffing a small deformity in his mouth, "but they'll do."

"Have you earned your supper, Miss Marcher?"

"I have, Mr. Smith. Have you?"

"Only you can be the judge of both," he answered. A place had been set for her at the head of the table, with all the proper cutlery and linen set out. Rupert held her chair for her and draped the napkin over her lap while Tom poured water from a jug into a glass. Malcolm placed a soup bowl in front of her and ladled their creation into it.

"You are talented," she said to all three of them.

"A man learns a lot in a prison camp," Tom said, taking the seat Rupert indicated.

"Were you all in Cahaba with Rupert?"

Her fiancé gave her a long glance before shaking his head in amused wonder. "You don't miss a trick," he murmured, sitting beside her.

"A woman learns a lot in a military hospital."

Tom and Malcolm stared at her for a moment but recalled their upbringing when she blushed and the two of them engaged in a quiet exchange at the other end of the table.

"Is that gown ready to go to Mrs. Lowell?" Friday arrived together with the last day of May and the appearance of her fiancé a few minutes after dawn.

"I need to remove some of the tacking and inspect the seams."

"How long?"

"An hour or so."

"Good. I'm going to Portland in the afternoon. I'll take it to Mrs. Lowell for you."

"I can't ask you to do that."

"You can ask me to walk into a burning building and I would," he said, "But I have to go to Portland to see my bank manager, so this will give me two good reasons."

"Only if you're going. This isn't a special trip just because I didn't remember the change Mrs. Lowell mentioned, is it?"

"No, my love. I have to go and I'd rather be doing something for you as well."

"I could go to Portland with you," she offered. "That would not be as much trouble as this."

"I can't take you with me—as much as I would prefer your company." He met her gaze for a moment before he said, "I have made arrangements to accompany Mrs. Miller today. We have an appointment with the bank to go through her late husband's accounts."

"You won't have time to see Mrs. Lowell—I don't want Susan to go there with you. I'll go myself."

"Why shouldn't she know how hard you work?"

"She doesn't have to know where. And it is also none of your business."

"You are my business and you have no reason to hide anything from that woman."

"It's my business and my privacy and, if you can't accept that, you can go."

"You don't mean that, Cathryn."

"I do, Rupert. I have had the privilege of living my own life in my own way since my parents passed away. Any mistakes I have made have been mine and my responsibility. I cannot—will not—abdicate my freedom."

"Never?"

"Never."

"I promise you I will compromise. Do you want to tell me why you didn't want me to know you are the Evie I have been looking for?"

"When you come back from your business in Portland with Susan."

For a moment, they stood holding one another in that miraculous state of trust and acceptance, understanding that the person in their arms felt and wanted the same.

"I will be back in an hour for the gown," Rupert whispered in her ear, loosening his grip, lingering as he caressed the muscles along her spine to her waist and stepped back. "I had better go so I can keep that promise." He hugged her once more and released her.

"I'll be here."

After Rupert had disappeared from view, all along the woodland trail, the slight movement of the long grass and the swish of the low branches ceased. Her doors and windows were locked but the only person who had ever breached the security of her home had left. "How strange." She unlocked her doors. She had taken care of herself for eleven years. She knew of only one person who could or would enter without permission. But she mattered to him. And he mattered to her. He, more than she, was threatened. Jericho had used his influence to have Rupert arrested and held in jail but Cathryn could not understand how Jericho thought this could help his cause in her eyes.

He must know Rupert would tell me who did this. He must know I would not like him any more than I did, for abusing his power in this way to hurt Rupert.

Once the woodland gave her no more pleasant connection to her fiancé, Cathryn started all her usual daily tasks including her vegetable patch. By the end of the afternoon, she had harvested all she needed to make a big pot of stew for her helpers' supper, only remarking on their absence as she prepared their meal. *The doors are supposed to be locked. They'll believe there's no threat.*

Although the explanation satisfied her, before she washed the rutabagas and turnips, she locked the front door and set the latch on the screen door. While the soup simmered on the range, she prepared a bath, locking the inner door of the bath closet, in case her fiancé returned early, glad she had taken the precaution when two men conversed beneath the small window above her head. The curtain was thin but the lamp light was dimmed. She lowered her body deeper into the water, shivering, straining to hear their words.

"Cathryn? Are you here?" Jericho called from the back of the cabin. Another man stepped onto the front porch. For several minutes there was no other sound, until the screen door latch ripped from the frame and something scraped against the lock on the back door. "Cathryn?"

She held her breath, keeping as motionless as possible in the cooling water in the wooden tub. A chair scraped along the floor in the kitchen and one of the men sat at the table, asking, "Did you check the front room?" Another man lifted the lid on her soup pot. "She's here somewhere."

"Can't have gone far with her supper on the range."

"There's enough in that pot for—she's waiting on company."

"We'd better get out quick."

"I know the men she's expecting and there's a good chance none of them will be here for at least a couple hours. We can wait a while longer."

Cathryn held back the groan and the shiver. The water in the tub cooled degree by degree but still too fast for comfort. If she had thought to bring clothes into the closet with her, she had a good mind to get out there and tell Jericho Colson where he could go. The linen towel draped over the chair was far too skimpy to cover her decently and she was too mad to confront him reasonably.

"You have no reason to worry, John. Smith's in the company of some fine distraction for the evening, most probably the whole night if Mrs. Miller is half the woman she claims to be."

"Women have a way of over-estimating their charms where men are concerned, as you know, Mr. Colson. And my only reason for being here is to keep Smith from any happy ever after he ahn't entitled to. That done, I'm gone and that madman will be history."

"Just tell Miss Marcher all you told me and I'll do the rest."

"After what he did, it'll take more than spoiling his wedding plans to make me happy, Colson."

"You won't be disappointed, I promise."

Cathryn's teeth chattered like ice and she stuffed her fingers in her mouth to keep quiet but Jericho and the man she believed to be John Falmer stayed in her kitchen, drinking her coffee and tasting her soup, until the closet was dark and the water was colder than her core.

"Let's see if she's on her way," Falmer said, "I don't like all this waiting around."

"I tell you, there's no reason for concern."

"You don't know Rupe Smith. He's probably out there right now, watching, waiting for one of us to make a mistake."

"I see nothing extraordinary about this sorry excuse for a man—."

"Smith'd sooner cut a man in half as look at him. The only reason I ahn't dead is 'cause his friends tore him off me. And they had to do some serious hurtin' to do it. If you want to be in the same room when he finds out we been sniffing around his honeypot, be my guest but I'm goin'."

She pressed her lips together to contain the sob of relief when Falmer left her house but Jericho stayed in the kitchen. She covered her mouth and imagined the sonata and how her fingers moved over the keys. That kept her from screaming when Jericho shook the knob on the door of the closet.

"I know you're there, Cathryn. You have no reason to hide from me. I'll be here when you decide to come out but if you don't, you'll have a long wait if you think that wastrel will be coming here tonight."

He sat again at the table. The chair creaked under his weight as he stretched and hooked his thumbs in his waistcoat armholes in triumph—a gesture she had seen once and never forgotten. The kitchen cooled faster than her bath when the sun dropped below the roof of the sawmill but Jericho waited for her to succumb to the drowsy, compelling need to surrender. She braced her hands on the edge of the tub but her legs had no power to help her stand. The water sloshed and Jericho leapt to the door, a hoot of laughter answered her dismay. Just as soon, he yanked on the knob and kicked at the flimsy door.

"Open this damned door, Cathryn, or I'll break it down." He kicked again so hard that the lower panel cracked. "If I have to, I'll rip this door apart, then I'll come after you."

For a moment, his heavy breathing filled her ears.

"Cathryn, darling, you know I mean you no harm. I want to talk with you. We have important matters to discuss. Please open the door."

She refused to speak, to give him the satisfaction of a response. She would not beg him to go or to have decency enough to leave her house. She had no expectation he had her best interests at heart. She had no expectation he had no intention of hurting her.

"Come out, you little—."

Trollop? Vixen? Harlot? Tart? She could think of many more words that she suspected he might use for a woman who had given her body so easily. *Had I ever been as low as he believes? Am I?*

"Cathryn, please. I need to talk to you. With you."

When she made no effort to respond, he gritted his teeth. "You leave me no choice." With one thrust of his boot heel, the door splintered below the knob.

"That's no way to treat someone else's property, Colson. Step back."

Cathryn sobbed aloud but Colson's shout drowned her distress. Cathryn dragged her arms to the top of the wooden tub and flailed until she pulled out of the icy water. Once she was up, she pounded on the door, pleading to be heard over the fight. Furniture crashed against the walls. A man hissed. Another man growled. Her kitchen table thudded against the iron range. The screen door screamed, ripped off its hinges as someone landed on the back porch.

"Let me out, Rupert!"

"You'll pay for this, Smith!" Colson scrambled past the cabin barely keeping his footing as he escaped.

Rupert dragged air into his lungs, collapsing against the wall outside the closet.

"Cathryn?"

"Let me out!"

"You have the key," he said between deep breaths.

"Is he gone? I'm freezing."

"How'd he get in? Come out, there's no one here to hurt you."

"I can't."

"No one's going to hurt you, Cathryn." His voice was low, labored. "I won't hurt you, you know that."

"I need something to put on," she snapped, "And if you don't hurry I'll be as solid as Bryant's Pond in January." She unlocked the door and thrust her hand toward him. "Give me your coat."

"I'll get you a blanket."

"Rupert, give me your coat! Now!"

As soon as the last button was open, she snatched it from him and ran through the kitchen and the back yard. When she came back, he avoided looking at her bare legs as he straightened the few pieces of undamaged furniture.

"You're not staying in this cabin one more night, not another minute."

"Rupert…"

"No."

"No one has ever done that to me. Ever…except you but this was different. I don't understand. Why would he do this?"

"Get dressed, Cathryn." He yanked a chair over to the table and slumped into it. When she returned, twisting her hair into a knot at the back of her neck, he looked up at her. "I should have been here."

"No, Rupert. *He* should not have been here."

He shrugged, shaking his head. "I told Mal and Tom to come by, stick around, but something went wrong. Mort…"

"This isn't their fault. It's no one's fault but Jericho's. He did this." She turned away to stoke the embers in the firebox. "Did you see Mrs. Lowell?"

Rupert stared at her for a moment before his mouth twisted into a grin. "She gave me your fee and asked when I'd be delivering the other gown. Something of a slave-driver, your Mrs. Lowell."

"Did she say anything else?"

"She gave me a parcel for you."

"But—."

He went into the front room and retrieved a brown paper wrapped package he'd thrown to the floor when he came in and attacked Colson. "It's a bit rumpled but I think whatever's inside survived."

"I haven't paid for this," Cathryn sighed as he pushed the package into her arms.

"Mrs. Lowell said she could depend on you to finish the other work on time and apologized for changing the schedule with Mr. Blanchett. The customer wanted the gown early. She said to consider this payment in advance."

"She's never done that before," she said, narrowing her eyes at him.

"Change of heart."

The exhaustion apparent in his manner stopped Cathryn from arguing any more. "I'm hungry and you need some coffee."

When she rose, he reached out for her hand, drawing her into his lap. "If I'd thought, I'd have told Mort to come to be with you."

"Rupert, this is not your fault. If anyone is to blame for Jericho's behavior, it's Jericho. I had locked the door. But I trusted him to be a gentleman. I was wrong. I refused to believe your warnings." She pressed her brow to his temple. "I foolishly thought he *hadn't* changed from the sorrowful man I knew in Boston."

"He's ambitious."

"He wasn't when I knew him. My heart broke for him and others like him—they had suffered so much…"

"That's the least of it, my darling." He raised his head to gaze into her eyes. "While I was in Portland, I had another meeting with an old friend up in Augusta. He says Colson is standing for office."

"What can that have to do with me?" She lifted a wave of his hair from his forehead and pushed it back. He caught her fingers and held them to his lips.

"That's not all the talk about him," he said. "Mrs. Moffatt was aching to talk at the opera. Do you remember?"

"And you were very rude to her."

"To protect you, my love. Colson's wife asked for a divorce about four years ago, some say she broke her heart over a scandal about his behavior during the war."

"He told me she was indifferent, there was no scandal—I can tell you exactly what happened if you must know."

Rupert set her feet on the floor and stood. "I don't need to know. Mrs. Moffatt thinks she knows but he's lied to her. My friend tells me that Colson kept mistresses wherever he was stationed and is desperate to dispel the story by whatever means. Mrs. Moffatt prefers to believe he wants to marry you."

"He doesn't. He never did." Cathryn broke away and returned in a moment, thrusting Jericho's letter into Rupert's hand. "And neither did I. It's all there. Read it."

Rupert stared at the letter, read the signature and met her gaze. "Does he know you have kept this?"

His eyes held another question and she answered that one, the one he didn't want to ask. "He wrote what he had never said, sentiments and compliments I was never likely to hear again. This was, is, the only love letter I have ever received."

"Never let him know. He'll want it destroyed." He pressed it back into her hands. "He'll be afraid you'll use it to blackmail him."

"I would never do such a thing."

"Of course not, but *he* would. He's using your relationship with him to blackmail you, isn't he? He's told you lies about my past to injure me."

"Not a very nice man, is he?" she lamented.

"No, my darling, he is not."

"Perhaps we could use this to make him a better man." He laughed. "If he's so ambitious, he'll want to behave well."

"Cathryn," he murmured, wrapping his arms around her, "even so, it is still blackmail."

"As are promises of heaven and hell."

"Keep that to yourself when we stand before Mr. Jorgens on our wedding day."

"Do you still want that?"

"Want that? I'm staking my life on that, Cathryn."

Sixteen

The soup bubbled on the stove and her sour milk biscuits steamed on the table. Rupert washed his hands and face at the sink, his coat returned, sleeves pushed up while he dried his hands. Reflected in the black glass of the window, Cathryn marched from pantry to stove to table. Something churned in his belly with the thought she would be his wife. It was fear. Dread. Disbelief and elation. Fear predominated. Fear something would get in the way. Fear she would change her mind.

The words she needed to hear to believe in him, to make her believe if he had written her a love letter, had ever put into words what he felt—. He choked. He wasn't that man. He was another kind of man—a different man to what he thought she needed, a different man to the one she knew before the war. That man loved her, not the arrogant boy she held in her memories and her heart. And the man he had become was afraid everything he did was a mistake.

"Cathryn, I know you've said no before, but I don't want you staying alone in this cabin anymore."

She pulled her back straight and took a deep breath, letting it go in a decisive huff.

"It's my fault, I thought I knew better. I was foolish."

They faced each other from opposite corners of the room. She folded her arms. He braced his hands on the edge of the sink, opened his mouth to propose his plan.

"After you left for Portland, I was so mad—."

"I didn't think. I'm sorry."

"Let me finish., Rupert. I got into a state. Mostly about you. So, I unlocked every door and latch to be just the way I've always had them, to turn my home and my life back a few pages. But I can't do that, can I?"

Rupert bowed his head, fighting the urge to cross the room, make her understand, knowing this would only confirm her suspicions that he was no longer the man she believed him to be. "The only way is if I go. I don't mean now. I mean——."

"I know what you mean, Rupert." She stepped closer to him. "This is what *I* mean. Thankfully, I came to my senses but they broke in. How could he do that to me? I don't feel safe here and it has nothing to do with you unless you aren't here with me."

For the final practice before the Summer Solstice charity concert at Susan's Oslo Women's Auxiliary, Cathryn walked through the village, enjoying the mild, mid-June summer day, as she had on the previous two days of practice. Her living arrangements weren't ideal but she had, as she told Rupert, always gone to the Smith House when she was in any difficulty, found strength and comfort there even when all she did was sit on the back porch because entering broke her heart.

She had been there since the first Saturday of June, she told Mrs. Moffatt, because Rupert was not able to prepare the house for sale as well as attend to his business. She moved into the back lower room as she had while the Peggy and George Smith were alive—a servant, a housekeeper, no one of any special importance or concern—at least to the outside world.

Still protective and inclined to indulge her protégé and fond of Rupert Smith, still convinced he was engaged to Susan, Mrs. Moffatt vigorously, and sometimes vehemently, defended Cathryn. Although Jericho protested that Cathryn should not be allowed to besmirch her good name in association with Smith, the matriarch was unconvinced and since Jericho still claimed to wish to marry Cathryn, Mrs. Moffatt saw no problem when, in her estimation, "They are like brother and sister, school friends, children who grew up together."

Anyone entering the house, saw nothing in their behavior toward one another to dispel that opinion. Rupert kept to his business in the front offices and Cathryn kept to hers in Peggy's sewing room where the sewing machine had been restored to its place. Mary Cook visited often during the three weeks since the wedding announcement, for her fittings and the second gown needed one final examination before Mr. Blanchett was scheduled to come to collect it, this time on the originally appointed day.

Mary's young man entered at the front door, banned from venturing anywhere near his bride-to-be while she indulged in the secrets of the sewing room but they exchanged pleasantries and had moments of privacy in the dining room while Rupert made coffee for anyone who needed a boost. Mort and the Arne brothers befriended North like a younger brother, including him whenever possible in their escapades, regaling him with tales of adventures in the west.

The piano remained at the cabin, there being no time in Cathryn's day to indulge in music for pleasure. Morton Pierce's return to the house and the Arnes' move into the cabin further confused the gossipers but the preacher's visits served to strengthen the Miller-Smith engagement as did Morton's frequent walks with Cathryn to the Miller house and back again.

On this day, Cathryn walked alone. Rupert had preceded her to practice with both of them for the first time. When Cathryn arrived, he was singing a charming tune, while Susan played the piano. Until the housemaid opened the door, they continued for several minutes after she rang the bell. She hung her linen jacket on the rack at the back of the hallway and followed the maid to the parlor.

Susan jumped, as though caught in some compromising activity, when her voice teacher entered. Rupert stood ramrod straight at the far end of the grand piano. Susan patted her cheeks. Cathryn approached the pair, noting the copies of the song they were to sing lay on the chair farthest from the instrument.

"Shall we start?"

"Would you like to join us for coffee, Cathryn? Rupert and I have fairly sung ourselves dry all morning."

"I have had coffee, thank you."

"You won't mind if we leave you to practice, then." Susan grasped Rupert's arm and transported him to the far corner, giggling and sighing while they waited for the maid to pour a beverage that had no aroma strong enough to be a decent brew for a western man. Cathryn warmed her fingers, playing scales and prepared her music as it would be on the night of the concert, played through at various *tempi* to feel the piece but liked it no more than when Susan first proposed it.

While she waited for the singers to finish their coffee, she played the piece she had chosen for Megan Giles and the dance tunes Mrs. Moffatt had suggested she contribute to the fundraising effort. When Susan and Rupert saw fit to join her, Cathryn was confident that nothing she did or had failed to do would spoil the performance planned by her fiancé and his presumed paramour.

Rupert stood opposite her, but Cathryn barely glanced in his direction. Despite Susan's urging, he was rooted to the spot. Susan stood behind Cathryn to see the music. She hadn't learned her words but Rupert sang his part as though the words were his own. They sang through several times until Susan expressed her satisfaction though Rupert was impatient with her after the second time. Susan cajoled him, teased and flirted, threatened to make his life difficult if he so much as hinted he was not delighted to practice a third and fourth time. Cathryn kept her eyes on the music, blocking every sound but their voices and the notes.

After the fourth effort, Rupert stepped back. "I am beyond endurance and have matters of business." He collected his wide-brimmed hat and strode through the hallway to the door, his boot heels striking the polished floorboards with a determined gait. To the housemaid, he said, "May you have a quiet evening after all this caterwauling."

When Susan insisted on a fifth run through, Cathryn warned, "You will strain your voice."

"You can sing Rupert's part," Susan commanded. "After all, I am paying your fee so I shouldn't think you'd have anything to complain about."

Although her concern had been for her pupil, Cathryn determined not to contest Susan's complaint. "You will know the truth of that, sooner than I." She played the introduction again but Susan sank into the chair Rupert had vacated.

"I have sung enough. Now, stay and have some tea with me. We haven't chatted about inconsequential notions in many months. I quite hoped we could while Rupert was here but I can see he's had more than enough of our company. He must find these arrangements a strain now you are under foot at every turning."

"Mr. Smith and I do not collide often, Susan. The house is big enough to accommodate my presence."

"All the same, you are there continually."

"Mr. Pierce is also."

"Whose company do you prefer?" Susan asked in a casual tone.

"I see neither of them with any regularity."

"Do you take your meals separately, Cathryn?"

"Neither gentleman is inclined to keep to any precise schedule, so meals are not communal as a rule."

"I asked if you ate alone."

"Often," Cathryn answered, "yes, I do."

Susan smiled, glancing down at her small hands, delicately covered by lace half-gloves. "We—Rupert and I—spent a charming afternoon in Portland last month. We shared hot chocolate in that café by the docks."

"I know of several in the area."

"Rupert visited an establishment nearby. I'm sure you know it. He delivered something and brought a parcel away."

Cathryn returned her music to her satchel, employing all her powers of pretended nonchalance.

"He seemed very pleased with his purchase but since he was so reluctant to reveal his enterprise I can only speculate."

If she said a word, Susan was poised to flay her. Cathryn buckled the strap of her satchel.

"Of course, I know what he bought from Mrs. Lowell—that woman should be arrested."

"Why do you say that?"

"Rupert allowed me a glimpse of the items."

All her strength of restraint and self-control cracked. Their crescendo exploded. "Rupert would never do that!"

"And what is that to you? What do you know about it? If my fiancé chooses to show me such things and delights in giving me gifts—."

"Rupert is not your fiancé." Cathryn crushed Peggy's hat on her head, dashed for the door with her satchel flying behind her and Susan's laughter chasing her down the porch steps.

"And I suppose you'll tell me he has made you his fiancée?"

If not for Morton's hand on her arm, Cathryn would have flung the satchel back at Susan Miller's head.

"Guess if you had a gun, you'd shoot her."

"I would not give her the satisfaction," Cathryn said, passing her hand over her eyes. "Are you here to make sure I get home?"

"Appears so, Cathryn. Rupe said I'd best be damned quick or he'd be up here after you with a whip."

"For me?"

Morton's bellowing laugh filled the street and turned heads. His eyes sparkled. "I can think of a few things he'd rather do with you than that. I've never seen a man so tied up and branded. Pure joy to behold."

"Why is that, Morton?"

"He's a good man, Miss Marcher, but times come when he can't believe it. Loving you proves it."

Though puzzled, she didn't ask him to elaborate or explain. "Will you be here for the summer concert, Morton?"

"You're stuck with me until Rupert decides otherwise. Least I can do to help get the house cleared, shoot some wild turkeys—."

"You won't find many of those in these parts. But Noam Snyder raises find specimens these days."

"Ahn't the same. Farmed turkeys are about as tasty as sawdust."

"And I suppose you have some experience of sawdust."

"Finest fare there is in a prison camp."

Cathryn received this information in silence, knowing as soon as he uttered it that he spoke of Rupert as well. She accepted the confidence as a gift, to help her come to grips with her fiancé's behavior. When they reached the Smith House, Rupert was in his office and, though they weren't quiet, he gave no indication he was interested in their return or eager to see how Cathryn survived the hour without him.

He had waited at the window as they walked up the street but disappeared as soon as they turned onto the walk. Morton retreated to the kitchen while she removed her jacket in the hallway, hanging it on a hook in the narrow cupboard. She glanced at the office door and listened but there was no sound despite her conviction that Rupert was on the other side of the paneled door, as intent on her as she was on him.

He struggled to live with the horrors he had survived but sharing them with her was not a solution that would satisfy any need. His friends carried that burden. Hers was of a different kind and even more crucial. She was not his savior. She was his future, but only he could save himself.

Cathryn turned on her heel toward the parlor. At the door, she realized Peggy Smith's piano could not offer her any solace or diversion while it remained in the cabin.

"Rupert, I have no piano."

Instantly, he flung open the office door and came to her side. "You shall have it back, I promise you."

"When? When, Rupert? Everything has changed. I can't live in my own house. I can't have any of my—it's all different because of you—." She slapped her hand over her mouth but there was no changing the look in his eyes or the searing rip through her heart, as she reached out to embrace him. "Rupert, I love you."

Morton fell back against the table as Rupert thrust past him and slammed through the kitchen door. By the time he was on his feet again, Cathryn had run out the front door. He ran after her, stopping at the edge of the porch as she ran along the darkening road and turned to follow his friend into the woods.

When he caught up to Rupert all he got for his concern was a growl.

"Go back to the house."

"What for?"

"For her."

"She ahn't there so what's the point of me staying in an empty house?"

"Go after her, Mort."

"You go. She's your sweetheart."

"She doesn't want me."

"Like hell she don't. You two are the damnedest love birds I ever saw with the damnedest funny way of showing it."

"Go after her or I'll take your head off," Rupert growled, crouching ready to spring.

"You tried that once, Rupe. Didn't get far, won't now, so you'd best get it through your skull. That woman is yours so you gotta learn how to handle your temper and not always be running off."

"Not my temper, Mort," Rupert said, standing with his shoulders square and his glare giving way to a soft grin. After a moment, Mort's laugh filled the darkening woods and birds shot from the tree branches all around them.

"I'm damned sure your bride-to-be will be mighty glad to know that but right now she needs to know something else."

"What?"

Morton shook his head. "I never figured I'd have to teach you anything about women," he lamented. "Seems you ahn't the sweet talker in this partnership."

"Just tell me." Rupert slumped against the tree, his head bowed.

"I know what you're scared of, Rupe. Seems to me Cathryn has a pretty good idea too. But what she needs to know ahn't got nothing to do with that. She's not scared of you. She's not scared you're going to lose control, if she was a mind, she'd just hit you—or shoot you."

"She should shoot me. Save us both a lot of trouble. I tell you what, Mort, you shoot me." He was serious.

"Go back to the house, get your horse and get your woman back where she needs to be, Rupert. There's no other way."

"She won't come back."

"She won't come back if you don't show her why she'd be a fool not to."

"How'm I supposed to do that?"

"Don't ask me. You're the one loves her."

Rupert closed his eyes. When he opened them again, he stared through the leaf-laden branches to the dark sky, fixing his eyes on Orion's sword. "Everything to lose," he murmured before he walked back to the house.

Cathryn stopped running at the junction with the road that led down to town. She had always been able to walk through her home town with her head square on her shoulders. She had always been able to meet her neighbors gaze. She had accounted to and for herself, lived as she wished, counted a handful of good friends—until Rupert Smith returned.

When she had caught her breath, she turned onto the road but headed in the opposite direction, toward Snyder's chicken farm and her cabin. She refused to be afraid of anyone. She refused to care what anyone else thought of her. She refused to blame Rupert for any of the changes in her life. She refused to leave her home or be anyone other than who she had always been.

At the foot of the path to the front porch of her cabin, she turned at the sound of galloping along the road behind her. Walking up the path to the first step, she faced the rider from the porch. "I shouldn't have said that," she told him. Rupert's hair was blown back, damp around his face.

"You're either coming back to my house or I'm staying here with you."

"I'm staying here."

"Good. I didn't like the idea of riding back with this storm threatening." He slid from the horse's back and tethered the animal to the porch rail. "Is the door locked?"

"It was," Cathryn answered, pulling the screen door open with ease. A small smile lifted her cheeks, growing to a giggle when he opened the door with a twist of his penknife. "Are you leaving your horse there?"

"You don't have a barn," Rupert commented as he searched the cold room with narrowed eyes "Are you afraid of what people will think?"

Cathryn opened her mouth to speak but remembered her pledge. "I'm concerned for the horse. This storm looks bad."

"Not half as bad as the one brewing here," he said, urging her into the front room, "and that animal's stood up to every terror life with me has to offer. Can you?"

"I'm not afraid of you, Rupert Smith."

"Good. That's good. You're going to need courage where we're going, Evie Marcher."

"Rupert, I'm not going to Wyoming."

He bowed his head for a moment before giving her a sidelong look and a crooked smirk. "We'll see about that when we've got this sorted." He glanced at his mother's piano. "Play something, Evie. It'll help us both."

She needed no urging to sit before the instrument and run her hands through the scales. Rupert sat at the small table, watching her in the cool dusk, soothing his weariness with the confident strikes of her fingers, absorbing the sound to the depth of his soul as the practiced movements evolved into a tune he knew somehow but had never heard before.

"Pretty," he murmured, closing his eyes as the tune came to an end.

"It's new. From Pennsylvania," Cathryn said, turning on the bench to study his face in the moonlit room.

"I like it, Evie."

His eyes remained closed but the traces of tears glistened at the corners. She had nothing to offer to take away the pain of his loss.

"Play something else," he requested.

The sudden rush of rain on the tarred roof and the wind beating at the windows accompanied the first bar of the 'Emperor' piano concerto, every note struck in memory, physical and assured, from practice but when the movement shifted its focus, she faltered and dropped her hands to her lap.

"Where are we going, Rupert? What storm has brewed?"

He leaned forward and clasped his hands between his knees. "I love you, Cathryn. I have loved you since you were a firebrand schoolgirl. I have loved you through all these years, you have given me hope. I came back to know with certainty that I had lost you."

"Did you want that, Rupert?"

He answered her question with a short laugh and covered his face. "No. But the chance I hadn't was eating me alive. I thought about you night and day. When Allan told me you had never married, I found every reason I could to be near you."

"The oak survived," she murmured with a laugh.

"I've done everything possible to protect you, Cathryn."

"I don't need protection."

"You do and you'll be better protected if you know me—what I've done, what I'm capable of doing."

"I know you almost killed someone. I know you saved the lives of a lot of men, they've told me."

"They didn't tell you what I did to save them."

"You don't have to tell me. I know you'd rather forget."

"I can't forget, Evie. I will never forget."

"Then tell me." She stood and strode through the passageway to the kitchen. "Tom and Mal haven't kept the fire going. You'll have to get the kindling if you want coffee."

The chair creaked as he unfolded his long legs but a long moment passed before he came to stand in the kitchen doorway. Cathryn kept her back to him, her arms folded across her chest as she stared into the dark, wet garden.

"I'm not—it's nothing heroic, Cathryn. Nothing to make a man proud or a woman to think well of him."

"You're not the best judge, Rupert Smith." She hunched her shoulders against the growing chill. "The kindling hasn't moved since you last had to start a fire for me and it's just getting colder in this house."

"Sit down, Cathryn. This is going to take more than one cup of coffee."

Rupert built the kindling frame in the stove and brought in an armload of firewood while she drew water and set the big kettle on the hotplate. He wrapped a blanket around her shoulders and when they both had a cup of her coffee in their hands, he said, "We all started out thinking we'd be home in a month, in plenty of time to resume our lives. I was all set, had my offer in chambers ready to take my first step up the political ladder, change the way things are done, the way my future wife thought they should be."

His smile was brief and self-mocking. Cathryn resisted touching his hand, not wishing to stop him from releasing his demons. The only light in the room came from the grated door of the firebox.

"We didn't change our minds," he continued. "They were changed for us at Bethal and Manassas. I stopped counting the number of bullets I loaded into my pistol. About the time I stopped watching men die."

"Could you do anything else?"

"Not without betraying what I thought was right."

Cathryn sipped at the edge of her cup but the hot liquid didn't reach her lips as she gazed at Rupert's averted face.

"I and half my unit were cut off from Sherman's army in August, a year after Gettysburg, and taken prisoner. The Johnnies had their own reasons for treating us like trophies but most of us made it to Cahaba—if not in one piece, at least alive. John Falmer was already there and had set up his survival hierarchy. I didn't like what I saw—what I could see from the pit they called the infirmary."

He studied her face for a moment. "You were a nurse, Evie. I don't have to tell you the details, do I? The filth, the stench. The screams."

Cathryn shook her head, staring at the surface of her coffee before she said, "I can imagine."

"When the butchers got to me, all they said was 'Amputation'. Didn't even look at my wound. I crawled into another corner, where they'd already been. The orderlies never noticed," he laughed. "I should be dead. Hundreds died that summer. More from disease than any wound."

He drank the rest of his coffee and took both cups to the stove, keeping his back to her when he said, "Pure cussedness kept me alive. I was not going to let them kill me in a prison camp. By the time I could stand up, Falmer was setting men against each other to survive."

Rupert leaned his hips on the stove when he faced her again and folded his arms across his chest. "A kid, no more than fifteen, right as rain, no mark on him, was Falmer's scapegoat. Any little thing went wrong, the kid got the blame. The Johnnies were dragging him back to the hole. The only thing distinguishing him from any of the other Union soldiers was his regiment."

Cathryn took the cup he offered in both hands, still watching his face in the glow of the flames.

"Tuck was a drummer with a Kentucky militia that fought with the Army of the Potomac. When he got separated from his unit and ended up with a West Virginian bunch, taken prisoner soon after. Once Falmer found him, that boy was the target for the Confederate soldiers. 'Traitor. Turncoat. Must have been that Kentucky renegade.' I didn't have a choice and Falmer didn't like my interference. The boy still ended up in the hole but he had company. Came to where there was more value in taking their anger out on me but they used him to get to me. One night, they took this boy out of the stockade for some entertainment, broke him down to begging, crying for his mother——."

He covered his face as his voice cracked. Again, Cathryn wanted to touch him but he went on. "A handful of us broke out of the stockade and went after the Rebels. A lot of men got hurt and I made a bargain with the guards—me for all the rest of them. I knew what I was doing, that kid didn't. Plenty of them offered but, being such an arrogant sod, I wouldn't let them. Falmer had a lot of fun after that. He'd rile a few enough so they'd put up a fight, stand back and watch the show. Once I'd stepped up, the Rebs made damned sure I kept my word. If not for the decency of the Arne boys and a good few others, I'd be dead."

Seventeen

He was silent for so long, Cathryn thought he'd finished his tale and reached for his cup. Rupert caught her hand and pressed her palm to his lips, staring at her, his eyes shimmering in the darkness. "I promised if I survived, I'd come back and, no matter what, I'd have you. I figured God would make that possible. You'd be here and you'd be waiting for me. Everything would be worthwhile then."

"I was here, Rupert," she assured him. "I did wait for you."

As if she hadn't spoken or he hadn't heard her, he laid her hand on the table and scraped his chair back.

"I crawled out of that camp on my belly, the lowest, slimiest creature in all God's creation. Months before I got the stench off me. A whole year went by before I could lift my head to look another man in the eye. Then I came across Falmer, riding high, decorated war hero, boasting how he'd survived that camp and kept his dignity."

He turned his back to her, facing the black window, staring up at the moon, his face bathed pale and stark. "He recognized me after a while. I could see his mind working. Before he said a word, I was on him. Took Mort, the Arne boys and that kid to pull me off. The way I felt, I knew I'd never be right again, not for a pretty girl with nothing but goodness in her heart and I was glad they threw me in jail."

"I wish you had come home, Rupert," she said, "as soon as you came out of the camp. You could have. I was here. I wanted you to come home."

"I'm going mad knowing Falmer's here. Right now. He's talked to you."

"He was in my home. I heard what he said."

"Did you believe him, Cathryn?"

"Yes."

A groan hissed from him as his body slumped.

"He said nothing I couldn't believe of any man subjected to the horror and humiliation of war. He said nothing I hadn't seen in other men's eyes, Rupert. Things I see in your eyes when you think I'm not looking. Nothing he said made any difference to the fact I love you but it made a powerful difference in what I think of Jericho."

"Do you believe what I've told you, Cathryn?"

"I've never known you to lie, Mr. Smith." With a tired sigh, she pushed away from the table and stood. "The rain has stopped. Time I did something about those pumpkins."

"You're a wonder, Evie."

"So your mother always said."

"She'd be happy to see us married."

"I don't know about that, Mr. Smith, but there is little she can do to stop me getting what I want now."

"My father wouldn't have allowed that. He had his eye on you for me from the day I enlisted, never let me forget. Evie."

The way he said her nickname stopped her heart. He raised his hand from his side and she dashed to clasp it.

"Cathryn, let me raise those pumpkins for you."

"You may if you want to. But," she said, catching his wrist, "you have to promise you won't reveal my secret method for growing them so big."

"All your secrets are safe with me, Evie."

When her expression crinkled in doubt, he caught her around the waist and whispered, "Even the fact that you wear silk pantaloons and French bodices."

"Susan seemed to know."

"Mrs. Miller makes suppositions based on narrow-mindedness—knowing is quite different."

"Mrs. Lowell told you."

"No, my angel, I investigated."

"You spied."

"If I wanted to spy, Cathryn, you would never know. I wanted to know so that I made no mistakes and you never said you kept secrets."

"What I wear is my own business."

"I admit to being surprised, pleasantly so, but when I thought further, your choice of undergarments was in keeping with your practical nature."

"How so?"

"Quality and comfort."

Cathryn hid her smile with a toss of her head. Rupert pressed her head against his chest with a tender sigh and she remained still, listening to the steady thud of his heartbeat until he raised his hand from her hair and stepped back.

"Pumpkins," he murmured. "I remember now."

The light of the moon etched his silhouette against the dark woods as he picked his way through the patch and crouched by the largest specimen of her crop. He caressed the ribbed surface for a moment and felt along the vine. From his pocket, he brought out the knife that helped him break into her home. He snipped twigs of pine from the pile of kindling and built cross-hatched platforms to keep the fruits above the soggy soil.

Cathryn stepped back from the window when he turned and waited for him at the open door when his boot heel struck the porch step.

"I love you, Rupert."

He lifted his gaze to her face, standing half in the yard and half on the porch, meeting her gaze without a flinch. "I love you, Cathryn Marcher."

She turned on her heel to light the lamps. He scraped the mud from his boots and kicked the door closed behind him.

"There's a beauty out there. Blue ribbon if I ever saw one."

"He's not perfect," she said, studying her effort from the window above the sink. "He'll be big but he's lopsided. I didn't see that. I should have noticed."

"What will you do, Evie?"

If he hadn't asked, if he hadn't called her 'Evie', if he hadn't lifted his gaze, she would have taken her hoe and chopped through its life cord and sacrificed it to the compost pit. She had never lost the pumpkin show when she entered. Other years, she had made pies, delicious pies for the contestants to mangle, but this year, she had planned to do both. The biggest most perfect specimen. The creamiest, most tantalizing pies.

"He may not be perfect but he will be grand," she said. "If we don't win on perfection, we will on stature."

"We, Evie?"

"You've done most of the hard work."

"Joint entry? Miss Marcher and Mr. Smith?"

"Has a nice ring to it," she answered, lulled by his expression into an embrace.

"Not as nice a ring as Evie and Rupe Smith."

"Sounds nice too," she mumbled as he kissed the corner of her lips and his arms clenched around her tight enough to stop her breath.

He gave her another kiss as she pressed closer. "This is where I have no choice but to leave you," he said, pulling back and searching her eyes.

"Must you?"

"You know I must."

"I hoped you would help me pick the berries to make pies for the Church Bazaar pie-eating contest."

"How will it look to young Aurelius Cook if I've helped make the pies he's expected to eat in competition with me?"

"Collusion?"

"Yes." He stepped away and caught her hand. "Let's go home, Evie. You can bake your pies in peace tomorrow. Mal and Tom will be back."

"Where have they been?"

"Buying supplies in Freeport."

"You know the boy you told me about? Where is he, Rupert."

"Tuck is back in Wyoming. Near man enough to be looking after the ranch while I came here to get you."

"Rupert—."

"I know, Cathryn. Wyoming is a subject we'll have to talk about but right now I want to walk you home, see you get to bed and have a good night's rest."

"Am I going to need one?"

"Tomorrow's another day, my angel. Bound to be trouble with me around."

Cathryn was at work in the cabin's kitchen at sunrise on Friday. Rupert had cooked her porridge and poured the coffee, sent her off with Morton to make her pies where she knew where all her ingredients and utensils were. The church fete and the fundraising concert were later in the day but she had enough time to make her pies and walk with Malcolm and Tom to the church common, each of them carrying baskets with two pies in each.

Rupert had entered the pie-eating contest, under the name 'Drummer' in honor of the Kentucky boy. At noon, Rupert arrived with Mrs. Miller and the Giles Family, Megan holding fast to his hand. He studied his youngest opponent for the pie-eating contest, half his weight and less than half his age.

Aurelius wore the appearance of a boy who had fasted for a week and looked at the table set out with raspberry, stewed apple and rhubarb pies as though he could devour every one of them. Though Rupert figured he had the boy beat on stamina, he wasn't as confident otherwise but winning wasn't his intent. He was in the contest for Cathryn Marcher's pies and he was going to enjoy every bite.

He hadn't reckoned on there being pies baked by any other ladies. The array set out on the long tables, behind which the eight contestants were ready to begin, was a motley display of elegant and disreputable. He recognized his intended's pies by the dishes in which they had been baked but only one had been placed at his position and it wasn't rhubarb.

Aurelius had one of Cathryn's rhubarb pies and Noam Snyder had another. Damnedest thing and there was no switching to be done. He had an apple pie—a fine specimen she had put her best effort into but the rhubarb pie he would have to swallow was a pasty, milky affair that was bound to choke him. But what really stuck in his craw was that Colonel Jericho Colson was standing a man down from him with Cathryn's third rhubarb pie waiting for him to sink his teeth in.

Morton clamped his hand on Rupert's shoulder, looked him in the eye and nodded once in the direction he meant Rupert to look. What he saw practically brought the Wyomian to his knees but instead, he squared his shoulders as his bride-to-be walked across the church lawn wearing his mother's purple coat and hat, over a pretty summer dress, with her hair in a chignon, her eyes bright and a shy smile on her lips, staring straight at him until Aurelius Cook stepped into her path.

Cathryn's knowing grin brought a similar expression to Rupert's face. "There ahn't anybody I'd rather say this to than you, Miss Marcher, so, if'n I win, may I share my prize with you?"

"What is the prize this year, Aurelius?"

"It's a buggy ride up the river and a picnic at the lake. My grandma's gonna make up the picnic basket. She said it'd be special if I win."

"In that case, I'm honored, Master Cook. Grandma Arnold is the finest cook in Oxford County."

"She also said, if *he* wins," Aurelius nodded toward Rupert, "and asks you, the picnic won't be much less special 'cause it be you he'll be askin' too."

"Your grandma is very kind."

"She likes you, Miss. And him." He scuffed his toe in the grass. "'Course if North was competing, he'd be winning hands down, no contest. You ahn't never seen a man can put away a meal Grandma made like Mary's beau."

The beau in question stood tall in the crowd, his sweetheart on his arm, still haunted but without the shadow in his gaze as he pressed Mary's hand and winked at his younger, soon to be brother-in-law.

"I will be cheering for you, Aurelius. And Captain Smith, of course."

The boy nodded and took his place at the table. The master of ceremonies explained the rules to the contestants. Though seeing Jericho among the men participating surprised her—risking his dignity was unlike him—she acknowledged him with a nod. She took a place with the onlookers that put her between Aurelius and Rupert to cheer them equally.

Mrs. Moffatt came to stand beside her. Cathryn smiled, taking the older woman's arm when Susan Miller joined them and waved at Rupert with a smile for him that Cathryn wished she hadn't seen.

In moments, the men and boys were chomping their way through pies. Rupert chose to eat the least attractive of the pies first and, at a pace that put him last in the first round. Jericho came second but, to Cathryn's relief, Aurelius was first. Rupert spoke to his young opponent. The boy gave him a quick, quizzical nod as they reached for the second pie.

Again, Rupert selected another poor specimen and finished last. Jericho first. Aurelius second. She began to suspect Rupert was deliberately lagging behind and was certain of it when the third pie and round were finished and he was no further up the ranking. Though most in the crowd were cheering for Noam and Aurelius, Jericho waved in acknowledgement of the cheers.

When Rupert rejected the pie she baked for his fifth and asked for another, Noam Snyder leaned back in his chair saying "You're a better man than I am, Smith."

Aurelius remained only a half of a pie behind Jericho and Cathryn urged him on but within minutes of starting his sixth pie, he eyes bulged and he ran in the same direction Noam had taken. Rupert, finally on his sixth pie, with two other men, one from Oslo Hill and one from town, and Jericho were the remaining contestants.

Jericho finished first and pulled one of her rhubarb pies toward him, with a glance at her she also wished she hadn't seen. When she turned her attention back to Rupert, he had pulled another pie toward him and sank his teeth into a quarter slice.

He kept his gaze on her as he quietly, steadily munched through half the pie and lifted a third quarter into his hands. The man from town had started on the first quarter of his seventh pie when his face lost all color and he toppled from his chair. The man from the Hill was less obvious but collapsed back from the fray staring at the half-eaten pie as if he'd eaten poison. Jericho had started an eighth. A crowd of cheering onlookers gathered at his end of the table, urging him to beat the Oslo Hill record of eight and a quarter pies.

Cathryn glanced once at him and turned pleading gaze on Rupert. He smiled back and chose another pie—her apple pie abandoned in front of him. Jericho tied the twenty-year champion record when he finished eight and a quarter pies and sat back. Rupert remained behind, cutting smaller slices, slowing to a crawl and Cathryn held her breath as Jericho reached for another slice to deafening cheers and glove-muffled applause from his lady-admirers. Mrs. Moffatt patted Cathryn's hand with a smile. Cathryn clamped her lips together. Rupert cut another, narrower slice.

"That's my raspberry pie," Susan said in Cathryn's ear, "made especially. Colonel Colson doesn't seem to have enjoyed your concoction."

Jericho's face was red but he was on the third quarter slice of her pie and another waited. How he had gotten so many of her pies, she couldn't guess but ungenerously hoped he choked when Rupert finished the last quarter of his ninth pie a few bites ahead of Jericho with only Cathryn, Mrs. Moffatt and one of the judges to notice.

Colson put the last morsel of her pie in his mouth to a triumphant cheer but neither chewed nor swallowed. The judge at his end of the table reached to lift his arm to declare him winner when Rupert said, "Bring me that rhubarb pie."

Aurelius leapt at his command, whisking Cathryn's pie from in front of Jericho and placing it, with reverence, before Captain Smith.

The judges conferred and stood back as Jericho's eyes widened. Rupert cut a thin slice and slid it into his mouth.

"Now that pie is worth the waiting," he said, savoring every chew before he cut another thin slice and winked at Cathryn. Jericho's hand trembled as he dragged a stewed apple pie from his neighbor's station but his face paled and his eyes drooped when Rupert cut a third slice of Miss Marcher's rhubarb pie.

When Jericho bowed his head in defeat, vacating his seat, Aurelius whooped and war-danced in victory celebrations for Rupert who still ate and enjoyed every crumb of his fiancée's contribution.

"I regret Captain Smith—Rupert," the first judge said, "but another gentleman has demanded a recount."

Rupert smiled at the judge and gave a shrug with only his left shoulder, extending his open fingers toward Cathryn. Though restrained by Mrs. Moffatt, she broke free and took the seat vacated by Aurelius and scooted closer to her fiancé.

"Whatever the result, Evie, you won't be going on any picnic with Colson."

"Yes, Rupert."

"You'll be with me."

"Yes, Rupert."

Aurelius stopped dancing while the empty pie plates were counted and all the slices left were measured. The three judges conferred and bowed their heads together, weighing the relative dangers of declaring one or the other the winner. After one judge broke into a sweat, dabbing at his brow, and another threatened to resign, the first judge stepped forward and said, "Ladies and gentlemen, under these unusual circumstances, we have made a thorough recount and precise calculation of the quantities consumed by the finalists. Our decision has come with difficulty and due consideration."

"Out with it," Noam Snyder called, shushed by his eldest daughter.

"While the number of pies consumed by Captain Rupert Smith exceeds those consumed by Colonel Jericho Colson, the length of time, the duration of this feat has been taken into account and we declare a well-fought draw—."

Shouts and whistles drowned the rest of his judgment, followed by an equal volume of insults until the Reverend Mr. Jorgens brought peace to the assembly.

Rupert cut another slice of her rhubarb pie. "You know, Evie, I don't think I've ever had the pleasure of eating a pie this perfect."

"Mind you don't make yourself too ill to sing your duet with Susan this evening," she replied with a frown at her wayward jealousy.

"You will keep me on the straight and narrow, Miss Marcher, I have no doubt."

"Am I such a tyrant, Mr. Smith?"

"Anything but, Miss Marcher, except when it comes to music." He met Colson's glare for a long moment, vaguely aware he had said something that riled the Colonel.

"As the judges have made their decision and you, sir, are in no fit state nor a fit companion for a lady, I will escort Miss Marcher."

Colson clutched Cathryn's elbow. She stared down at his hand, his grip on her fierce and painful. Rupert staggered to his feet and blanched but threatened Colson with a growl. Cathryn tugged at her arm, pushed at Jericho's fingers and finally ripped her arm from his hold.

"A lady has a right to make her own decisions. In this case, I have music to prepare for this evening's concert." She turned to the Arne boys and Aurelius. se that my fiancé arrives home safely and finish that pie before he makes himself too ill to perform this evening."

"Yes, Miss," the three said together.

"And no shenanigans at all."

"No, Miss."

She returned Jericho's stare with a scolding glance and walked away. Allan Giles joined her at the edge of the lawn but the unexpected appearance of Morton Pierce relieved her of any similar scenes of male presumption. She took the sergeant's arm and smiled, heading in the direction of her cabin.

"There's nothing down that way for you, Cathryn."

"My piano?"

"Where it should be."

"Are you sure of that, Morton?"

"If I wasn't, I'd take you back to your camp and leave you there. And if you ahn't sure, all you have to do is look over your shoulder right this minute."

Cathryn laughed as she turned her head back to the road in front of her. "He ate a mighty number of pies to come up with a draw."

"Seems he figures he won."

"Seems so," she agreed, glancing back once more at the triumphant scene, her fiancé surrounded by friends and villagers, glad-handed and back-slapped, Mary's beau keeping Falmer and Colson at bay. Cathryn raised a hand to her own beau before they reached a bend in the road and the Hamlin House blocked her view.

At the Smith House, Cathryn slid onto the piano stool and caressed the length of the cover over the keys. Before she opened it, she pressed her hands together and laughed again at the image of a grown man hoisted onto the shoulders of his friends. A part of her remained sorrowful for Jericho Colson, but so much of her respect for him had faded when he befriended John Falmer, her regret was tinged with a sense of justice.

Trusting Rupert with the safe-keeping of the letter Jericho had sent to her, she accepted, if he read it, he would understand the circumstances. He would not hold her accountable for Jericho's condition. He would not blame her or be jealous. Cathryn knew this as certainly as she knew she could not blame him for Susan's flirtatious nature or for her own jealousy.

"I will defeat this demon," she laughed. Her hands floated over the surface of the keys, the crescendo of the scales reaching the *forte* and returning to *pianissimo*, until her fingers tingled with warmth and excitement anticipating a performance, even as unremarkable as the Oslo Hill Women's Auxiliary Charity Fund Raising Concert.

Morton made coffee in the kitchen and her fiancé was enjoying his victory with friends. She had chosen her gown for the concert from among Peggy's favorites and her familiarity with the pieces was certain. All she had to do was limber her hands, change her clothing and walk to the town hall. Susan was as well-prepared as she would ever be and Rupert would have no difficulty, even if he was overfed.

When the time came to prepare for departure, she drew a bath. Morton called up to say he would return as soon as he could to escort her.

"I'll be going to the hall at six:thirty."

Morton grunted an answer and the house was silent again. At the appointed time, Cathryn donned her borrowed hat and coat, beginning the walk to the hall alone, soon joined by other participants in the concert. Susan Miller's usual tardiness concerned her less than her soprano's complaint, "What have you done with Rupert?"

Morton had not returned from town and Rupert had not been wearing the clothes he chose for the concert at the fete that afternoon but Cathryn put all her worries to the back of her mind while she accompanied the ladies' choir. Susan and Rupert's duet was scheduled for more than half way through the concert program and she had three other performers as well as her own contribution to occupy her mind.

Megan Giles held her hand so tight for the few minutes before her piece that Cathryn's fingers cramped until she flexed her hand several times over the keyboard. The little girl sang from her heart, with her heart in her throat but, as Cathryn predicted, no one criticized the child except her own parent.

Cathryn's baritone sang a hymn and the piano duet performed by Polly and Prissy Snyder delighted everyone, especially when the sisters huffed at each other for missing beats. Mrs. Moffatt fretted about the program and the missing tenor until Jericho offered to take his place to partner Susan, to save the lady any embarrassment.

"Thank you, Colonel Colson, but that will not be necessary. Mrs. Miller and Captain Smith will not be required until after the interval," Cathryn replied, certain her fiancé would appear.

"My dear, there is no reason for you protect this man. You are not expected to carry the responsibility of his unreliability—."

Dressed as he should be in his best formal attire, clean and shaven, Rupert entered at the back of the church hall, surrounded by his friends and all the young boys of the village, still the victor, still the hero of the day.

"My good gracious," Mrs. Moffatt crooned. "That man could stop a train looking like that. If I were a younger woman, you would have serious competition, Susan."

"Thank goodness you have not been taken in by Cathryn's flirtation with Rupert, Mrs. Moffatt. Although he has been circumspect about such matters, a perfect gentleman…. Cathryn persists in this fiction, even in polite company, regarding *my* fiancé's affections. He certainly cannot be possessed of any strong attachment to her, not while she courts the attention of his friends."

Mrs. Moffatt turned to look at the widow for a moment, folded her hands at her waist. "Susan Josephine Hamlin Miller, I never realized you were so much like my dear departed husband's cart horse."

"Whatever do you mean, Mrs. Moffatt?"

"No need to put blinkers on her. She was blind to every single thing, even in front of her nose. Of course, Cathryn and Rupert are close. After all, she took exceptional care of his parents during his long absence. To suggest anything else is wicked."

"The whole village is aware of how blinkered you are where Cathryn concerned. She does nothing wrong in your eyes, even though we all know what she did in Boston."

"The only person who truly knows that is Cathryn," Rupert said, coming to stand behind his fiancée, close enough to sense her anger. "And, Mrs. Miller, no one takes kindly to folks who whip up tales, especially those that serve no useful purpose."

"Why, Rupert, I have no idea what you mean."

Rupert turned his back on Susan Miller, catching Cathryn's hands and studying them for a moment. "Are you tired, Angel? You've worked hard all evening."

"There are only a few more items."

"Will you play the Pennsylvania piece?"

"At the end of the concert."

"May I sing it with you?"

"Of course, if you wish, Rupert."

"I do wish, Cathryn. Nothing will please me more."

Although Mrs. Moffatt stepped away to give Cathryn some privacy to speak with her tenor performer, Susan stood rigid at her accompanist's side, grinding her small teeth. "Why haven't I been told of this song? Surely, such a duet is more appropriate for me."

"Why do you think that, Mrs. Miller?"

"Rupert, there is no need for that attitude. I am your acknowledged singing partner. Cathryn is a competent pianist, but—."

"She has obviously not heard us together, my angel," Rupert said, kissing Cathryn's fingertips.

"And *she* has no desire to," Susan sneered, whisking her skirts away from Cathryn and tossing her head as she minced to the side of the stage.

"Was that wise?"

"Perhaps not, but satisfying." He kissed her fingers again. "I will cajole the widow, for your sake."

As Cathryn drew her hand out of his grasp to walk onto the stage and take her place at the piano to accompany the duet, she stood face to face with his duet partner.

Susan smiled with benevolence as she leaned forward and whispered, "That dress makes you look as common as your heritage."

"Peggy Smith loved this dress. Rupert asked me to wear this in her honor."

"I wouldn't put too much faith in that, Cathryn. He knows a wanton when he sees one."

"Perhaps, but I know wickedness. Your singing voice is your only redemption."

Cathryn swept the voluminous skirt of the red ball gown over the piano bench and played the opening bars of the duet. When she paused, the audience expressed their approval of the coming item with applause that reverberated in the high ceiling of the hall. Rupert led Mrs. Miller onto the stage with a flourish of his hand and a deep bow to her and to the audience. Cathryn took her cue from him, her hands poised above the keys, took a long breath and repeated the opening bars.

Rupert's perfect entry and Susan's responding echo relieved their accompanist. Through all the verses, Cathryn had no cause to regret her pupil's musical ability but Susan's flirtations caused her considerable heartache, setting her a weary struggle to hold up her side of the performance and her determination to conquer her jealousy. The applause at the end of the duet sent a chill through Cathryn's spine and she could not restrain the shiver that passed over her.

She remained seated as the singers accepted the accolades and did not see Rupert extend his hand to her and applaud her achievement. Cathryn sat square, facing the sheet of music propped in front of her ready for the calls for an encore. She missed Susan's impatient dismissal and departure as well as Rupert's approach until his hand appeared before her eyes and he grasped her elbow to encourage her to stand, face the audience and accept their appreciation.

She glanced often at Rupert but when she found him always looking at her, she smiled at her friends in the seats and worked her way off the stage. It was unseemly for the worker to take more credit than the performer. Before

Rupert followed her into the wings, Susan had already made her feelings known to the concert organizers.

This was of less concern to Cathryn than watching Rupert burst through the back door of the hall and run out of sight into the bricked streets. She searched the faces of friends in the audience. Mary Cook leaned on her mother's shoulder. Her younger brother stared in the direction Rupert had run.

That he may not return to sing the Pennsylvania song was apparent when Cathryn took her place at the end of the concert at Mrs. Moffatt's insistence and played the charming melody of Parry's [17] "Good Night." No strength of will induced her to sing the simple words of the three-part harmony. Her voice was locked in her aching heart. *Good night. To each weary toil-worn wight—Now the day so sweetly closes, Every aching brow reposes—Peacefully till morning light. A soft good night. Good night, good night.*

At the end of the song, she bowed her head to the polite clapping and walked away behind the curtain, slipped into her coat and hat, leaving the concert hall in the direction she had seen Rupert disappear, eager only to be away from the cheerful self-congratulations of the fund-raisers and their willing performers.

"Miss Marcher!" Aurelius called, running to catch her before she had reached the walk by the river. "Captain Smith asked me to see you got home."

"Where has he gone this time?"

"North's gone off and he and the others are looking for him."

---

[17] **Joseph Parry** – a celebrated Welsh-American composer whose many tunes became popular during and after the Civil War (*American Star, Make New Friends, Annabelle Lee, Myfanwy*), perhaps most famous for his hymn tune, *Aberystwyth*.

"What's happened?"

"North's folks sent a letter to my sister saying they ahn't coming to the wedding 'cause they don't want their son marrying her. Pa thinks North's taking it real hard, so he asked Captain Smith to find him. Mary's mighty upset."

"I'll come with you to your place."

"My folks have all gone to the Smith house, Miss, except Pa. He's gone to the sawmill to look for Mary's beau there."

Cathryn took the arm the young man offered and retraced her steps, sure to meet everyone she had hoped to avoid.

As though they knew she would return, Allan and Nancy Giles stood at the corner of the hall with their daughter, each holding one of Megan's hands, speaking to one another over the girl's head. Megan looked from one to the other as they hissed in the lamplight. When she saw her teacher, the child yanked out of their grasp and ran to Cathryn.

"Did I sing all right?"

"Yes. I was very proud of you." Cathryn glanced at Aurelius, silently asking for a moment. The boy shrugged.

"They don't think so."

"Did you do your best, Megan?"

"I did the best I could but I was scared."

"As long as you did your utmost, even though you were frightened, I can ask no more, nor can anyone else."

"Did Mr. Smith hear me? I didn't see him."

"I didn't see him either but I'm sure he would not have chosen to miss a single note." She glanced up from the child's face as the widow, Mrs. Miller, descended the front steps of the church.

"Isn't Master Cook a tad young, even for you, Cathryn?"

Nancy sniggered. Aurelius's chest expanded, ready for a retort.

"I am sorry you have to hear such ugliness, Master Cook."

"Ahn't nothing, Miss Marcher. No one pays *her* any never mind."

"Well!"

Cathryn patted her escort's arm and turned toward Lincoln Street. Mrs. Cook met them at the door, Mary's sobs echoing through the hallway.

"She's breaking her heart," Mrs. Cook choked. "See what you can do, Cathryn, while I make some strong coffee. Aurelius, you keep a watch out for your papa and any sign of that young man."

"Yes, Mama."

Eighteen

"He's a convicted criminal, did you know?"

Mrs. Moffatt gazed at the questioner, lounging comfortably in her parlor with his teacup balanced in his hand.

Allan Giles spoke with a hush, a tone of conspiracy, as though he feared he was overheard. "I know this news must come as a shock to you but, as Cathryn's friend, I felt I had no choice other than to give you warning. She may listen to you."

"Have you told Cathryn what you know?"

Allan looked away, through the heavy lace curtain, onto the sun-spattered lawn. "She knows."

"In that case, why tell me? Cathryn has always followed her own mind."

"But he's a violent man. He nearly killed his superior officer—without cause—attacked him with no provocation at all. It took four men to pull him off."

"I must say," Mrs. Moffatt fluttered over her slice of cake for a moment. "I must say, I am surprised to hear this." She fell back into the cushions of her wing-backed chair with a deep sigh. "Very surprised, indeed. He has always been high-spirited but this.... Are you certain Cathryn knows the full story? Perhaps he kept some details to himself. I would be sorry to leave Cathryn in the dark."

"Exactly as I thought, Mrs. Moffatt," Allan said, lurching forward from the waist and righting the teacup before the contents spilled. "That is exactly why I arranged for Miss Marcher to hear the truth from the victim of this wicked assault."

"Did you? When was this?"

"A few weeks ago."

"And her response?"

"She said she knew, had known for some time."

"Yet, she has not ended their friendship."

"Far from it, Mrs. Moffatt," Allan continued, "Cathryn has a stubborn loyalty to this mad man."

"I believe so. I believe they have been friends since before the war, because of their commitment to helping runaways escape to Canada."

"There is talk they are planning to wed."

"I do not condone such silliness. I have not received an announcement of their engagement and certainly no invitation has arrived. The Hill understood Rupert was engaged to Mrs. Miller before the war. I'm sure her decision to wed Joshua Miller wounded him deeply."

"He has not mentioned that to me. I certainly hope he is not using Cathryn to wound Mrs. Miller."

"Rupert is many things, but I believe his heart is above such meanness. As Cathryn's friend, I'm sure you will receive an announcement."

"If so, Nancy will make an appropriate response."

"No doubt you have done all you could to prevent this misfortune. Cathryn has a mind of her own. That does often lead to errors of judgment. We will have to continue our efforts to protect her."

"I'm relieved you see this as I do, Mrs. Moffatt. I hope you will be more successful in dissuading her from this course."

"Rest assured, Allan, I will do all possible for Cathryn's sake. I'm sure her long acquaintance with Colonel Colson has been a factor in her unwillingness to believe Rupert to be the man you portray."

"Colson? She is to wed the officer she met in Boston? The man who ruined her?"

"Yes, of course, who else? That is only the proper thing, is it not?" the matron enjoined. "Surely you ahn't one of those who extends her friendship with Rupert Smith to such an absurd outcome. They are like brother and sister, as I have always said."

At the first squeak of the floorboards outside her room, Cathryn's eyes opened. Not just one pair of boots and not just one voice relieved the silence of the old house. Leaping from the bed, she pushed her arms into her robe, ready to question Rupert and his friends, until she heard another voice she had never expected to hear in Rupert's house.

"I'll admit he's done well for himself. Conniving his way into the good graces of decent women, some pretty ones at that."

"Just who do you think you are?" Mrs. Cook demanded of John Falmer, the speaker. "You may be known to Captain Smith but you're not welcome in this house when he's not here. Out you go."

Despite the days and nights of waiting for news, Cathryn smiled at the woman's forthright manner with a man no one in the village seemed to like. Mary Cook lifted her head from the bed she had shared with Cathryn since North disappeared Friday night. The young woman's eyes were red and battered with weeping long into the three nights he could not be found.

"North?" the bride-to-be gasped, rushing toward the door to the kitchen. Cathryn caught her, shook her head and wrapped her arms around Mary as she sank, with a low wail, into the embrace.

"Is that you, Cathryn?" Jericho demanded, striding toward the kitchen and her bedroom door.

"Out you go!" Mrs. Cook snarled at the intruder. "You've no right to barge into this house. Out. Out." From the scuffling, Cathryn surmised that Colson had met a formidable challenger to his authority. Despite protests, rattling of crockery and huffing, the front door slammed and peace, such as it could be while they awaited news of Mary's beau, was restored.

Mrs. Cook rapped quietly on Cathryn's door and peered into the room. "Mary, all that crying will spoil your photographs after the wedding. Come out and have some of the porridge I've made."

Mary slid from Cathryn's embrace into her mother's arms. Mrs. Cook, stroking her daughter's disheveled hair, guided her to the table, pushed her into a chair, slipped a steaming bowl in front of her daughter and said, "Eat or you won't be strong enough to stand up when you say 'I do' or 'I will' or repeat your vows."

"Oh, Mama, what if—."

"Ahn't no call for you to go imaginin' what you can't and won't know until that young man plants his big feet on that front porch."

"But—."

"Hush. Eat your breakfast. I don't cook anywheres like your Grandma Arnold but you haven't touched even a dry crust since Friday night."

"How can I eat?"

"You gotta, that's all. And you'd better start trustin' that man you love like nobody's business or you're goin' tah have a tough time livin' with him."

Cathryn tied the robe's sash around her waist and poured coffee in Mary's cup, added the thickest cream and a pinch of sugar. The young woman looked from one to the other, a trembling, weak smile lifting her cheeks for a moment before tears spilled over them again.

"Seems he has a way with women of all sorts," Falmer sneered at Mrs. Cook's treatment.

"Some women cannot resist that type of scoundrel," Colson replied, standing his ground in the hallway.

"You ahn't here to commend my success with ladies, Colson, and I won't give you the satisfaction of blowing a hole in your head, so what do you want?"

The three women in the kitchen held their breaths as the owner of the house entered from the front porch. Mary had to be held down by her mother.

"You have no authority to grant permission. I am here for a word with Miss Marcher. Five minutes."

"Your reason?"

"That is not your concern."

"Any matter concerning his fiancée, concerns Rupert," Morton said. "Ahn't no concern of yourn."

"I *will* speak to Cathryn."

"We have had the one and only conversation we will ever have, Jericho," Cathryn strode from the kitchen into Rupert's arms, her hair tied back with a ribbon, hurriedly dressed in her work clothes.

"You have something that belongs to me. I am here to collect it."

"You are mistaken. I have nothing belonging to you."

"You know to what I am referring, Cathryn. I require that you return it."

"I believe my fiancée has given you her answer. Please leave my house, Colson."

The colonel took a long breath, turned the brim of his bowler hat for a moment. "I have been patient. I have asked with all due courtesy. The return of this item is essential, Cathryn, for my future. I do not believe you are the kind of woman who takes pleasure in vindictive actions or spiteful revenge. Not after all we shared, all we meant to one another. If not for your unselfish love for me, you know I would not have survived. You were once a loving, generous woman, warm-hearted and capable of making a broken man want to live just to hold you through the night, surrender his heart to your passion. Do you not remember how we made love, inflamed by our need to be joined, as only a man and a woman who share love for one another can be joined?"

Rupert's expression hardened, his eyes darkened, threatening slits below a rigid brow. The arm around her waist tensed with rage.

Cathryn turned her head to glare at Colson but his steady gaze never faltered. "None of that is true."

"You came to me, Cathryn. When I most needed you. Do you turn from me now because your heart is hardened by bitter years without me? It pains me to see you so reduced—this life of base servitude to even baser men. I cannot bring myself to condemn you or to give this condition any name. Nor can I lower myself to make even a cursory atonement for what my desperate need has brought you to."

"Then do not. I have no need of your atonement so stingingly offered."

"I have come to you as an officer, a gentleman, to ask you to return to me property you have in your possession that was not intended for any purpose other than to express gratitude. I ask you again, Cathryn, if you are still the good and generous woman I have always believed you to be, to return what is mine."

"As I told you, Jericho, I have nothing belonging to you. I have not kept even a scrap of the smallest order nor of any value. I have kept nothing belonging to you or written by you."

Colson drew a sharp breath as though she had struck him. A gradual smirk marred his handsome face. "You say these unkind words in front of these felons. And do yourself a disservice. No lady would speak so falsely to gain favor among thieves. You are a trollop of the worst order—." Before Rupert reacted, Colson turned on him, "And you, sir, are a scoundrel for taking advantage of this woman's fallen state and her moral turpitude."

"If I was a killing man, Colson, you would be lying in the dirt with all the rest of the poisonous men of this world. As it is, I can promise *you* will never be governor of this state."

Had she not clamped her arms around Rupert's chest and Morton had not been the first to grab Colson by his starched collar, popping it from his shirt, Cathryn had no doubt that her fiancé would have succeeded in throwing the former Union officer through the beveled glass panel of the front door.

"To whom did you give my property, Cathryn?"

Before she responded, Rupert, quelling his fiancée's immediate attempt to silence him, said, "To me."

"You are no gentleman," Colson sneered. "You are a scoundrel, of the worst order. And you will be driven from this state before you have any opportunity to make good your threat."

"I make no threat, Colson. I state a fact."

Rupert responded to his friend's grin and Cathryn's worried stare with a gentle kiss on her temple.

"You have no honor, Smith, or I would call you out for your impertinence toward a superior officer."

"Ahn't one of us in the Army anymore, Colson," Morton said. "And you oughtn't be challenging a man in front of his future wife."

"Wife? That is absurd. Cathryn is a fool but not—."

Morton took Jericho by the throat, flipped him onto his back on the credenza and threatened him with a burly fist. Rupert grasped his friend's wrist but did nothing to free the colonel. They stared at the captive with malevolence, exchanging a non-verbal communication.

Cathryn moved away, leaving the decision of Jericho's fate to the men while she returned to the kitchen to prepare a pot of coffee for those who survived the altercation.

"Have they given up looking for North?"

"I don't know, Mary." The old house, its kitchen and pantry were as familiar to her as her cabin, with the same comfort to be derived from useful implements hung where they were most convenient. She had only to stretch her arm to the side to have the kettle to hand, a mere inch or two more gained her the tin of coffee. She glanced at the bride-to-be's mother, pressing her lips together.

The three women listened to the voices in the hallway. Jericho's growls and noisy exertions drew no concern from any of them until another man said, "I say the pond."

Mary leapt, knocking over her chair. Her mother caught her, pressed a finger to her daughter's lips. "Let the man be for now."

"If we could be sure no one saw him come here," Rupert said, "I'd agree but that's hard to know."

"Knock him on the head," Morton said. "He'll drown quicker."

Cathryn lost count of the ways Morton and North discussed how the gubernatorial candidate could be killed. She had no concerns for Colson's safety. Rupert shook his head, a quiet grin on his face as each method, each more gruesome and sure than the previous. She didn't begrudge them their fun at the Colonel's expense.

"If'n you want to live, get your sorry self out of this house," Morton growled, shoving Colson, stumbling and grumbling, down the hallway and out the front door, landing on his belly on the gravel pathway, in full view of Rupert's neighbors.

He scrambled to his feet, dusting his clothes and yanked the flapping collar free to shake it in the big man's direction. "Expect the constable, you——." He shook his fist, looking around him at the staring onlookers. His henchman, John Falmer, had disappeared. "You will be driven from this state, Smith, before you have any opportunity to make good your threat."

"As I said, I state a fact, Colson. Best seek other employment, far from the great state of Maine."

Morton slammed the door. The walls of the house trembled and the painting of red lilies jerked to an extreme angle. Cathryn collapsed against the sink board, covering her face.

"Forget every word he said, Angel."

"How can I when you and everyone here heard them too?"

Mary broke her mother's hold and lunged into the hallway, squealed and sobbed at the same time.

"What's this?" North asked.

"How could you scare me like this?" his bride-to-be demanded.

While Mary and North settled their differences, surrounded by her mother, father and younger brother, Rupert assured his bride-to-be, "Nothing he said matters to me. I know what he's doing and why." He clasped her hands and raised them to his lips. "I read what he wrote to you." When she tried to free her hands, he said, "You have no reason to be concerned. For a man in his position, confessing his love for a woman not his wife, and because his wife has since sought a divorce, will ruin his political future. That is the only reason he wants that letter back. He can also use them to keep you from speaking against him, should you ever consider doing so."

"What have you done with the letters?"

"I have them. I'll keep them, as you intended. He'll never get them, I swear to you, and he won't be able to hurt you."

"How will you manage that, Rupert? How are you going to keep him from being Governor?"

"John Falmer."

"Not the letter?"

"How could I use that without hurting you?" He caressed her cheeks with his thumbs, pressed a kiss on her brow. "Colson's association with Falmer will destroy him."

The question in her expression demanded a substantial explanation but Rupert avoided giving her a better answer.

"Are you sorry we'll be married with only these ruffians to witness?"

"They are your friends."

"And your friends, Cathryn. All the people in this house. And many in this village."

"And my friends." *But not that many in this village.* "Rupert?" His searching gaze pulled at her heart. With the obvious exceptions, people she had counted as friends for much of her life would not stand by her if she needed them. Morton, the Arne boys, were all she had, all she could depend on—only because they, like her, loved Rupert. And he, for want of good sense, loved her. "When will you go to Wyoming?"

"What did we miss now?" Tom Arne grumbled as he came through the kitchen door. "That Colson fella, pretty darn mad he was, stomped off like a little boy."

Malcolm pulled a chair from under the table, gesturing for Cathryn to sit. "Should've thrown him down the quarry, say he jumped."

"Pushing won't pass for jumping, Mal," Rupert laughed, offering Cathryn a cup of coffee, "North had the same idea. Are you ready for breakfast, Angel?"

"You haven't answered my question."

"Which one, my darling?"

"When are you going to Wyoming?"

He clasped her hand, dropping into a chair facing her and stared at the floor. "I had planned to start back before the end of August."

Tom and Malcolm backed toward the door to the hallway, stood there between the two soon-to-be-wed couples, grimacing at Morton who shrugged.

"So soon?"

"A friend from college is interested in the house but won't be able to move on the purchase until after those two are married."

"And what about *our* wedding?" Cathryn tugged her hand free and clasped the cup of coffee.

"By then, all the legalities should be over. The weather will still be favorable."

"So soon."

"The trails will still be passable. There'll be enough water." Judging by her stare and reluctance to meet his gaze, his effort to convince his bride-to-be was far from successful. "And, now the Union-Pacific[18] Railroad's joined up all the way to Utah, you can travel like a lady as far as Laramie. From there, the ranch is a day's ride." Cathryn remained silent. "Your piano will travel in cargo, on the same train, and the Singer, my love." She nodded. "Maine is beautiful, Cathryn, I know. Wyoming is breathtaking open country. Will you think about it? That's all I ask."

For answer, Cathryn stroked his cheek before sipping from the cup.

"Malcolm has his orders and Tom will be here at your service."

"Where are you going, Rupert?"

His brief smile accomplished his intention. She was distracted. He and Morton were gone again. The front hallway was empty.

Cathryn sighed.

"Miss—."

"Oh, I know, Tom. I understand there are always good reasons for everything he does."

"Ay-yuh, Miss," the loquacious brother replied. "He don't let folks down 'less it's unavoidable." Tom dropped

---

[18] **Union-Pacific Railway** promoted by President Lincoln to strengthen the sovereignty of the United States, and hold the Union together, was completed four years after the end of the American Civil War, greatly assisted by the need for timely transportation of troops and supplies.

into the chair beside her. "That North was sure mad. Took all Rupe's fine way of talkin' to convince him tweren't a good idea to walk all the way up to wherever his folks live to tell 'em how mad he was."

"Castine. They're from up there."

"Pretty place, North says, but he won't be goin' back now," Tom continued. "Best thing coulda happened's my way of thinkin'. Knocked the bitter war right outta him."

Malcolm nodded and set to work making a meal for all the folks in the house.

"He's not sure what he wants 'ceptin' to marry that fine girl," Tom laughed. "Boy's got a head full of being wed to Mary, didn't stop talking about her all the way back from Augusta."

"He went that far on foot?"

"I told yah he was mad." Both men laughed, slapping the top of the table in admiration. "Nah, we couldn't get him turned around. Even Rupe was getting tired of talkin' him back to thinkin' straight."

On the Saturday before Independence Day, Cathryn chose a dress from among the few Sunday best that belonged to her mother, a pale blue muslin print, with four tiers—old-fashioned but in season, and a reminder of her mother's love of summer. Mary Cook stood in the middle of the upstairs bedroom, eyes brimming with happy tears as her mother set the lace veil over her loosely pinned hair.

She held a nosegay of harebell and fern, picked that morning by her younger sisters, both of whom wore blue and yellow dresses made for them by their older sister under the tutelage of her own dressmaker. There was no procession to the church common, accompanied by her father or younger brother. Pastor Jorgens awaited the bride, as did her husband-to-be, in the large front parlor of the Smith House. Grandma Arnold held court in the dining room, directing the Arne boys and Morton where to put the many dishes she had spent the morning, with Malcolm's willing help, preparing and slapping Tom's fingers when he was tempted to sample the offerings.

Mr. Jorgens tapped his spectacles on the Bible opened on the lectern substituting for a pulpit as Morton pushed the double doors into the walls. Cathryn descended the stairs alone. Mary's groom and Rupert, stood to the side of the shoulder-high mantel. Both men stared at her until the groom stretched to raise his gaze to the landing where his bride stood with her father.

Cathryn took her place at the piano and played the bride's chosen music for her procession following her two little sisters—tossing petals every which way over the parquet floor and her youngest brother, Edgar, bearing the ring. The simple *pavane*, suggested by the pianist, kept pace with the step-hold of the bride's procession to meet her future—eager yet hesitant. The pianist held her breath as the young woman entered the parlor, not daring to look at the man in her own future, though he was intent on her.

Many more petals were thrown over the newly-wedded couple as soon as Pastor Jorgens pronounced their union before God and Man. The little girls threw their bounty as hard as possible at the youngest member of the Cook family until Papa Cook took charge, rescuing Edgar with a swoop of his arm at the same time as he swept his eldest daughter away from her husband for a farewell embrace. North shook his father-in-law's hand, bowing his head as he listened to the stern orders to take care of his wife.

The photographer engaged to memorialize the occasion in tintype captured the image of the once-haunted veteran with his joyful bride, indelible in their witnesses' misty-eyed memories. Cathryn pressed the backs of her lace half-gloves to the corners of her eyes and followed the bride and groom into the dining room where Grandma Arnold, Mrs. Cook and Malcolm Arne presided over the wedding meal. Rupert stood beside her for a moment before taking his turn to congratulate the couple.

After the celebratory meal, Malcolm Arne joined Cathryn in the kitchen, opening the pantry to reveal a frosted cake and a bottle of whiskey.

"It ain't that bubbly sweet drink for ladies. It's good Kentucky[19] bourbon."

"Please do the honors, Mr. Arne."

"Yes, Miss."

Tom and Malcolm raised glasses to North's future, clapped him hard on the back as he swallowed the whisky, laughing as they took advantage of his choking to kiss the bride.

Cathryn sipped the whisky, wrinkling her nose, and Rupert took advantage to kiss her.

"Seems we'll be having another wedding afore long," Mrs. Cook remarked, receiving a wink from the owner of the house as Aurelius peered through the dining room window, and called his father's attention to the street.

"Mr. Giles is on his way," Mr. Cook murmured to Captain Smith. "Looks madder than a rooster."

Rupert closed the doors to the dining room and opened the front door as Allan stomped one foot on the porch, stopped and held his friend's gaze for a moment.

"Mary Cook didn't come to work today and I believe your house guest has something to do with that. Mrs. Giles has heard a rumor that set her off like a firecracker." He stepped into the hallway. "And, I wouldn't be surprised if you didn't instigate this travesty, Smith."

---

[19] **Kentucky bourbon**, one of the most famous bourbons was the creation of the Welshman, Evan Williams. His *1783* blend is still revered today. His distinctive black and white label was copied by his apprentice, Jack Daniels, whose Tennessee sour mash became a well-known imitator.

Allan Giles shouted Mary's name. North filled the dining room doorway, backed by Tom and Malcolm. Rupert joined the group and Allan craned his neck to see over their heads, meeting Papa Cook's glare as North stepped forward.

"What can we do for yah, Mr. Giles." He grinned over his shoulder at his wife. "Might yah be wanting a word with my missus?"

"Your what?"

Mary giggled, proud of her husband's sense of humor, silenced when the master of the Giles's household glared over North's shoulder with a severe frown, not for her but for Cathryn Marcher.

"Have you any idea what trouble you've caused?"

"Thank you for coming so soon to congratulate Mary and her husband, Allan," Cathryn replied. "We were aware that Mary and North's decision to wed in a private ceremony might upset a few on the Hill, however, I think *trouble* is too strong a word."

"You can jest if you wish but Mrs. Miller and Mrs. Moffatt will ensure you fully grasp how absurd this…this move is, *will be* for everyone concerned."

"Just you wait a minute, Giles," Papa Cook said, stepping forward, straightening his spine. "My Mary has every right to be married to a decent man and there ahn't no reason she has to ask your permission. So I suggest you turn right round and take yourself down the road. We have some celebratin' to do and we don't need no lawyer to do it."

Allan glared at the man blocking his entry to the room to accost his paid servant but Papa Cook and North stood solid, the younger man flexing the muscles of his back. Mary sighed and Cathryn giggled—for once, not embarrassed to be a giddy, giggling girl.

"Unless you've come to celebrate with us," Rupert intervened, "and share in Mary's happiness with a slice of wedding cake, I suggest you'd be more comfortable at home. My guests are about to offer another toast with a fine

Kentucky whisky." Rupert extended his arm in the direction of the front door.

"Cathryn," Allan sneered, "I cannot believe how you've changed since this man returned."

"My fiancée is not your concern, Allan. Please leave or I'll have to throw you out."

"*This man* is the love of my life. He is also the best man I and his friends have ever known. Thank you for visiting." She turned away to salute the bride with another sip of whisky.

North pushed his chest out to force Giles backward. When the lawyer failed to move, Mary's husband gestured toward the front door and prodded Allan's shoulder. With the support of Rupert, Morton and the Arne brothers, the groom convinced the visitor to retreat.

"I hope North isn't sorry he married me," Mary whispered.

"If he is, he's a bigger fool than I'd've thought, even for a Yankee," Tom Arne declared.

The laughter from the women chased Allan Giles down the steps of the Smith house, a grim scowl clouding his vision. He stumbled at the edge and his discomfort brought another round of chuckling from the veterans standing on the veranda, making sure he went in the direction of his home.

Barely an hour later, the newly-weds walked to the summer cottage deep into the Smiths' woodlands— prepared for them by the bride's mother and grandmother. Rupert Smith kissed the back of his fiancée's wrist, turned on his heel and rode away on his horse.

Early the next morning, Cathryn attended to her duties as the Sunday School teacher although several of her usual students were absent. Megan Giles was most remarkable among the absentees. One or two of the other girls were known to be away visiting grandparents and the youngest absentee, Edgar Cook, had been excused by his older brother as having a fever but Aurelius confessed the younger boy had eaten all the remaining wedding cake.

Lila Snyder deposited her girls at the door of the church hall as usual and a few of the rest of the children dawdled along the road, taking advantage of the hot, dry day to venture their talents as dandelion puff warriors. The sun, though bright and glittering, had no effect on the children enjoying the sweltering church grounds. Cathryn called them in and Mrs. Miller followed, shutting the door between the Sunday School room and the outside door.

"I wouldn't put vindictiveness beyond you, Cathryn. You've always been jealous of my friendship with Rupert, but I never believed you capable of stooping so low. What terrible trick did you play on the poor man?"

There were so many responses crowding into Cathryn's thoughts that she was overwhelmed by silence.

"Did you expect me to hide away, cry myself to death in shame?"

"Of course not, Susan. But I fail to understand what cause you have for this tirade."

"How could you do this? Rupert and I were meant for one another. Everyone says so. There is not one person in this village who doesn't think you are the most hateful of all the people they've ever known. To steal your best friend's fiancé like this, behind my back. I can barely endure their sympathy, their pity!"

"Rupert and I—."

"Don't deny a word, Cathryn Marcher. Everyone knew you were setting your cap for him when you tricked his parents into trusting you...and how did you repay them? At their lowest moment, stealing from them, accepting gifts that rightly belonged to him...and his lawful wife."

Everyone?

"You may believe whatever you like, of course, but as far as Rupert and I are concerned, I will not allow you to spoil one of the happiest days of my life. And I have no reason to explain or defend what Rupert and I have planned."

"Oh, so high and mighty! I'm surprised Reverend Jorgens has allowed you to teach Sunday School today."

"He has and I have left the children to their own devices long enough."

When she skirted around the widow and opened the door, the quiet in the room was ominous. All the girls sat at the low table, each with a sheet of thick paper with the tin of watercolor tablets in the center. The breeze from the open windows cleared the stifling odors of the week-long closed room. Aurelius Cook encouraged the younger boys to sit while he read the child's version of that week's Lesson.

Cathryn closed the door and leaned against it. Her assistant glanced at her, winked and went on with his reading, embellishing details as only a young man with an energetic imagination could. Cathryn retreated to the small kitchen and wondered how Rupert Smith, with so little effort, could spin the world on a different axis and not one person besides herself, a chosen few good men and a group of Sunday School children recognized the change.

Monday morning, Mary entered the kitchen with a shy blush heightening the healthy glow on her cheeks.

"North's gone with Malcolm to your Mrs. Lowell. Why it takes two men to deliver a ball gown, I am sure I don't know, but that means I can help you with your wedding gown."

Though they made the most of the daylight hours, working in Peggy Smith's south-facing dressing room where she could depend on the sun from midmorning, her thoughts were far from her task.

Malcolm returned in the evening without any new projects for her. North whisked his bride away to the cottage without a word. Tom and Malcolm had given up residence in the Snyder's cabin for the newlyweds to move in as soon as they wanted. Lila added a few new furnishings and Noam had agreed happily when North expressed an interest in helping on the farm in exchange for a reduction in the rent, since work at the sawmill didn't pay as well as teaching singing and offering piano lessons.

Within days, rumors spread that Captain Smith had left the county, possibly the state, and talk of any other explanation was a feeble attempt to shield his so-called bride-to-be from his second thoughts. And, if the rumors were true, the accusations against him were false. Whichever explanation was put forward depended on who expressed it and to whom.

Cathryn heard whispers of Augusta and Portland between Tom Arne and North but neither willingly confirmed what they knew. Unfamiliar with boredom and idleness, the thought of another day of making work to keep her spirits from sinking even further, Cathryn wandered through the silent rooms of the house, stared at the painting of red lilies, as her expectation of hearing the stamp of boot heels on the front porch faded with each passing moment.

But on the day after Independence Day, Friday evening, still cherishing his newfound freedom as a working man with a summer job in the mercantile store in town, Aurelius Cook returned to the village and called by the kitchen of the Smith House.

"Someone better get up to town, 'cause I just saw Captain Smith get himself arrested by that McLain feller and hauled off in a wagon like a peddler."

All Cathryn had to do was glance in Morton's direction and he tossed the rest of his evening coffee down his throat and took off on one of the horses.

"Where are you going, Miss?"

"To find the man who is supposed to be my husband."

"Please, Miss. Cathryn," Tom stumbled through the forms of address.

"Please don't make excuses, Tom."

"Cathryn, Rupert won't want you to put yourself in harm's way."

"He's not here."

"He will be."

"When? He's been gone for days."

"As soon as he's released and done what he set out to do."

She stood in the wide hallway, staring from one to the other of her jailers. "Don't any of you have anything better to do than gawk at me?"

"No."

"I'm going to the church to arrange flowers."

"We're coming with you."

Since there was no point protesting or refusing Tom's declaration, Cathryn donned her shawl and sun bonnet. The Arnes slapped on their cowboy hats.

The summer heat had doubled its efforts and there were few villagers on the road to impede the long walk. Neither of the brothers questioned her change of direction when Cathryn turned at the crossroads away from the village and church. Once within sight of her cabin, Cathryn's spirits sank even further. Even in a short time, the small house was as forlorn as its former occupant. Malcolm exchanged a sharp glance with his brother.

Neither spoke before they went to work to repair some of the ravages of the heavy rain and the heat of early July. Though the cabin was no longer her home, Cathryn entered through the kitchen door. Her cry brought the Arne brothers to her side in a heartbeat.

"Who could have done this?"

They stared first at her, dumbfounded, then at the destruction around them.

"Falmer."

"Jericho," Cathryn added to Tom's pronouncement.

"Don't touch anything. I'm going for the county sheriff."

"Why?"

"This is what Rupe was afraid of," Tom said. "I'm gonna make sure that constable from town sees this. Should keep that Colson fella from the Governor's Mansion for sure."

"There's no evidence—."

"There will be," he assured her. "Guaranteed he left his mark."

"How do you know?"

"A man like that wants Rupe to know where he's been."

Cathryn collapsed against the rim of the big sink. "I didn't want any of this."

"Miss Cathryn!" Mary Cook gasped as she burst into the cabin from the road. "I've run all the way."

"What are you doing here, Mary?"

"Mr. Giles told me to go. I don't have a job there anymore!"

"Why did he do such a thing?"

"Because North and I are married. He doesn't want me in his house. He said I had betrayed his family. What am I going to do without a job?"

"You'll have enough to do helping me finish my wedding gown."

"We better be going back to the house," Tom said.

"Before I left, Mrs. Giles gave me this for you." Mary thrust an envelope into Cathryn's hand.

"Let's all go home," Cathryn said, conscious the word warmed her heart. "We have work to do this afternoon."

Nineteen

The handwriting on the unsealed envelope belonged to George Franklin Smith. Cathryn stared at her name, flipped the envelope to the back, stared again at her name. She had put off the moment of discovery until she and Mary had worked to the last of the daylight, fitting and pinning the skirt of her gown. While Mary happily took on the task of tacking the hem, Cathryn made an excuse and, in the seclusion of her bedroom at the back of the kitchen, she slid her finger under the flap and worked the single sheet of paper free. After a deep breath, she unfolded the letter.

Tuesday, September 17
The Year of our Lord, 1867

Dear Evie,

If you are reading this, please do not feel sorrowful for either Peggy or myself. We are together. Whether you grieve because our son has not survived this terrible war between our fellow citizens is not for us to know or judge.

I have entrusted to our attorney, Mr. Allan Giles, Esquire, an addendum to my and Peggy's Last Will and Testament, with instructions that pertain to you and your future.

Although Mr. Giles will no doubt apprise you of the details, both Peggy and I wish you to know why we have made this change.

You have been with us, as a friend and support in our darkest & most hurtful moments over the past six years and we have no doubt that, with your kind heart and generous nature, you will continue to do so through however many years our Lord grants to us.

Whether or until our son, Rupert, returns to his home from this war, Peggy and I have agreed that, as we have no other heir, all our possessions, including our family home, should be yours to enjoy in his absence, with our deepest gratitude for all you have done to lessen our sorrow and bring some joy to our later years.

With great respect and appreciation,

George & Margaret Smith

Cathryn held the letter in her hands for several long moments, caressing the folded edge as though she could comfort the two people she had loved as parents after her own mother and father had passed away. They had left life not knowing whether their only son had survived. She could only imagine their pain in writing such a letter. Bequeathing their only child's inheritance to her must have broken their spirits even more.

She gazed upwards, pressing the letter against her heart, wondering what had caused Nancy Giles to betray her husband's trust. That did not surprise her, Allan's failure to inform her of the letter, or let Rupert know who Evie was or the contents of their Will did. *Perhaps, if Allan believed Rupert to be alive…*

"I have no time for this," Cathryn murmured. After folding the letter back into the envelope, she walked into the kitchen to join Tom and Malcolm. After North left to walk to the honeymoon cottage with his wife, assuring her that he could take care of her, the two men settled at the table, huddled over cups of coffee, the grated door of the firebox open to heat the darkened room. She grasped the back of the chair at end of the table as both men sat erect and faced her.

"While I'm having words with Mary's former employer, I'll be grateful if the two of you start packing."

"But—," Tom began, leaping from his chair.

"There's a lot to do, Tom, and there will be very little time after Rupert and I are married next weekend. I have no idea what will be needed. Use your best judgment."

Before either man responded, Cathryn grabbed her heavy shawl from the coat rack and trotted down the front steps to the road.

Nancy Giles, with no housemaid to perform the task of opening the front door, stared through the lace curtain, shaking her head at the late evening visitor. For answer, Cathryn raised her fist to the door frame and pounded the wood.

"What are you thinking?" Nancy hissed, yanking the door open only enough to be heard.

"If you did not want me to come here, why go to the trouble of making sure I had George Smith's letter?"

"I have no idea what you mean."

For a moment, Cathryn held her breath, self-doubt waging war with her certain knowledge of Nancy Giles's lazy relationship with honesty and her penchant for using whatever method arose to inflict a wound on her equally disingenuous husband. "You know exactly what I mean, Nancy."

"I'm sure I do not, Cathryn, but please come in. The evening has turned extremely unpleasant."

"It certainly has," Cathryn agreed, bursting over the threshold, shaking the evening mist from her shawl and thrusting it at the lady of the house.

"What has come over you? I'm sure I have never seen you so...so—."

"So angry?" She tossed the shawl on the seat of the coat rack since Nancy had made no offer to hang the garment.

"So distressed, Cathryn. This is not at all like you. You are usually quite even-tempered, even docile, under all circumstances."

"You mean servile."

"I have never thought of you as *servile*," Nancy laughed. "Anything but. Calm certainly, never haughty, as you are now."

"Rising above my station."

"Cathryn, that is unlike you. You know very well *I* do not think of you in that way."

"But others do," Cathryn replied, striding past toward the door of Allan Giles's office.

"And you know very well who those others are. Take your grievances to them." When Cathryn lifted her hand to rap on the lawyer's door, Nancy said, "My husband is not at home. I would be grateful if you left my house. My daughter has had enough unpleasantness these passing few days."

"Where *is* Allan?"

"I do not see how that is any of your business."

"The letter you gave me makes his whereabouts my business."

"I still have no idea of any letter or how that could be of any importance regarding Allan. However, if you must know, he is at his lodge meeting and will not return for several hours."

"That lodge never meets this late, Nancy."

"I might have known you would be well acquainted with the schedules of the men of this village," the lawyer's wife sneered. "If you know so much, you will have no trouble locating him without my assistance. Please leave."

At the top landing, Megan Giles cried out and immediately covered her mouth with both hands.

"Go to your room!" Nancy's hands shook with rage at her daughter before she turned to confront Megan's teacher.

"And you will leave this instant. Take your accusations and your evil tongue where they will be welcome—I hear Rupert Smith has a room at the jail. He will no doubt welcome *your* company."

Cathryn glanced at her student, struck motionless on the landing and staring down at her mother. Giving the little girl a sad smile, she turned toward the still open door.

"Don't go, Miss Marcher!"

"She is no longer Miss anything to you and I told you to go to your room!"

Minutes after Cathryn left the Giles House, Morton Pierce returned to Oslo Hill alone. The clop of his mount's hooves echoed along the road as he passed the Miller residence. The curtain of the front parlor shook as the inhabitant concealed herself again but Susan Miller's presence had already been noted by the lone rider. Though tempted to confront her, Morton tipped his hat in her direction and chuckled softly when the curtain snapped shut in response.

At the front yard of Rupert Smith's house, he dismounted as Malcolm came onto the veranda. The Southerner took the reins, leading the bay toward the stable at the back of the house.

"Cathryn?"

"Out."

"Alone?" he snarled.

"Tom's watching."

Morton nodded, slapped his hat on his thigh. "It ahn't good news I've got for her, but it can wait 'til morning. Meantime, a cup of coffee and some of your cake would go down pretty good right now."

"Ain't none left."

Morton lowered his voice as the two men walked through the front hallway. "Afore you ask, Rupe's okay. Colson's wanted to have him taken up to Augusta but that little constable, bless his soul, is hungry for a bit of notoriety. Wants to keep his prisoner 'til the judge comes 'round."

"What they got agin' him?"

"Next to nothin'. Some complaint, most likely from that dog, Falmer, about a threat of violence. Blackmail maybe."

Searching the village for Allan Giles on any evening was a much simpler task than Nancy imagined. Cathryn strolled along the road until she reached the Miller house and walked into the front hallway, following the light sounds of laughter and glasses clinking. Without knocking, she entered Susan Miller's back parlor and met the stares of the four people she expected to find there.

"To what do I owe this honor, *Mrs.* Smith?"

Cathryn ignored the sneer and walked directly toward Allan. "Unless you want your friends to know why I'm about to have you thrown in jail, I suggest you come outside."

Allan Giles attempted a scoffing laugh that ended in a choked cough.

"Considering your *husband—*."

"Susan, you do yourself a disservice by opening your mouth." Cathryn strode from the room, conscious that neither Jericho Colson nor John Falmer had moved or spoken when she entered. "You kept this letter from me. Why?" Though gratified that Allan stumbled after her and stared dumbfounded at the sheet of paper she thrust at him, her words were less harsh than she had rehearsed them.

"Where did you get this?"

A day before her inclination would have been to shield everyone but herself. "Your wife sent it with Mary North."

"Mary read it?"

"Of course not. Unlike her former employer, she is a young woman of integrity."

"You have no call to impugn my honor." As he lurched backwards, his complexion reddened and turned a curious shade of blue.

"I believe I do. I want to hear your reason for keeping me ignorant of George and Margaret Smith's wishes. For ensuring that I continue living in poverty, indebted to you and others in this village, for my livelihood."

"That is harsh, Cathryn. You know I have only *ever* had your best interests at heart. I've protected you, ensured you had employment—."

"You have no idea of how harsh my life has been. I have no doubt that if this letter had been brought to light at their deaths, some in this village would have found reason to condemn me but even that possibility is no excuse for your withholding this bequest from me. Mr. and Mrs. Smith made their wishes clear to you. Should Rupert have returned at any time after their deaths, the disposal of his property would have been entirely up to him."

"You have certainly circumvented any possibility of losing their property and wealth by marrying him," Allan sneered.

"Oh, that explains everything!" Susan exclaimed, rushing from the back parlor doorway. "You really are a low creature after all."

"And you would be the first to say so," Cathryn replied, her voice cracking on the last word. For a moment, she turned away from them, gathered her strength from her love for the two people who accepted her and for their son who loved her in return. "Think as you want, Susan. You will never have the happiness I enjoy."

Though she received no satisfactory answer from the lawyer, she strolled through the village as though no care or trouble had ever touched her heart, greeting some of her neighbors with a broad smile, as they enjoyed the pleasant evening for a constitutional. The walkers nodded and smiled in return, leaning their heads toward one another after they had passed her.

"Where did Rupert go?" Cathryn asked as she came through the front door.

"That ahn't nothing to do with him not being here now, Cathryn," Morton replied, gesturing her toward the kitchen. "After North and Mary's wedding, Rupe intended to be back in time for cake."

"Morton, tell me what he's planning. I have a right to know."

"He made an arrangement to meet an agent, to get the house sold and your piano packed up."

"To send it to Wyoming."

"That's about the way of it."

"Why does he do this? Make plans without discussing anything with anyone, especially me?" Although she expected no answer, Morton's discomfort made her laugh. "Why do I even ask?"

"You got a right, Cathryn, now you're marrying him—."

"There's no assurance of that," she commented, accepting the cup of coffee from Malcolm.

"—But I ahn't got much of an answer for you." He winked at Tom, coming onto the back porch. "It's the way he is. The way he's been since the war. He ahn't had anyone to be answerable to 'cept his own self and getting through day after day. He sees somethin' needs doing and he does it."

"That will have to change."

"Yes, ma'am."

McLain stamped his feet deeper into his low-heeled boots and stood when the three men opened the door to the constable's office in the Oslo Township Jail, a brown brick box at the junction of the road to the Hill. Allan Giles strode forward and slapped a sheaf of papers on McLain's desk.

"We have a warrant to take your prisoner."

"By whose order? And take him where, gentlemen?" The stout man folded his arms across his chest. "The judge hasn't considered the charges brought against him yet."

"This is from the district court, McLain, not the town magistrate."

McLain opened the sheaf, scanned the documents for a moment and tossed them back on his desk. Reaching into the middle drawer of his desk, he took out his ring of cell keys.

"I will take full responsibility," Giles said.

"I have no objection if you wish to see your friend. All the same, whose custody is for the town magistrate to decide, Mr. Giles."

The brawny man with Allan Giles stuck his hand toward the constable. McLain ignored Falmer's request, tossing the ring back and forth in his hands.

"Smith's my responsibility. Whatever happens will be on me, regardless of that piece of paper."

"If you read that document, McLain, you'll see that Smith is to be released into my custody," Jericho Colson sneered.

"I did read it, Colonel, but ahn't a one of yah holds any authority in this township. So don't be thinkin' I'm goin' tah let yah take him. While yah visitin', Smith's your responsibility, Colonel. Whatever happens will be on you."

"Come now, McLain. You cannot think any harm is likely to come to your prisoner in our custody. The charges brought against this man are serious."

"No need to tell me, Colonel. I've already had trouble with him and his big friend. Not to mention Noam Snyder and the Pastor."

"Regardless, this is signed by the district court. I will take full responsibility for Smith's appearance in court, whenever that is appropriate."

McLain shrugged. "His friends had a warrant signed by the town magistrate, Mr. Giles."

"Rupert's gone?" Allan demanded.

"I'll tell you what I told them. He must be a mighty headache for all you folks to come down here on a Monday afternoon, disturbing the town magistrate and a district judge, to get Captain Smith out of here," McLain said. "You tell me Smith is a dangerous criminal. You say you'll be held responsible for losing him if his friends decide to help him escape. Is that what you're attempting?"

"That is unlikely," Colson replied. "We know Mr. Pierce has been here."

"You know that for certain?" the constable asked.

"Although I doubt he has the intelligence, has he or his Reb friends made such attempts?"

Constable McLain remained silent, a slow smirk twisting his mouth.

"If Sergeant Pierce had attempted anything of that nature, I'm sure you would not be talking to us. In fact, I would expect that your effort to recapture your prisoner would take precedence."

"Well now, Mr. Pierce did present me with that possibility," the constable said. "I'm doing my job, Colonel. Pierce has posed no threat to the execution of my duty. He's keeping Smith nice and quiet. However, your own man," McLain nodded in the direction of Falmer, "told you, in my hearing, 'Pierce better not get in my way when Smith's in my hands.' Are you thinking of causing harm to my prisoner, Colonel Colson?"

"I give you my word, Mr. McLain. No harm will come to Smith while he is in my custody."

"Like I said, Colonel, I'll hold you responsible for the safety of my prisoner."

"Captain Smith will be in no significant danger."

"His court hearing is scheduled for this Wednesday morning. I expect you to see he gets here, on time and in one piece."

"I can assure you of that, Constable," Morton Pierce declared, grinning at the three men.

McLain tossed the ring of keys to the sergeant and hitched his shoulders into his overcoat. "Glad to be getting out of here myself. Listening to you two reminisce all night long was getting on my nerves. You ahn't the only ones in this township with war stories."

"Thank you," Morton said.

"Don't thank me, Pierce, thank that bag of wind, Colson. Never met a man more sure of himself with less reason."

"I object to your tone, McLain. And why have you given the keys to Smith's cell to that man?"

"Pierce is my deputy, Mr. Giles. Has been since he and Smith returned to the Hill."

"Then why did you lead us to believe you'd give Colonel Colson custody," Giles demanded.

"Just the pure fun of it," the constable laughed. "'Bout time someone took him down a bit." He donned his peaked cap. "I'll be having my suppah now. Don't expect you'll be here when I get back. If'n yah stay, gentlemen, expect to share a cell with the drunk who'll be startin' up his singing any second now."

Later on that hot evening, Cathryn announced, "I am going to the township jail, will you come with me?"

"Yes, ma'am, but—."

"There is no alternative, Tom. I know who has brought these charges against Rupert and I know they are false. Allowing Rupert to endure another night in that jail is exactly what these vicious men want. Whatever I must do to have him released, I will do. Will you help me?"

Both men stood, shrugged into their jackets and went to the barn to saddle the horses. Cathryn returned to her room, changed into her dungarees and jacket, twisted her hair into a bun under her straw hat.

Tom Arne led one of the geldings to the back porch and held its head while Cathryn mounted from the top step, throwing her leg over the saddle and taking the reins from the Southerner. When Malcolm brought the other two horses, Cathryn rode toward the township of Oslo. The sun reflected back at them from the windows of the houses as they passed. The shimmer of heat rising from lawns and the creek hissed as they descended the sloping highway from the Hill.

Cathryn blocked misgivings and doubts as the street lamps from the township flickered into view ahead. The whitewashed walls of the stone jailhouse shone in the dusk. Before the three riders reached the corner of the building, the door of the jailhouse opened, the harsh light flooding over the street and blinding Cathryn for a moment.

"This is a pleasant surprise."

She knew the voice and shivered. Tom joined her, helping her to dismount at the sidewalk. Malcolm came alongside his brother, gathered all the reins, wrapping them around his big hand as he calmed the horses with a low whistle.

"Keeping company with traitors now, I see."

Cathryn glanced at her companions, exhaling as though she counted each modicum of air as it left her lungs. Though she opened her mouth to retort, she closed her lips on the angry words.

Allan Giles joined Jericho in the doorway and stepped toward her. "Cathryn, what are you doing here?"

"I have come to see Rupert."

"You must know that's not possible this time of night. You should have come this afternoon."

"I don't think that is your decision, Mr. Giles. I will present my case to the constable."

"Mr. McLain has better occupation than to entertain the whims of a foolish woman."

"Regardless, Jericho, I will speak to the constable and if you prevent me from doing so, these friends will ensure that you and Mr. Giles will not interfere."

"Let me deal with her," another familiar voice growled. John Falmer pushed forward, knocking Allan aside.

"Keeping company with cowards, I see," Tom drawled.

Before Falmer lunged at the Southerner, Malcolm brought the horses forward. "You ain't no gentlemen. None of yuh. Get out of the way so Miss Marcher can have a private conversation with her fiancée."

Constable McLain beckoned Cathryn toward the door of the jailhouse, nudging Giles and Colson to stand aside. Falmer stood his ground until Malcolm Arne brought the geldings to snort in the henchman's face.

"These gentlemen have been after me for days to release my prisoner," McLain said, escorting Cathryn through the narrow passageway to the cells. "Claim they have documents proving he was blackmailing Mr. Colson but none of 'em could produce a single scrap of evidence."

"Mr. Smith is too honorable to even consider doing such a thing."

"But he has documents that will incriminate Colson," McLain murmured.

Cathryn returned a weak smile as she stepped ahead of the constable, looking through the bars of each heavy-planked door. "Whether they are damaging is irrelevant, since no one else will ever see them."

"That's none of my business, Miss Marcher, anyhow. You've come a ways on a fool's errand. Don't let on, but your man ahn't here."

"Where have they taken him?"

"Old Judge Coffin let him go this morning, after a little talk, so Rupe could get what he had to do done." He walked through the cells hallway. "Get on out through the back,

Miss, I'll send your friends thata way. I've been keeping those villains pacin' in my office all afternoon. Be glad to shut up shop tonight." The constable unlocked the door at the rear of the jailhouse, pushed slowly to silence the creaking hinges. "Hear you two have a wedding coming up."

"We do."

"Then you best get on home."

"Thank you, Mr. McLain."

"No call to thank me, Miss, my missus has been naggin' me you need to get this fella under your wing."

After another lonely, worry-filled night, Cathryn sat in the company of the brothers but was at a loss for any occupation while Malcolm assumed all the kitchen tasks, her mind wandered to the absence of her husband-to-be and the uncertainty of any future—either in the home she had always known or a faraway territory, part of a vast lawless wilderness.

To make her misery complete, Susan Miller arrived, sweeping through the front hallway into the kitchen and waving her hands in Malcolm's face to demand a cup of tea. In her wake, Allan Giles and Jericho Colson barged past Tom, into the kitchen.

"This is outrageous, Cathryn." Allan stormed forward, thrusting a copy of George Smith's letter in her face. "You have made accusations and demands without the courtesy of waiting for an explanation."

"Can't be any worse than this," Cathryn murmured.

"I'm glad to hear you say that, my darling," Rupert said, standing in the open front door, arms folded across his chest, dressed in his wedding frock coat, trousers and gray silk brocade vest. His boots gleamed and his broadcloth shirt was starched, as though he had not spent nearly a week in jail. Cathryn remained silent, too surprised and relieved to react.

"Rupert," Susan cooed, gliding toward him, her hands outstretched. "We have been so worried since hearing the ridiculous tale you had been arrested."

Rupert brushed past her and pulled Cathryn into his arms. "Forgive me?"

For answer, she pressed her brow against his shoulder, no question or answer coming to mind and hundreds of them all at once. *Where have you been? How are you here? What is happening? Why did you leave me?*

Rupert took his father's letter from her, read through it and put it back in her hand. "A curse disguised as a blessing," he murmured.

She nodded and leaned away, folding the envelope and its contents into the pocket of her dress. "Coffee?"

"You know I do, my angel." He kissed her temple. "Mort tells me you've ordered these boys to pack up."

"To pack."

"Cathryn, I demand a hearing."

"You might have your day in court, Giles, but my fiancée will not be at a disadvantage because your incompetence— and I use that term as a kindness—has been exposed. My best advice to you is to clear up your business with the few clients who still trust you and find another profession. Perhaps, Colson will hire you to manage his campaign, but I daresay he will require a much better attorney than you are once *his* villainy is known."

"How dare you?" Jericho Colson demanded as Cathryn and Rupert returned to the kitchen.

"Where do you intend for Tom and Malcolm to go?" Rupert asked, leading her away from the coffee grinder and stove toward the blossom-festooned woods.

"With us. To Wyoming. If they've a mind to do that."

"That's a pretty big decision, my love. Why the change of heart?"

"Not heart, Rupert, mind." A breeze trembled in the branches, dusting them with petals, and Cathryn halted to breathe in the fresh scent. "Those who had been important to me in this village are gone. Those kind people who remain will never begrudge me my heart's desire. Those who would, for spite, will go on as they are now."

"Wyoming will have the same mix of good and bad, Cathryn."

"I do not want my children raised where it is certain they will be sneered at for who their mother is."

"Or their father," Rupert added, reminding her of their equality of disfavor.

"I know nothing about Wyoming, but I am willing to join in this adventure with you, for the sake of our offspring."

"A fresh start?"

"A fresh start with familiar—and beloved—friends."

The house echoed with heavy boot heels on the floorboards as Rupert's law school friend paced his new home, measuring the dimensions of the rooms in strides.

What furniture hadn't been shipped to the Portland rail station had been sold or given away to neighbors. The piano, Singer and the decadent *Red Lilies* Peggy Smith loved had been specially crated and carted away to be loaded onto a railroad car bound for East St. Louis, then Laramie, wherever that was.

Cathryn stood before the one remaining full-length mirror, as Mary North and Mrs. Cook assessed Lila Snyder's progress arranging the bride's veil over Mrs. Lowell's handiwork, an elaborate chignon.

"Most unlikely I will ever appear as elegant as this any time in the future," Cathryn giggled.

"You will have the tintypes to remember," Mrs. Cook assured her, "and the look in Captain Smith's eyes when he sees you."

Mary crawled around the three-foot length of the ecru lace train, straightening the fabric, examining the edges, inch by inch, to ensure there were no stray threads to mar the embroiderer's work.

"Captain and Mrs. George Rupert Smith," Lila sighed, stepping back to admire her own effort. "This is truly a wonderful day."

"Not yet," Mrs. Lowell remarked. "Best not count a blessing a certainty, in case—."

"No need to worry," Mrs. Cook declared. "Ahn't nothin' going to keep these two apart. Am I right, Cathryn?"

"We all hope and pray," Mary said, "you'll be as happy as I am, Cathryn."

"Thank you," the bride murmured, hardly daring to look at her reflection or into the faces of the women who surrounded her.

Footsteps on the stairs sent Lila scurrying to the door and onto the upper hallway, barring the door with her arms folded across her chest. "No never mind who sent you snooping around, Sergeant Pierce, neither you nor any of those other gentlemen are going to get a peek at the bride. You will all have to wait."

"Any notion of the time, Mrs. Snyder?"

"No. Miss Cathryn will appear when she's good and ready. But there is no doubt Captain Smith won't be in any way shape or form disappointed, no matter how long he has to stand at the altar."

"As long as you can assure me, so I can calm him down, that Miss Marcher will, indeed, arrive."

"After all she's been through, how can he doubt for even a moment? Ahn't no way in all tarnation that girl's changed her mind."

Morton's familiar chuckle as he descended the stairs reassured Cathryn more than all the kind words and embraces she had received throughout the morning and early afternoon that day. The women in the front bedroom treated her like a daughter, a close friend and a sister—all the ways she felt about them in her turn. If either her own mother or Peggy Smith had been alive, she could not have been better loved and pampered. For a moment, she covered her face with trembling hands.

"Now, now," Mrs. Lowell cooed, "you don't want to make your eyes all red, Cathryn. Stand up straight. You have no reason to be anything but proud."

"I am. *So* proud to have such good friends."

"There will be many more in your life, no need to worry about that, my dear." Mrs. Cook held a handkerchief out to her. Cathryn dabbed at her eyes.

"Buggy's here," Aurelius shouted from the front hall. Jacob, taking a day off from Mrs. Moffatt's beck and call, stood, erect and at attention, near the door of the open landau, dressed in his Maine militia uniform. The carriage, rented for the occasion, was draped in white lilacs and satin ribbons, hand-picked by the Mary's little sisters that morning. Noam Snyder and Papa Cook waited on the lawn, both dressed in their Sunday best. Rupert's friend, a man in his forties, joined them and lit a cigar.

All the women preceded Cathryn down the stairs and were helped into a second carriage. Noam offered Cathryn his arm at the top landing, patted her fingers and walked onto the veranda. "By rights, Cathryn, I'm proud to be standing in your papa's place today. He and your ma would be proud beyond measure to see you so happy."

"Thank you, Noam. I am happy." With shaking fingertips, she touched her mother's lapis lazuli earrings. *Something blue.*

"As you have a right to be." He looked her over for a moment. "You'll do."

The youngest Cook, Edgar, stood behind her and lifted her lace train as they descended to the front walk. Flower girls, Prissy and Polly, wiggled in the carriage, beside Mary, the matron of honor. Cathryn's bride's maids, Mary's two younger sisters, sat opposite, facing the driver, excited and giggling, exactly like the giddy girl walking down the front path. Once the bridal party were settled, Jacob clucked at the horses, turning them in a graceful arc in the middle of Lincoln Street and kept them at a stately walk to the church.

As the doors into the sanctuary swung open, Rupert met the gaze of his bride, over the heads of Snyders' girls, calmly scattering rose petals along the carpet in front of her. The quaking in his heart settled to a heavy thump in his throat. If not for the proximity of Mort at his elbow, his unsteady stance might have seen him prostrate in the aisle at his bride's feet. Above him, in the organ loft, one of Cathryn's students played the same *pavane* she had played to accompany Mary North's procession. For a moment, Rupert lowered his gaze, recalling the expression on that groom's face.

At his bride's first step into the church, Pastor Jorgens, joyful and grinning, stepped forward. Rupert drew a long breath, straightening his spine, shoulders back at parade stance, his dress uniform as impressive as on the first, and also the last, day he wore it.

As Cathryn reached the half way point between the empty pews, Rupert took two steps toward her, extending his hand. Noam Snyder guided the bride's hand to the groom and moved back to take his place beside his wife and daughters.

The ceremony was over before Rupert had taken a full breath. Cathryn had not worn the veil over her face nor had her gown been white but when the Pastor gave him permission to kiss his wife, Rupert first kissed the palms of her hands, clasped both to his heart and leaned forward to kiss the corner of her mouth. He leaned back, gazing into her eyes for a moment, then encircled her waist, drew her close and kissed her lips, holding Cathryn as though she was as delicate as the petals that had been trampled under the little girls buttoned-up slippers, sealing the vow he had spoken to cherish her as a solemn oath.

The tears that had threatened to redden her eyes while she dressed took their revenge, gathering in pools and spilling over her cheeks to the corners of her mouth. Rupert handed her his linen handkerchief and swept her into his arms, threatening to run with her out of the church. Instead, he whirled so that her veil whipped through the air above Edgar's head and the little boy chased it.

The laughter in the sanctuary was accompanied by the melodious chords of the hymn tune, *St. Denio*, as Peggy & George Smith's son led John & Hazel Marcher's daughter toward the open doors of the church. At the entrance, Cathryn held back a moment and Rupert came to a halt, turning to face her.

"Have you changed your mind already?" The question was serious and told her all she needed to know.

"From this step onwards, Rupe Smith, you are not going anywhere without my knowing where and why."

"That's good." He kissed her fingertips. "That's good."

And then, she kissed him, with all the love in heart, held back for all the years he had been away, held back for fear her past would condemn her, held back for fear her desire was unrequited.

The love of her life held back a moment, swallowed hard and met his wife's passion with the love he had kept hidden, for fear his need was too great, for fear his ardor would offend and overwhelm her.

"There's a cake waitin', folks, and a train to catch. Let's get rollin'." Sergeant Pierce donned his braided cap and rubbed his big hands together. "I ahn't missin' out on Grandma Arnold's cookin' this time since it's likely to be the last time for a long time."

That being true did not dampen the enthusiasm of any of the men who had packed their scant belongings that morning. Nor did it lessen the sadness of the newlyweds who had signed the bill of sale for the house they both loved or their relief that the buyer now had enough evidence to present to Judge Coffin for an indictment to be brought against the would-be Governor of the Great State of Maine.

Those loving souls who meant the most to Captain and Mrs. Smith gathered around the cobbled together dining table in the Cook's house on the Oxford Sawmill and Lumber Yard road, joined hands and bowed their heads as Aurelius Cook said *Grace* for his Sunday School teacher and the man who had shown him living proof of what his own father had taught him.

> '*...One equal temper of heroic hearts,*
> *'Made weak by time and fate, but strong in will*
> *'To strive, to seek, to find, and not to yield.'* [20]

---

[20] *Ulysses*, 1842, Alfred Tennyson, the final three lines.

About the Author

Leigh Verrill-Rhys is a native of Paris Hill, Maine and the author of four previous novels. *Pavane for Miss Marcher* is Leigh's first American Historical novel and her fifth work of fiction. Her third book is also set in her home state, *Nights Before: The Novel* which is the print edition (2015) of the *'Twas the Night Before* six-novella series published between 2012 and 2013. Leigh's debut novel, *Wait a Lonely Lifetime* (April 2012), an Avalon and Amazon/Montlake publication, set in Florence, Italy, is a story of lost love recovered. Her second novel, *Salsa Dancing with Pterodactyls*, (2014) is a multicultural, interracial novel of love healing the wounds of corruption, set in San Francisco. Her fourth novel, *This Can't Be Love*, is set in Edinburgh during the Fringe Festival for experimental performing artists.

As a founding member and director of the Welsh Women's Press co-operative, Honno, Leigh edited several collections of women's autobiographical essays: *On My Life* (now out of print), *Parachutes & Petticoats* and *Iancs, Conshis & Spam*.

Throughout her long writing career, Leigh has published essays and short stories, winning several awards for both her fiction and non-fiction. Her blogs, *EverWriting*, at everwriting.wordpress.com and *Ink on the Carpet*, at inkonthecarpet.blogspot.com feature articles about Leigh's books and books by authors in her many professional networks as well as essays about her writing experience.

Leigh is also a contributing author on the *Classic & Cozy Books* blog, classicandcozybooks.blogspot.com where she posts on the fourth Thursday of the month. Please visit LeighVerrillRhys.com for more information about Leigh's books and novels, forthcoming publications and works in progress.

All Leigh's previous novels are in print as well as digital editions, available at all major online booksellers.

Leigh welcomes your thoughtful comments on her novels, non-fiction and articles. Readers' comments are below.

Thank you for reading *Pavane for Miss Marcher* and we hope you will return to read *Dance by the Light of the Moon*, an "Americans in Love" novel set in Wales, Montana and Arizona, with visits to Cardiff, Chicago and San Francisco!

Comments about Leigh's debut novel,
Wait a Lonely Lifetime

"This was a most enjoyable book to read - a romance novel for 'mature' women! Romance can recur. The ex-husband was very credible, unfortunately - gain the 'unattainable goal' then - dump her. Loved the setting in Italy and enjoyed the extended Italian family. Fun reading!"—Mrs. Charles W.

"An excellent read! I was fortunate to get a sneak preview, very much looking forward to the next release."—I.D.

"This book is a well-thought out romance novel which shows how life can often come around full circle and complete itself. Fate, destiny, call it what you will, the connection between the two lovers in this book is highly believable. The setting in Florence adds atmosphere and is beautifully described. It's gratifying to read a book where the lovers are mature people embarking on a new phase of their lives at a time when they believed their future lives were already set.

Understated, and far more effective than graphic detail, this author can certainly write about passion!"—Mrs. Rochester

"The book is very good. I am enjoying it…. Thanks"—Shelba H.

"It is the sweet type of romance I was looking for. Sometimes the dialogue is choppy and silly (by design, I'm sure) but it didn't make me want to put the book down. It's worth the read."—Mbl1959

"Read for 6 solid hours. When I turned the last page I was so disappointed, I wanted the story to go on. I want to know more - how did they handle the Ex's threats, did Eric & Sylviana have a baby, what happened with Enid & Eva? If I'm really lucky, maybe we'll get a sequel."—Martha

"*Wait a Lonely Lifetime* was an enjoyable read. It made me want to read other books by this author. I liked her characters."—Barbara J.

"This was definitely a five star! Thanks for the opportunity of reading this book. I could hardly wait to see where the story was going. The first time I have read her writing."—JimCGrn

"I always hope for a good ending to a book. There were so many times and ways throughout the book that something awful could have happened, it kept the reader on the edge of his/her seat. I won't reveal whether or not there was a good ending, but it's worth reading the book to find out."—Dixie Silcox

"I enjoyed the story and since Florence is probably my most favorite city in the world, I loved visiting all the wonderful sites of that city."—Amazon Customer

"I had read a few pages in the free part before I ordered the book! I felt I wanted to read the rest of the book. I was not in the least disappointed. It was sad in parts, but so is life. I am always satisfied with the condition of the books I receive and the timely way they arrive. They usually arrive before the day expected!"—Rochelle

"A sweet story about true love. Fill the tub for a warm bath, light some candles, and enjoy some quiet time."—FBH

Forthcoming Novels by
Leigh Verrill-Rhys

Dance by the Light of the Moon

Colette Ilar had one career ambition until a retired American running back turned team-building trainer captured her heart; ambition paled in comparison to the man she wanted to forget.

Marshall Gregory had one rule regarding trainees until a Buffalo Gal taught him a thing or two about the language of heaven and dancing by the light of the moon.

That Kentucky Boy

A sequel to *Pavane for Miss Marcher*.

Tuck is left in charge of the Singing Creek Ranch while Rupert, Morton and the Arne brothers journey to Oslo Hill in Maine, to convince Cathryn Evelyn Marcher to leave the only home she has known.

Elswyth Emmaline Bishop, fighting off the unwanted offers of dance partners from ranch hands, is rescued by *that Kentucky boy* and leads Tuck on a hunt into Montana Territory for her mother's closest friend.

Novels in Digital & Print Editions

Wait a Lonely Lifetime, 2012, Avalon & Amazon Montlake

Salsa Dancing with Pterodactyls, 2013 & 2014, Eres Books

'Twas the Night Before (novella series), 2012-13, Eres Books

This Can't Be Love, 2015, Eres Books

Six Novellas *'Twas the night Before…,* 2014-2015

Nights Before: The Novel, 2016, Eres Books

All of Leigh's books are available online at all major booksellers and in some independent bookstores. Signed print editions can be ordered directly from the author through her website: leighverrillrhys.com/contact/

ℬibliography

This is a partial list of titles, in print and out of print, of books used for background material in *Pavane for Miss Marcher*. Most can be found in libraries, bookstores and online.

Alcott, Louisa May, *Civil War Hospital Sketches*
Batty, Peter and Parish, Peter, *The Divided Union*
Bennett Jr., Lerone, *Forced into Glory: Abraham Lincoln's White Dream*
Desjardin, Thomas A., *Stand Firm Ye Boys from Maine*
Foote, Shelby, *The Civil War, Volumes 1-3*
Katz, Harry, "Bringing the Civil War to Life," *National Geographic*, May 2012
Morris, Jan, *Lincoln*
O'Reilly, Bill, *Legends & Lies: The Civil War*
Seabrook, Lochlainn, *Everything You Were Taught About the Civil War is Wrong*
Shaara, Michael, *The Killer Angels*
Swan, Susan Burrows, *Plain & Fancy: American Women & Their Needlework 1700-1850*
Tobin, Jacqueline L. & Dobard PhD, Raymond G. *Hidden in Plain View: A Secret Story of Quilts and the Underground Railroad*

Online Sources Include: *AboutNorthGeorgia, AntiquePianoShop, CoffeeChronicles, DaleHospital, HackettstownHistoricalSociety, HistoryofCowboy Boots, HistoryofWyomingCattleRanches, HowtoHarvestRhubarb, JosephParry.org, PartsofaCarriage, VehicleCollection, Wikipedia*